Changeling ILLUSION

MARINA FINLAYSON

FINESSE SOLUTIONS

Cover design by Karri Klawiter
Editing by Larks & Katydids
Formatting by Polgarus Studio

Published by Finesse Solutions Pty Ltd
2019/01
ISBN: 9781925607048

Author's note: This book was written and produced in Australia and
uses British/Australian spelling conventions, such as "colour" instead
of "color", and "-ise" endings instead of "-ize" on words like "realise".

A catalogue record for this
book is available from the
National Library of Australia

1

Moonlight silvered the room, shining through the open wall of the pavilion. Outside, a lone frog croaked somewhere in the garden, but that small noise wasn't what had woken me.

My naked back felt chilled. When I rolled over, I realised Kyrrim was gone, though the place where he had lain was still warm from the heat of his body. I was still blinking in confusion when a figure appeared in the black rectangle of the door into the hallway—Kyrrim returning, the long length of Ecfirrith glinting in his hand.

Not a midnight jaunt to the kitchen for a snack, then. Not unless he was using his sword to cut bread these days.

Still groggy from sleep, I sat up, my heart rate picking up. "What's wrong?"

He crossed to my side on silent feet. All he wore was a pair of jeans and, even in my alarm, I took a moment to appreciate the way the moonlight fell on the sculpted muscles of his chest and torso. What could I say? This was only our third night together; it would be a long time before his beauty didn't knock me for six every time I saw him.

"Someone is in the sith. Where is the cloak Raven gave you?"

Several someones were in the sith, of course. Willow owned it, and she and Sage, my best friends, lived here, as did the three servants that Willow's parents had felt necessary to support her station in the appropriate style. Clearly, that wasn't what he meant. He wouldn't be prowling the grassy halls with a naked blade in his hand otherwise.

I slid out of bed, hastily throwing on his discarded T-shirt, which was just long enough to cover my bare arse. Raven's cloak of shadows was on a shelf in the walk-in closet. I moved as quietly as I could in the dark, locating it by the feel of the slippery black feathers.

"Put it on." Kyrrim was right behind me, breathing the words into my ear with as little sound as possible. "Stay out of the way."

I shot him an incredulous look, but he was already moving, ghosting out into the garden so silently I lost track of him almost immediately. Stay out of the way? While there were intruders in the sith, threatening the people I loved most in all the world? Not bloody likely.

But I put the cloak on, because that, at least, was a good idea. It was very short, hardly worthy of the name "cloak", but its value wasn't in its appearance. It clung to my shoulders, fastening itself and, as soon as it did, I became invisible. Handy little doodad. Every girl should have one.

While I was there, I grabbed two throwing knives. Who could be in the sith? How was it even possible that we could have intruders? Siths were magical pieces of the fae Realms that had been broken off—self-contained little bubbles that many fae living in the mortal world used as retreats and places of safety. They were safe because they were impregnable—they couldn't be entered without the invitation of the owner.

But I trusted Kyrrim's warrior instincts. He was a Knight of the Realms, sworn servant of the king, and only the best of the best rose so high. If he said we had intruders in the sith, the knives were coming with me.

He'd gone outside, and I was tempted to follow him, but concern for Sage and Willow drove me into the hallway instead. Willow might well be awake, since most fae preferred the night hours. But living in the mortal world as we did, many of us had adapted to the diurnal rhythms of humans, working during the day and sleeping for at least part of the night. Sage had work tomorrow, and would probably be asleep and vulnerable just down the corridor from us.

The sith was a large one, which boasted extensive gardens. Willow was from Spring, so gardens were really her thing. Her home followed the Spring style of construction, being a series of interconnected pavilions, all partially open to the surrounding gardens. That was great for enjoying their beauty, but not so hot from a security point of view.

Of course, the security was meant to be in the fact that no one could enter a sith without the permission of the owner.

The short grass was soft on my bare feet as I padded down the hallway, invisible in my feathered cape. Sage's door was shut. I eased it open just wide enough to allow me to slip inside, then closed it behind me.

Her room was similar to mine, huge and airy. One whole wall opened onto the garden; one door led to her bathroom, and another into her walk-in closet. Both were closed. The harp the king had given her stood in a corner near the enormous bed, whose gossamer curtains were draped from the posts like fairy wings. Her cropped head poked out from under the sheet, which was snuggled around her neck.

So far so good. A little of the tension unwound from my limbs as I stood, listening. The croak of the frog was louder here—that was a good sign. Nothing had disturbed him. The only other sound was the soft trickle of water from the fountain outside her room—a simple arrangement of rocks piled atop each other with water welling from the top and falling down into a wide pool at the bottom. Very Zen. Perhaps the frog lurked in the low-growing plants that surrounded it.

I watched the garden for long moments, but nothing stirred out there. Quietly, I moved to Sage's bedside. Up close, I could hear her breathing.

"Sage," I whispered. "Wake up."

She came awake in an instant, unlike me, her brow furrowing as she looked around the dark room and failed to see any sign of me.

"I'm wearing the cloak," I added. "Kyrrim says someone's inside the sith."

Her frown settled into a scowl as she slid out of bed. She

was wearing short black pyjamas with Teenage Mutant Ninja Turtles on them. Someone had been shopping in the boys' wear section again. Silently, she opened the top drawer of her bedside chest of drawers and removed a gun. Suddenly, she looked a lot more grown-up.

"Is that thing loaded?"

Her teeth flashed in a brief grin. "Wouldn't be much use if it wasn't, would it?"

"You can't keep a loaded gun in your bedside drawer!"

"Says who?"

Why did she even have a gun? It was hardly the weapon of choice for a fae. She was only half-fae, but she'd spent most of her life in the Realms and had totally drunk the Kool-Aid as far as the fae way of life went. She was way more traditional than I was. Her motorbike was the only modern thing that she'd adopted with enthusiasm—or so I'd thought. Seemed I'd been wrong on that count.

"Where's Willow?" she asked. She and Willow were tight—more like sisters than friends—and had known each other most of their lives.

I shrugged, then realised she couldn't see me. "Don't know. I'm going to look for her next."

"Where did Kyrrim go?"

"Outside."

This time, her smile had a feral look. "Then that's where I'm going. He shouldn't get all the fun."

I rolled my eyes. She couldn't see that either, of course, but it was a habitual reflex around Sage. "You have a very strange idea of fun."

I didn't bother telling her to hide somewhere safe. That would get about the same response from her as it had from me.

We stepped out into the garden together, and she disappeared into the trees. I walked around the outside of the guest pavilion where we slept, keeping off the pebbled paths, passing the main one that housed the shared living areas. Behind it lay a smaller one reserved for Willow. It had a tiny stream running through it and trees holding up the roof. Inside, she had a bedroom as well as a separate lounging area and a small library that doubled as an office.

I slipped into the bedroom, which was open on two sides to the garden. Nothing stirred in the dark room, and there was no figure tucked under the covers. As I'd thought, she was still awake somewhere. A quick search of the other rooms revealed that that somewhere wasn't here. She must still be in the main pavilion.

I headed back that way, moving silently, as a childhood spent hunting in the forests of Autumn had taught me. There was no sign of either Kyrrim or Sage. The sith was as quiet as the grave.

As I drew level with Sage's bedroom, something pinged at my subconscious. My steps slowed as I tried to figure out what had alerted me. No one was moving anywhere in sight, and the only sound was the soothing trickle of water in the fountain.

Ah—that was it. The frog had fallen silent. I stiffened, every sense on high alert. Someone must have passed this way. It might have been Sage or Kyrrim, of course. The faintest scent of something unusual teased my nose, and I sniffed the air, trying to decipher the unusual aroma. That was the smell of an unfamiliar magic. Not one of my friends, then.

Moving like a shadow, I headed back towards my own room. Was someone checking the bedrooms for sleepers? Whoever had broken in was clearly fae—I hadn't needed that whiff of strange magic to know that. No mortal could break into a sith. I was still certain of that, even if I'd been sure before tonight that no fae could either. Who could they be after?

Willow herself could be the target. Anyone who kidnapped her could expect a massive ransom from the Lord of Spring for his beloved daughter. Sage probably didn't have any enemies, but Kyrrim had plenty.

And me? There'd been several attempts on my life in recent weeks, and I wasn't expecting that to change any time soon. Saving the king from captivity might have won me the king's gratitude, but it certainly hadn't earned me any brownie points with the Lord of Summer, who I still believed was behind the plot. Others had shouldered the blame for it, but nothing would convince me that Kellith wasn't angling to take the throne for himself. It wouldn't surprise me in the least to find that Kellith had stooped to sending assassins against me.

His motive just depended on how much he knew. Maybe it was payback for foiling his plans—but if he knew of my connection with the Illusion refugees, it could well be an attempt to stop me before he lost the territory he'd snatched from Illusion.

Not that my death would halt that. The king knew of the refugees' survival now. One way or another, Kellith was losing the captured territory, and I certainly wouldn't be shedding any tears over that.

I saw no one on the way back to my bedroom. Looking at the rumpled sheets gave me an idea, and I hastily stuffed a few cushions into the bed and pulled the blankets up, to make it look as though someone still slept there. It wasn't especially convincing, but at least the pillow playing the part of my head was fluffy enough to look like hair at first glance. Satisfied with the deception, I stepped back against the wall to wait.

Perhaps five minutes later, my vigil was rewarded. A slim man dressed in black appeared out of the darkness under the trees and moved along the path without crunching a single pebble. I'd spent years stalking deer through the woods, and I'd never learned the trick of walking on pebbled paths without making any noise. A faint whiff of that unfamiliar magic reached me—a smell like butterscotch or caramel. It was probably Air magic, and the intruder's feet weren't actually touching the ground at all, though they looked as if they were.

He stole across the grass and slipped into my room, passing close enough to where I stood concealed that I held my breath in case the sound of my breathing gave me away. But I needn't have worried—a subtle change in his posture told me when the man noticed the "sleeper" in the bed, and from that moment, he had eyes for nothing else.

Moonlight glinted on something in his hand, and I

carefully shifted my grip on my knife, raising it, ready to throw. I couldn't quite make out what he was holding—it wasn't a knife, but there could hardly be any doubt of the man's intentions. Still, I would wait and see what he did first. I was no Kellith. Never let it be said that Allegra Brooks was the type to shoot first and ask questions later.

He approached the bed, fading into the darkness of the room. I could have sworn the soft grass carpeting the floor didn't even bend beneath his feet. He loomed over the bed, lifting the thing in his hand, and I saw it was a syringe. A white-hot rage filled me. Iron? Some other kind of poison?

He stabbed down in a swift motion, burying the syringe in what would have been the sleeper's neck. The resistance provided by the pillows must have felt all wrong, because in the next second, he hurled back the blankets, exposing the deception.

That was my cue. I threw the knife across the room, but his reflexes were amazing. He sidestepped so quickly I barely saw him move—one minute he was by the bed, and the next he was halfway across the room, thrusting the syringe back into the pouch he wore at his belt and drawing a knife instead.

That was fine. I still had another one, plus the advantage of being invisible. And I might not have Air magic at my disposal, but I could certainly manage to sneak across the soft grass of the floor without making any noise. I crept closer. The knife would be visible the moment it left my hand, so the closer the better.

He raised a hand, and a stiff breeze sprang up from

nowhere, making my short hair stream back from my face. So I was right—he *was* using Air magic. But he'd have to do better than that if he meant to discourage me.

As if he'd read my mind, his hand darted out in a sweeping gesture, and I crouched reflexively. He had to have a fair idea where I was, even though he couldn't see me, because he'd seen the direction from which the knife had come.

Damp earth rose from the nearest garden bed at his gesture, then hurtled in my direction. His expression was intent, his gaze roaming all over the general area he'd targeted.

Shit. I realised what he was doing in the same second he made his move. Most of the soil had fallen harmlessly to the floor—but some had clung to me, making me partially visible.

He launched himself at me, knife arm extended, and I rolled aside, swinging one leg out and catching him right in the gut. The breath whooshed out of him as he landed. *Try to Air magic your way out of that one, arsehole.*

But he wasn't done—he was rolling to his feet at the same time as me, breathing in harsh rasps as his eyes roamed the darkness. We were half-in, half-out of the pavilion, and I snatched a rock from the nearest garden and hurled it behind us at a low angle. Hopefully the bushes would shield where it had come from.

As I'd hoped, his head whipped around at the sound of it landing, and I launched the second knife while he was distracted.

His reflexes were good, I'd give him that—he must have caught the movement in his peripheral vision, because he started to turn. The knife caught him in the junction between shoulder and neck instead of in the jugular as I'd planned. But he still went down.

Not for long, however.

What did it take to stop this guy? He hurled his own knife in my direction, close enough that I felt the wind of its passage. Pretty bloody impressive, since I was largely invisible. A few bits of soil still clung to me, but in the dark—and at this distance—they weren't making much of a difference. I bent for another rock.

A shot rang out. The guy slumped backward, a neat hole right in the centre of his forehead, and Sage stepped out of the darkness under the trees.

"Holy *shit*, Sage." I snatched off my cloak of shadows and glared at her. "Is it really a good idea to run around firing guns when your friends are invisible? You could have killed me!"

"Don't be such a sook. I knew where you were."

I frowned at the cloak, its feathers crumpled in my fist. Surely, she couldn't see through it? "How could you possibly know that?"

"I can smell your magic. You're giving off fumes like a kid hitting puberty."

My magic. It was so strange to think I actually had magic now. Not that it would do me any good here. The only things I knew how to do so far were create a ball of faelight and take on the appearance of someone else.

But taking on this guy's face would probably get me mowed down by Kyrrim, even if it might have been useful for sneaking up on his colleagues, if there were any others here. That possibility was now my biggest fear. Kyrrim hadn't reappeared, despite the sound of the shot, which made me worry that he was busy somewhere else, fighting off the dead guy's buddies.

"Have you seen any more of these guys?"

"No, and I haven't seen Willow yet, either." I could tell she was worried. She crossed to the body and nudged it with her foot, as if to make sure he was really dead. Not that there could be much doubt after taking a headshot like that. Fae were hard to kill, but some things were impossible to survive. "You'd better put that cloak back on if we're going hunting. I don't want to be the one to tell the Hawk we got his new girlfriend killed."

Invisible once more, I hurried back towards the main pavilion. That gunshot should have alerted everyone in the sith. Where were they all?

A knot of anxiety settled in my stomach. Was Willow all right? Was *Kyrrim*? And what about the servants? Kyrrim was lethal enough that worrying about him was probably a waste of time, but Nevith and Zinnia and Yarys didn't have his expertise in killing people. Zinnia was a mean cook, but that was about the extent of her meanness; Nevith never had a cross word for anyone; and as for Yarys, who tended to the extensive gardens, I couldn't imagine him hurting the tiniest bug—unless, of course, it was attacking his beloved plants.

Sage had gone the other way, towards Willow's pavilion, though I'd told her that Willow wasn't there. She didn't move as quietly as I did through the lush gardens, but she had her gun, and clearly she was a good shot. As I stole through the foliage, I listened for any sign of movement. I wished I knew how many intruders we were dealing with. Possibly the guy Sage had shot was the only one, and all this tension was for nothing, but somehow I doubted it.

A clang of metal inside the main pavilion confirmed we still had at least one. I moved faster, hurrying towards the source of the noise through the midnight garden. Deep pools of shadow could have been concealing any number of assassins. Thank the Lady for the cloak. At least I didn't have to worry about knives—or syringes—in the back when no one could see me.

Or thank Raven, I guess. I still had rather mixed feelings about my "benefactor"—particularly since I'd discovered it had been he who'd blown up my house. But his gift of the cloak had come with no strings attached, and had saved my skin several times already. If we all made it through this safely, I'd have to remember to thank him.

Suddenly, a man burst out of the pavilion in front of me. I raised the bloodied knife in my hand, but before I could loose it, Kyrrim appeared, hot on his tail, and nearly took his head off with a sweep of Ecfirrith. I held the knife throw, not wanting to skewer my new boyfriend.

This intruder was dressed in black, just like the other, and carried a long pole with sharp blades on each end, which he stabbed at Kyrrim as they circled each other on the grass. Not exactly a typical assassin's weapon. It seemed a little bulky for stealth.

A wild wind buffeted the open area on which they fought, and at first I thought it came from the assassin. But when he staggered back, I realised it was Kyrrim's magic.

Leaves whipped about us, and tree branches lashed the dark sky as the Air magic battered the assassin, pushing him off balance and diverting his strikes. Kyrrim fought without expression, his sword flashing through the air in a series of deadly swipes that were almost too fast to see. Obviously the man facing him had some skill, or he'd have been dead already.

Three more black-clad figures appeared out of the trees, and I cried out a warning that was lost in the noise of the wind, even as I loosed my knife at the nearest. He toppled soundlessly onto his face, but I only had one knife left.

One of the remaining assassins waved an almost casual hand in my direction, and a blast of icy air hit me, so cold it felt as if I'd fallen through ice into the winter sea. My suddenly numb fingers lost their grip on my last knife, and it thumped to the ground.

A second later, I followed it, paralysed with cold. My teeth chattered, and I felt as though the blood in my veins had turned to ice.

I curled into a ball among the bushes, trying to control my shaking limbs. I had never experienced Winter magic before, and I never wanted to again, either. I was lucky; because I was still invisible, it hadn't been a direct hit.

All around me, the foliage had shrivelled. An iris not far from me was coated in ice, its deep purple petals looking as though they had sugar frosting on them. The flower bowed toward the ground, its frozen weight too heavy for the stem to bear, then abruptly snapped off.

Wind continued to buffet the trees, tossing their

branches as if a wild storm had hit. I hoped that was Kyrrim, throwing the Winter fae off balance. If he managed to strike Kyrrim with his icy power, the fight would be over.

I couldn't turn my head to look; I'd lost control of my shuddering limbs. Now I almost wished I was a Summer fae. I could have blasted these assassins with the same ferocious heat that Blethna Arbre had used when she'd tried to kill me at the king's palace. My amazing new Illusion powers didn't seem so awesome right now. Being able to turn into a copy of someone else wasn't an especially useful battle skill. Particularly as I wasn't even very good at it yet.

A storm of frost-coated leaves, twigs, and blossoms whipped past my chilled face. I ground my teeth together, desperate to stop them chattering. In spite of being invisible, I felt like a sitting duck just lying there. And the sound of blade striking blade terrified me. I needed to get back into the fight before Kyrrim succumbed to the paralysing chill of Winter. Where was Sage and her gun when we needed them?

After what seemed an age, I got my shaking limbs under some semblance of control, though they still trembled with spasms of icy pain. I dragged myself into a sitting position and found that the garden had come alive with black-clad figures. Five of them now faced off against Kyrrim and, as I watched, a knife came whizzing out of the trees, so there was at least one more there.

Fortunately for Kyrrim, the knife was accidentally knocked aside by the backswing of the assassin's staff, otherwise it might have ended up in his throat. Wings burst from Kyrrim's back and he leapt into the air, obviously deciding that the odds had turned too bad to stay earthbound. The change of angle took his immediate opponent off guard, and Ecfirrith soon sent the man's head bouncing into the bushes, spraying blood as it went. The body crumpled, but no one but me saw it fall. The dead man's companions were all too focused on Kyrrim.

My winged knight sent a blast of Air among the assassins, whipping dirt and stones into their faces, then swooped at the closest one. I groped among the bushes for my knife, my fingers feeling as though they belonged to someone else, sluggish and stiff. When I found the blade, it took me three tries before I could close my hand around the hilt and actually pick the damn thing up.

The temperature dropped and more frozen flowers sagged as one of the assassins sent another blast of frigid Winter into the sky. Fortunately, Kyrrim saw it coming and managed to dodge in time, but how long could he keep this up? I tried to force myself to my numbed feet, desperate to rejoin the battle and even up the odds a little, but my frozen legs gave way, and I tumbled back into the bushes.

A faint rustle signalled that I'd caught someone's attention. An assassin crept from the shelter of the trees, knife in hand. Shit. It was pretty obvious from the way I'd flattened the greenery where I was, and his gaze was trained on the body-shaped depression I'd made. Adrenaline flooded my body, going some way towards banishing the bitter cold that gripped me, and I groped desperately for the knife, which I'd dropped again.

The man leapt, stabbing downward in a killing blow. I rolled aside in a panic, finally finding my damn knife. My fingers closed on it in relief, and I brought it up and sank it into the man's thigh, which was all I could reach from my position.

He grunted in pain, but his hand snaked out and grabbed mine, twisting and grinding the bones of my wrist until I was forced to drop the knife. Movement finally returned to my limbs, and I kicked and writhed like a mad thing as he brought his own knife around and lashed out. I managed to kick his hand away, but he still had hold of my wrist, so I wasn't going anywhere.

Something glinted darkly on the edge of his blade as I scrambled for a rock or anything with my free hand. It looked like poison, and I had no illusions about what would happen to me if he managed to get that knife into my body.

A lucky kick connected with the stab wound on his thigh, and he let go of my wrist and fell back with a grunt of pain. I scrambled away, the branches of the camellias leaving long scratches on my bare arms, but I didn't care. I'd take a hundred such scratches over one from that poisoned blade. I pressed myself deeper into the bushes, scanning the dark ground for my knife.

A high scream followed by a gurgling rattle behind me brought my head whipping around. Kyrrim had dispatched another enemy, but four still remained. One of those lifted a blowpipe to his lips as I watched.

"Kyrrim! Look out!"

But the man slowly lowered the weapon, a look of

surprise on his face. All at once, I realised there was something protruding from his stomach. Slowly, he folded in on himself, his hands going helplessly to the point of the weapon.

Only it wasn't a weapon. It was a tree branch, and leaves now waved incongruously in Kyrrim's Air winds, as if a plant were growing from the assassin's body.

I took an involuntary step back and looked around uncertainly. All around us, the trees stirred, their branches snaking around in search of prey. One looped a vine around the throat of another assassin, hauling him off his feet. He kicked and jerked, clutching helplessly at the vine as it slowly choked him to death.

A sound at my feet brought my attention back to my own opponent. The roots of a large oak had speared out of the ground and caught him in their grip. He struggled against them, the only sound his panicked breathing, until they drew him underground in a churning of earth. My last sight of him was of his eyes, wide open and terrified, before the soil closed over his face.

A new figure had appeared in the midst of our struggle. Willow. She held her arms spread wide, head thrown back, and the plants did her bidding. Dressed in jeans and a loose, comfy T-shirt, she didn't look like a mighty weaver of Spring magic, but the effects of her power were all around us. Every one of the black-clad assassins died as I watched, open-mouthed. And yet not a leaf touched me or Kyrrim, who landed at Willow's side, his sword still raised in case she needed protection as she worked her magic.

She didn't. I drew in a shaky breath as she lowered her arms and opened her eyes. Beside her, Kyrrim was soaked in sweat, his broad chest glistening. The jeans were incongruous, but with those mighty black wings rising behind him and the naked blade soaked in the blood of his enemies, he could have been an avenging angel.

"Everyone all right?" Willow asked, gazing around at her handiwork with evident satisfaction. She wasn't even out of breath.

I pulled off the cloak and crossed the lawn on shaky legs. "Still in one piece."

Kyrrim sighed, surveying the destruction, and bent to wipe his blade clean on the grass. "You might have left one of them alive for questioning."

Willow considered him without expression. "Oops."

3

Half an hour later, we assembled in the main pavilion, in the kitchen. Zinnia, the cook, had produced tea and cakes apparently out of thin air, declaring that we would all feel better with a little food inside us, but it wasn't until her husband, Yarys, offered whiskey all round that I felt a relaxing warmth spread through my limbs.

What a night. It took another whiskey to convince my body that I'd actually lived through it.

Kyrrim had wanted to do a sweep of the sith, to make sure there were no more intruders, but Willow had assured him there weren't. She would have felt them if there were. The only living creatures that remained were the ones who were supposed to be here—which begged the question of how the assassins had managed to get in in the first place. So, he had contented himself with ransacking all the bodies before Willow asked the tree roots to drag them under. Sure beat digging graves.

We gathered around a large table in the centre of the

brightly lit room. It was nowhere near as big as the long dining table in the formal dining room, but it was big enough to seat us all—though Zinnia was still fussing with food and hadn't sat yet—and small enough that we could feel close. That felt important after what we'd just been through. Any of us could have died. I appreciated my friends even more now, knowing how close I'd come to losing them.

The only person missing was Nevith, the young fae who served as a kind of jack-of-all-trades around the sith, helping Zinnia and Yarys with whatever needed doing. He was more comfortable in the mortal world than the older couple, and was often out and about running errands. Zinnia said he'd gone to The Drunken Irishman to meet with friends.

The rest of us stared at each other in rather stunned silence until Sage cleared her throat. "So, who do we think they were after?"

My gaze was drawn to the small pile of belongings on the table—weapons, mostly: knives, blowpipes, throwing stars, a garrotte, plus a couple of syringes and several vials of an unknown liquid. There was also a set of lockpicks and three masks. Our assassins had come prepared for almost any eventuality—except for the strength of Willow's power. The fact that they'd sent eight men suggested that they'd been aware of it, but they'd seriously underestimated her.

People didn't usually consider Spring dangerous. Spring powers were more often used for growth, to create pretty displays at feasts and beautiful gardens. Nobody feared

Spring the way they did Night or Fire, or even Winter. But in the right hands, Spring's powers could be every bit as wild and dangerous as those of ancient Earth. And some had feared that Realm so much that they had neutered it and renamed it Flowers before it was subsumed into Spring and disappeared forever.

"Could have been any of us," Willow said, "though we never had this kind of problem before the Hawk came to stay, so I vote we blame him."

The ridiculousness of the comment brought a gurgle of laughter to my lips and did more to make me feel better than all the whiskey I'd just poured down my throat.

"It's true I have plenty of enemies," Kyrrim said, "but I don't think any of them are powerful enough to break into a sith uninvited."

"I've never heard of anyone being able to do that." Willow tapped her fingers on the table, a doubtful expression on her face. "Surely I would have felt the assault on my wards."

"It shouldn't even be possible," Sage said.

We all knew that, and yet, here we were. Eight dead bodies rested under the soft grasses outside, and eight people's weapons glinted in the light, looking very out of place in the warm and homey kitchen.

Kyrrim glanced at Zinnia, who was cutting thick slices of fresh bread and slathering them with butter. "What time is Nevith due back?"

"I—I don't know." Poor Zinnia was a quiet woman who could happily spend hours perfecting a new dessert. She seemed overwhelmed to have us all huddled in her kitchen, and horrified by the night's events. She glanced at Yarys, her husband. "We're normally in bed when he comes in. I couldn't really say."

"The boy's of age," Yarys said. "He's free to come and go as he pleases."

"Of course," Kyrrim said with a grave nod. As the Hawk, he was known and feared throughout the Realms of Faerie. Perhaps it was his presence alone that had Zinnia so unsettled. His fearsome reputation hid the caring man I'd come to know. "But he is the only resident of the sith unaccounted for. I think we need to find him as soon as possible."

"Is he in danger?" Zinnia's eyes were like saucers.

"You think he has something to do with this, don't you?" I asked. I knew the way his mind worked. Kyrrim had made suspicion into an art form.

"I make no accusations, but before we go tying ourselves in knots trying to understand what new magics these killers could have used to gain access to the sith, it makes sense to eliminate more mundane methods."

"Are you suggesting that Nevith could have let them in?" Willow asked. Zinnia made a noise of protest, quickly smothered as Kyrrim's tawny gaze fell on her.

"It's a possibility."

"Or they may have forced him to let them in," Sage said, to reassure Zinnia, though that raised its own set of problems.

"Yes. Which is why the sooner we can locate him and ensure his safety, the better."

Sage picked up one of the vials. It was small, perhaps half the size of my little finger, and contained a few drops of a thick, dark liquid. "What do you think this is?"

"Be careful with that," Kyrrim said quickly.

She cast him an impatient glance. "I wasn't about to drink it."

"The one who attacked me had a knife," I said. "It had something dark smeared on the edge of the blade."

"Undoubtedly poison," Willow said. "Yriell would know."

Yriell was the king's sister, a powerful Earth fae. She could probably do more with potions and poisons than these assassins had ever dreamed of.

"Does it matter?" I asked. "They were obviously sent to kill at least some of us."

"Of course it matters," Sage said. "Different fae favour different poisons, just as different Realms wear different clothes or have different conventions for naming their kids. If we can find out what it is, that will narrow down our list of suspects."

"I don't think that will be necessary." Kyrrim's face was grim. "They looked to me like Vipers."

I thought he was talking about snake poison, and didn't follow, but understanding dawned on the faces of the rest of his audience.

"The Night Vipers?" Sage looked at the array of gear on the table with renewed interest. "I thought they were just a myth."

"Sadly not. They've been around for centuries. An

assassins' guild," he said, seeing my look of confusion. "They were supposed to have been wiped out in the reign of Ordrin, King Agar's son, but I've heard rumours of them for a long time and found the bodies they leave behind."

"Do they work for Night, then?" I might not have been too thrilled with Raven at the moment, but I had trouble imagining his family employing a guild of assassins to do their dirty work.

"No. They take their name from the night viper, a snake that is fortunately extinct. It made no sound, and its bite killed in seconds."

Willow chewed her lip in thought. "But that means they could be working for anyone, correct? They sell their services to the highest bidder."

"Yes." Kyrrim's lips were a grim line. As if we didn't have enough trouble with Summer trying to kill us, now we had to add a legendary guild of assassins to the list of our enemies. Though it was most likely Summer who'd sent them after us. I wouldn't put anything past that worm, Kellith.

Willow cast me a suspicious look. "Anything else you're not telling us? You're actually the long-lost ruler of Illusion?"

Willow was still sore that I hadn't told her I was fae as soon as I'd found out. We'd all been up most of the night before while Kyrrim and I filled my friends in on what had been going on.

I snorted. "As if. My aunt is apparently a healer, married to a skincrafter. And we all know Lord Perony has been dead for years, not lost."

"Maybe you're his secret love child," Sage said, joining

the speculation with her usual enthusiasm, "and that's why Kellith has this deep and abiding hatred for you."

"First of all, how the hell would Kellith know anything about Perony's love life? And second, Kellith doesn't need any more reason for hating me than that I managed to whisk the king out from under his nose. That makes me Summer Enemy Number One."

"You had a little help with that," Sage objected.

"Well, maybe the assassins were meant to kill all of us. Vengeance, wrapped up in one tidy package." I caught Zinnia's eye as I spoke. Hers were open wide in shock—all this was new to her, of course, since the servants hadn't been part of our discussions. "Except for you guys," I said to her and Yarys. "You would be more like collateral damage."

"I'm sure I don't need to know anything about it," she said faintly, bringing the plate of hot buttered bread to the table. "Jam, anyone?"

Willow caught her wrist. "Zinnia, sit down and have something yourself. You're too pale." Then she looked past Zinnia's shoulder, and her expression changed to one of loathing. "There's that damn cat again. When are you going to find another home for him?"

Kel stalked into the kitchen, tail waving like a flag above his fat, furry butt. He had belonged to Edgar, a changeling friend who'd died recently. Got himself killed, actually, throwing in his lot with the bad guys. I'd hardly known whether to mourn my friend or resent the fact that he'd tried to get me killed. But either way, none of that was his cat's fault, and it didn't seem right to just leave Kel to his own devices, even though we cordially loathed each other. So I'd brought him here while I considered what to do with him.

The little devil sauntered over to Willow, an insolent look in his eyes, and wound himself around her bare ankles.

"Why does he *do* that?" she demanded, ineffectually trying to shoo him away. "I don't even like cats! Can't he go wipe himself on someone else?"

"That's probably exactly why he does it," Sage said, grinning hugely. "Cats are arseholes. They zero in on the one person in the room who doesn't like cats, just because they can."

I wasn't exactly sure that Willow was the only person in the room who didn't like cats. Kel had always treated me with contempt, even though I was now the person who fed him. If my life would just stop being crazy for five seconds, I would be more than happy to find a better home for him.

Zinnia sneaked a bit of hot bread under the table and offered it to Kel. He sniffed doubtfully at it, then turned his little pink nose up in disgust.

"I don't think bread is quite up to his usual standard," I said. "But I gave him fresh salmon for dinner and he lapped that up."

"We'd be better off with a dog," Sage said. "At least that might have given us some warning."

Willow shuddered. "Please, no pets. I don't want them digging up the garden and crapping everywhere."

"Just think of it as free fertiliser," Sage said.

"I prefer to think of it as *hell no, not in my sith*," she said frostily, giving Kel a nudge with her foot.

He moved, but only far enough to allow him to jump up into her lap. The look of horror on her face sent Sage into a fit of giggles, and I felt my own lips twitching. Maybe we were all a little drunk on survival, but it seemed like the funniest thing I'd ever seen.

Kyrrim rose with his usual fluid grace. "I'll head into The Drunken Irishman and see if I can find Nevith."

I stood up, too. "I'll come with you."

"Me, too," Sage said, no longer smiling. She was closer to Nevith than any of the rest of us.

A look of irritation flitted across Kyrrim's handsome face. "I don't need an escort."

"What you mean is, you don't want us coming because you think you'll have to protect us," I said. His protective instincts, especially where I was concerned, were very strong. And a pain in my butt. "But we're perfectly capable of looking after ourselves, thank you very much."

He scowled. "You should stay here where it's safe."

"Who says we're safe here?" Sage objected. "We don't know how these guys got in—there could be another attack any time."

I could tell from the look on Kyrrim's face that he'd already discarded this as a possibility, but poor Zinnia looked horrified at the thought.

Willow laid a comforting hand on hers. "We won't be taken by surprise again if they do. I've got this. You guys go find Nevith and make sure he's safe."

"Will do," Sage said determinedly.

Kyrrim grunted, but seemed to accept that we wouldn't change our minds.

The three of us returned to our bedrooms to change. I slipped off the T-shirt I'd been wearing and handed it back to Kyrrim, still warm from my body. He sighed with appreciation at the sight of my nakedness and pulled me into his arms for a kiss.

"Damn you, woman," he growled, after a long, delightful moment in which I forgot all about assassins and plots and missing people. "I'd drag you back to bed right now if I could. Maybe that would make you stay here where it's safe. But you attract trouble like flies to roadkill."

"Oh, nice." Clearly, my refusal to jump to his commands still rankled. I punched his bare chest hard enough to make my knuckles sting, but he gazed down at me, unmoved. "Flies to roadkill? You couldn't have said bees to nectar or something?"

"I call it as I see it."

"Clearly, your mother didn't smack you enough as a child."

He shrugged his T-shirt on, a reluctant smile tugging at his mouth. "Perhaps you would like to remedy that."

"In your dreams, buddy."

He was still smirking as he buckled on the scabbard that held Ecfirrith. Once fastened, the sword disappeared from view, hidden by the strong and very specific Aversion he had on it. "You have no idea of the kind of dreams I have about you."

There was a hunger in his eyes that made me want to shove him down on the bed there and then. Instead, I pulled on jeans and T-shirt, too, lacing my boots with impatient fingers. My blood was up; I was sick of being Summer's punching bag. There would have to be a reckoning soon, before one of these constant attempts on my life succeeded. I had too much to live for now.

We met Sage at the entrance to the sith. She was dressed as I was, in black jeans and T-shirt, with sensible boots for running or delivering a swift kick where it was needed. There was a slight bulge under her jacket that might have been her gun, but I made no comment. My own jacket hid two knives, hastily cleaned of blood.

We stepped out onto the street. It was four o'clock in the morning and not a soul was in sight. Kyrrim's Maserati sat at the kerb where he'd left it, apparently untouched. I patted it absently as we passed; I loved that car. A couple of cars belonging to the neighbours were parked on the other side of the street. The only sign that something was off was the fact that the streetlight that stood outside the house two doors down was out.

A wind sprang up out of nowhere, picking up dirt from the neighbour's garden and whirling it down the street.

"Is that you?" I asked Kyrrim, hand slipping inside my jacket for a knife.

"Yes. Just checking for hidden assassins."

Just as that assassin had discovered where I was, even though I'd been invisible. Must be a common trick among Air fae. My cloak of shadows was in my pocket, ready to be used again if needed. I scanned the darkness around us, checking the shadows around parked cars and in people's front gardens.

Sage lifted her head, sniffing the disturbed air. "What is that smell?" She moved towards our neighbour's front yard, following her nose.

A coppery tang was in the air, and my heart sank. I knew that smell. The neighbour's yard had no front fence. Instead, a straggly hedge separated it from the street. Sage pushed through a gap and gave a wordless cry of dismay.

Kyrrim was at her side in a moment, and I wasn't far behind. My breath whooshed out in a troubled sigh as I stared down at what she'd found.

It was Nevith, and he was dead.

"Lady save us!" Zinnia breathed, her hands covering her mouth, as Kyrrim carried Nevith's body into the kitchen. We'd only been gone five minutes, and the others were all still there.

Willow leapt up, her expression stricken. "Where did you find him?"

"Just outside," I said. "They didn't make much effort to hide him."

"Forced him to let them in, then killed him as if he was no more than a bug to squash." Sage's fury was evident in her voice. "Where shall we put him?"

Willow pushed his soft, blond hair out of his face. Her own face was white with shock. She'd dispatched those assassins without blinking, but this was different. Nevith had lived here in the sith since she and Sage had arrived in the mortal world. He was—he'd *been*—a friendly soul, and nothing had ever been a trouble for him. He had also died shockingly young for a fae, at no more than thirty years old.

She glanced at Zinnia. "We'll have to take him back to Spring, to his family."

Zinnia nodded, tears running unashamedly down her face. "They would want to say goodbye to him."

"Put him on his bed for now," Willow said to Kyrrim. "Zinnia will show you where it is."

The mood was solemn as the two of them left, Kyrrim bearing his heavy burden with great gentleness. I went to the sink and washed some of Nevith's blood off my hands, watching the red swirl against the white porcelain in a kind of daze. I'd seen so much death lately, you'd think I'd be inured to it, but the shock of it never failed to rock me.

A deep hatred for Kellith rose in me. All of those deaths could be laid at his door. It was his mad lust for power that was driving everything that had happened in the past few weeks. He was a poison, a rotten piece of flesh that needed to be cut out of the Realms if they were ever to heal. The sooner he died, the better. That was one death I wouldn't mourn.

When Kyrrim reappeared, it was evident he'd stopped to wash his own hands and change his bloodstained T-shirt. There was a grim set to his mouth that reminded me of the hard knight I'd first met. If I was burning to put an end to Kellith, how much worse must *he* feel? Kellith's schemes had ruined the last twenty years of his life. When the day of reckoning came, Kyrrim would be right there, a winged justice ready to mete out punishment.

If we both lived that long.

He met my eyes, as if he'd heard my thought. "We need to plan our next move."

"You'll be safe here," Willow said.

Sure, as long as none of us went outside. The assassins could use anyone in the same way they'd used Nevith; all they had to do was catch us. Kyrrim's sword, Ecfirrith, could open gates for people to leave undetected, but he was a Knight of the Realms. He couldn't stay here forever on gate duty. At some point, he would be gone, and someone would have to venture out the usual way.

"I feel like my staying here puts you all in danger," I said. "I'm betting Kellith sent those bastards for me—so if I go, they won't bother you anymore."

"Maybe," Willow said. "Or maybe you've got tickets on yourself, and they came for me."

But she sounded as though she was arguing for the sake of it, rather than from any real conviction that she was right. Not so unusual for Willow. She did love a good argument.

"Where else would you go?" Sage asked. "To your new place in Autumn?"

The king had gifted me an estate in Autumn for services to the Crown. Things hadn't calmed down enough yet for me to check it out.

"Not there," Kyrrim said with a fierce look. "Not secure enough. You'd be better off on Oldriss." Oldriss was his own private flying island.

"But you'll be at the palace. You're a Knight of the Realms; you can't just disappear."

"But you can. You'd be safe there." His tawny gaze was intense. "Please. I need you to be safe. I'd join you whenever I could."

"No." I wasn't about to hide, alone, waiting for him to make time for me. That could be a long wait, considering how busy the king kept him. Sometimes I really wished he wasn't a knight. "I have a better idea: Arlo. I want to go there anyway. And no one can get past their wards." If they could, the lost island of Illusion would have been found long ago. It was currently hidden away in the depths of Night, its presence known only to a few.

I had two reasons for wanting to go there: first, I had family there, family I'd only just met and barely knew; and second, my injured bondmate, Squeak, was there. Morwenna had said he'd probably sleep for three days because of the drugs she'd used to knock him out. That was only two days ago, but I still itched to be with him. The little drake had wormed his way into my heart even faster than the knight still staring at me as if he'd like to lock me away somewhere safe and throw away the key.

"Very well," he agreed grudgingly. "That's not a bad idea. But first, we should visit the king and let him know what has happened here."

As if poor King Rothbold needed more bad news. But I nodded. "Perhaps we can set up a meeting between him and the Illusionists while we're there. That would make my welcome on Arlo warmer."

Morwenna, my new aunt, had been particularly unimpressed that I hadn't sorted that little detail already. Coupled with the fact that Squeak had been so badly injured on my watch, she was barely speaking to me, and I was keen to change that. I had so many questions for her, having grown up with only my mother. I'd had no idea that we'd even had any other family. My mother had never spoken of them. I had so much to catch up on.

"And if we show our faces at Whitehaven, the assassins will know you aren't here anymore," Kyrrim added. He glanced at Willow. "Will you be all right with getting Nevith home?"

"Of course. You go. We can handle everything here."

He nodded and drew his sword. Kyrrim was a man of action. Now that we had a course laid out for us, he saw no reason to delay. I considered asking him to let me change my clothes—we were going to see the king of all the Realms, after all—but decided against it. *He* was only wearing T-shirt and jeans. If it was good enough for him, it was good enough for me. Beside, jeans and sneakers were easier to run in than dresses, and there'd been so much running in my immediate past that it seemed wiser to be prepared.

I would have made such a good Boy Scout.

With the point of Ecfirrith, Kyrrim drew three quick slashes in the air in the shape of a doorway. The slashes glowed with light, lingering in the air as the space between them went opaque and suddenly billowed with mist.

"Ready?" Kyrrim reached for my hand with his free one. "We should get moving before the sun comes up. The king won't appreciate being kept from his bed."

"Ready." I took his hand, and together, we stepped through the gate.

We arrived, as always, outside the great, jewel-encrusted gates of Whitehaven. The wards wouldn't allow gating within the palace grounds themselves. The gates were as white as the walls, and taller than three men standing on each other's shoulders. Two dragons roared at each other from either side, with rubies as big as my fist for their eyes. Dolphins danced in the waters beneath them—the dolphin being the sigil of the king's house. The top of the gates was shaped like the canopy of the Lady's great silver Tree, spreading its leafy, emerald-studded boughs protectively over the kingdom.

The gates were closed at the moment, but the guards posted inside stiffened to attention as they recognised the Hawk. One of them stepped forward and opened a smaller postern gate.

"Sir Knight. Welcome back to Whitehaven." If he thought there was anything odd about a Knight of the Realms turning up in jeans and T-shirt, his dark locks still ruffled from bed, he made no comment.

Kyrrim nodded to him as we passed through the gate and made our way along the shining path through the gardens.

The world was pale and grey, showing how close dawn was. I'd never yet seen the fabled white walls of Whitehaven in sunlight. They were said to be so bright it was impossible to look at them directly. Perhaps this would be my chance to check out whether the rumour was true.

The many roofs and towers of the sprawling castle rose above the trees ahead of us. Kyrrim moved quickly, my hand still firmly tucked into his. He wasn't shy about letting people know about our relationship even though, to all but a few, I was still nothing more than a lowly changeling—albeit one with some notoriety. My part in rescuing the king had brought with it more fame than I was comfortable with, but Kyrrim took it all in his stride. He was comfortable in himself, and the strength that gave him was one of the things I loved most about him. That and the fact that he didn't give a damn what anyone thought of him.

We passed more guards as we climbed the wide marble steps and entered the main building of the castle. The sound of Kyrrim's boots on the white marble floors echoed as he strode through the hallways to the throne room, but when we got there, it was empty.

He stopped a man in the corridor—a higher-ranked servant, judging by the elegance of his dress. "Where is the king?"

"Walking in the gardens with the queen, I believe, Sir Hawk."

Kyrrim made a noise of impatience. "Which part of the gardens?" They were huge, of course. Searching for the king would be like looking for a needle in a haystack.

The man drew himself up. "I'm afraid His Majesty doesn't keep me apprised of his movements, sir. I merely observed him leaving the terrace earlier with the queen on his arm."

Kyrrim glared at him until the man dropped his gaze, then he offered a grudging thank-you. We turned at the next intersection and followed a new, smaller hallway that ended in a pair of glass doors. These opened onto a terrace, the same one Raven had plucked me from the night he kidnapped me. Kyrrim hurried me down the wide steps onto the path that led away, into the trees.

"Are we just going to wander around until we find him?" I asked.

"More or less. We'll try the rose arbour first; that's a favourite spot of his when he wants somewhere more private than the palace. If he's not there, we'll move on to wandering and hoping."

"Aren't there meant to be armies of pages whose job it is to run around finding people?"

"Well, yes—but this way I get to enjoy the gardens in the company of a beautiful woman."

His tone was light, but his eyes were constantly roving, keeping watch. It was certainly no leisurely stroll. He was a man on a mission, and I suspected at least part of that mission was keeping me away from hostile elements in the palace.

In the twenty years the king had been missing, the queen and her brother had stacked the place with Summer sympathisers. There was no knowing who was watching, or who they were reporting to—the best thing to do was assume that anyone you met within its marble halls was probably an enemy. The haughty way that servant had spoken to him, bordering on insolence, was a sure sign he was on Summer's side. He was probably already reporting to Kellith—if the Lord of Summer was still in residence—

that the Hawk and the changeling scum were back, seeking the king.

We walked beside a creek that burbled cheerfully over a smooth, stony bed. Ancient willows hung their graceful fronds over the banks. A pair of swans glided by, and I realised the sun was rising. Bird calls filled the trees around us.

It was a very pleasant setting, and I relaxed a little, despite the pace Kyrrim was setting. Any time I got alone with him was time well spent in my book. I was disappointed when the path curved away from the restful creek, though everywhere I looked, new beauty greeted me. We passed through a wood where hundreds of bluebells filled the spaces between the trees, then the creek reappeared, grown wider. Here, it fell in a series of small waterfalls into a lake. Stepping stones picked a path through water lilies in full bloom across the lake to a small island. I itched to explore, but our path led in a different direction.

At last, the rose arbour came into view. I'd been expecting something small, but the "rose arbour" was the size of a football field and contained a lot more than just roses. Artfully placed hedges formed privacy screens for the paths that wound through the gardens, and trees shaded small, hidden nooks where stone benches invited the wanderer to sit and admire the flowers.

Rising from the centre of the arbour was something that looked like a Spring pavilion, but made of a thin framework covered in climbing roses. The sweet scent of roses was everywhere, reminding me of Willow's magic as we worked our way along the winding paths. There were no straight lines here; visitors were clearly meant to take their time and enjoy each new vista as it opened up.

I heard the king before I saw him. A row of camellias, old and tall and absolutely covered with enormous pink blooms, blocked our way, but evidently the king was on the other side. He was making no attempt to keep his voice down.

"I see no reason to rush into this," he was saying, and there was a note of frustration in his cultured tones that I'd never heard before. Usually, Rothbold kept his cool whatever the provocation, at least in my limited experience of him. He had "kingly" down to a fine art. Now he just sounded exasperated and thoroughly pissed off with whomever he was speaking to.

We turned and followed the path to the end of the row of camellias. I glanced at Kyrrim, unsure if the king would welcome an interruption, but my knight didn't seem at all perturbed. If Rothbold was arguing with the queen, I'd rather be almost anywhere else. The queen already didn't like me; I couldn't imagine she would welcome me walking in on a private argument with her husband.

"We're not rushing. This has been arranged since I was born. The world didn't stop just because you weren't here, you know."

Well, that wasn't the queen's voice, which was something. The speaker was female and youngish, though "young" was often hard to pin down with the fae. She sounded just as exasperated as the king, but there was an added helping of outrage that made me suspect her identity. Besides, who else would have the balls to speak to the king like that?

We rounded the last of the camellias, me hanging just a little behind Kyrrim's broad back. Okay, maybe I was a coward, but royalty already made me uncomfortable—they were so far outside my experience. I'd grown up in a cottage in the woods, with no contact with any nobles apart from glimpses of Eldric, Lord of Autumn, and his brother a couple of times a year at festivals. Royalty in the middle of an argument was a whole new level of awkward.

The king stood beside a fountain, its gentle trickle totally failing to soothe any of the three people in front of us. His royal fists were firmly planted on his hips in the universal attitude of a man laying down the law. Queen Ceinwen sat on the stone coping surrounding the fountain, her hands folded decorously in her lap, but the black expression on her face spoke volumes. A third fae faced them both. She had dark hair halfway down her back, and wore a dress of palest pink, tiny pearls scattered all over the gossamer fabric. That was all I could see, since she had her back to me.

The king was too intent on her to acknowledge our arrival, but the queen caught sight of us and scowled. Great.

"Rothbold," she murmured.

Distracted, the king nodded at us. The woman in pink threw a glance over her shoulder.

I was right, she was young. Though I'd never met her

before, the shape of her face and her blue eyes made it clear whose daughter she was. This was the child who'd been born and grown to womanhood while her royal father was trapped in a dementia unit in the mortal world. She looked a lot more like him than her mother, the pale ice queen. I wondered if that bothered Ceinwen.

"That doesn't mean that every decision taken in my absence must stand, Lily. The disposition of your hand is no small matter for the kingdom. I will not have my choices dictated to me."

"What about *my* choices? Merritt and I *love* one another!"

Whoops. Looked like we'd walked into a major family battle. I remembered there'd been talk of a betrothal. The name Merritt rang a bell, though it took me a moment to place it. Right—he was the son of Kellith, Lord of Summer, which made him the princess's cousin. And she wanted to marry him?

Eww. I'd lived long enough in the mortal world to find that more than a little off-putting.

"We will speak more of this later," the king said firmly, glancing again at Kyrrim, who stood patiently waiting at the princess's back, his modern clothes an odd juxtaposition against the fae splendour of the royal family's garb.

"I don't care what you say. I'm marrying Merritt. Mama and I both want it. Everyone in the family wants it." Except the king, obviously, and that was no surprise. He would hardly be on board with a move that brought Kellith even closer to the centre of power. Lily glanced at her mother for support, but the queen only rose gracefully to her feet.

"Hush, child. Not in front of these people." The way she said *these people* made it sound as though Kyrrim and I were roaches. "Come back with me to the palace and leave your father to his visitors."

I was surprised she wasn't putting up more of a fight, since I was sure the idea to marry her daughter off to her brother's son suited her view of Summer as the supreme Realm nicely. And if she and her brother had hatched this scheme when the princess was born, she wasn't likely to give it up without a struggle. But the scowl was gone, her face closed off into her usual cold expression.

Lily threw us a scornful glance, as if our visit could have no value to the king, but she went with her mother, all but flouncing down the path away from the fountain. I watched her go. She was only a couple of years younger than me, but she made me feel old with her flounces and her scorn.

If this was what a real princess was like, I would never call Willow a princess again.

The king sighed and ran a hand through his dark hair. "I thought fatherhood would be easier than this."

"Most people have more time to get acclimatised, sire," Kyrrim said.

"True." The king gave a rueful laugh. "I missed all the teething and the toilet training. All I get is the teenage tantrums." He rubbed the back of his neck, looking like a man lost. He'd been running the kingdom forever, but fatherhood was a whole new experience, and feeling like an amateur probably didn't sit well with him. He was trying to make a joke of it, but I'd been there when he'd discovered that he'd missed his daughter's whole life, and I knew how much it had hurt him. He sighed. "She's a lot like her mother."

That was hardly surprising, given that the queen and her brother had had complete control in Lily's upbringing. She was a Summer creature through and through, and, judging by what I'd just seen, she saw her father as a hindrance to her plans.

Moved by the baffled misery on his face, I said, "She's the spitting image of you, sire." I bet that ground the queen's gears, too. She might have moulded her daughter into a Summer pawn, but every time she looked at her, she'd be reminded of the princess's Brenfell heritage.

"Do you think so?" he asked, his face softening. "She's so beautiful. I'm trying so hard to tread carefully with her, to build up some kind of a relationship. Yet I can't help feeling she would have preferred her father to stay missing."

"I'm sure she'll feel differently once she gets to know you," Kyrrim said.

"Perhaps." King Rothbold didn't look sure at all. "But it might take her a few years to get over me breaking off her engagement." He snorted. "As if I would allow Kellith to get his claws any further into this kingdom than he has already. I sometimes wonder if I should have made a different choice of wife. It seemed prudent at the time to ally myself with Summer's might, but …"

He shook his head, letting the thought trail off. I'd never

seen him so uncertain before. The argument must have really unsettled him.

"It's ridiculous, anyway. She's not even of age yet. These negotiations should never have been allowed to begin so early." He glanced at Kyrrim and straightened his shoulders, the grieving father replaced by the monarch. "Still, I'm sure you didn't bring our lovely Illusionist here to listen to my family woes. Has something happened?"

"Yes. The Vipers struck at Willow's sith tonight."

Rothbold stilled. "Casualties?"

"The servant they used to gain entrance."

"What happened?"

Kyrrim gave a brief report, and the king's expression grew thunderous as he listened.

"Any survivors?"

"No, sire. But you know they wouldn't have talked, even if we'd managed to take one alive."

"Who was their target?"

Kyrrim glanced briefly at me. "We can't be sure, of course, but it seems likely that it was Allegra. This is not the first attempt on her life."

The king turned stormy blue eyes on me. "Our Lord of Summer grows impatient for the crown. We must find a way to put an end to his ambitions."

That was fine with me. I was kind of over having arseholes popping out of the woodwork attempting to put an end to *me*. Interesting that the king had jumped straight to assuming Kellith was the one behind the attack. We were all going to look stupid if it turned out to be someone else entirely. But I suspected we were pretty safe on that score.

"Perhaps a meeting with the Illusionists on Arlo," Kyrrim suggested. "Bringing Illusion back into the game will weaken him."

"Yes," the king said decisively. "Set it up for tonight. The sooner my dear brother-in-law is reminded of his place, the better."

B ack through the gardens we went, retracing our steps to the gate. The sun was fully up now, and the pale walls of Whitehaven did indeed glitter in the light. Fortunately, the day was overcast, so my eyeballs weren't seared from my head by their glow. I'd gotten used to wearing sunglasses in the mortal world, and the fabled faerie palace would have been too much for me on my present lack of sleep. It had been a busy night.

And no sign of slowing down yet. I was eager to return to Arlo to see Squeak and to find out more about my family, but I hadn't forgotten Morwenna's attitude last time, and that tempered my excitement somewhat. I was also worried about what condition I would find my little bondmate in. Hopefully a lot better than when I'd last seen him, but even fae healing magic couldn't work miracles. I was trying not to think about it, because I didn't want to admit that a miracle might be required to restore poor Squeak to full health.

Kyrrim was leading me around the bulk of the palace, since there was no need to go back inside, but a figure on the terrace called out, "Hawk!" and hurried down the steps towards us as we passed.

Kyrrim stopped and waited for the man, though I could tell he was reluctant. I recognised the figure as he came closer; it was the Dragon, one of the other knights who served as the King's Chosen. There were only four of them at the moment: the Hawk, the Dragon, the Lion, and the Wolf. The Bear had been killed when the king was kidnapped.

The Dragon was taller than me—hey, wasn't everyone?—about Kyrrim's height but of a slimmer build. He had warm brown eyes that had a friendly smile in them as he reached us. I'd only seen him in his ceremonial armour before, and he looked much more approachable today, in a more informal tunic of soft green over brown trousers tucked into tall black boots. Despite the lack of armour, he still carried himself like a military man, and I imagined there was a weapon or two tucked away under his clothes somewhere. As Kyrrim had once said to me, knights didn't live long by being trusting.

"Is all well with you?" he asked Kyrrim. "I haven't seen you around the palace for a couple of days."

"Quite well," Kyrrim replied. I managed not to give him the side eye. If he didn't want to tell the Dragon of the Night Vipers' attack on us, that was his affair. "I've been on the king's business. Still am, in fact."

That last was so clearly a *get lost, I'm busy* that the

Dragon gave a small half bow and stepped back. "I won't hold you up, then." He smiled at me. "But I wanted to ask how your bondmate is. I heard he took some bad wounds."

"Yes." All my anxiety over Squeak came rushing back at the concern in those brown eyes. "He was burned quite badly, especially on one wing."

"Wings can be tricky things." His face was grave now. "Who has the care of him?"

I just stared at him, not sure how to answer that one. Clearly "a healer on the lost island of Illusion" wasn't an acceptable option. He might be one of the King's Chosen, but I was fairly certain that the king hadn't shared that information with anyone. I glanced at Kyrrim for support.

"The king's sister is an excellent healer," he said.

Well, he wasn't exactly lying. My heart swelled with pride at his quick thinking. Yriell was indeed an excellent healer—just not the one who was working on Squeak.

The Dragon looked troubled. "No offence to the Princess Orina, but I'm not sure she has the right skills for something so critical. But I will not interfere, other than to say that if you need my help, you know where to find me. Dragons have had more experience than anyone over the years in healing wing damage. You might say that it's something of a specialty. Our wings are our whole identity."

"You're very kind."

He gave that little half bow again as Kyrrim nodded at him and resumed walking. I hurried after my dour knight.

When we were far enough away, I said, "That was nice of him."

"Very nice." His grim tone belied his words.

"You don't like him?"

"I don't trust him."

It was true that the Dragon, the Lion, and the Wolf hadn't been supportive of the Hawk in his years-long quest to find the missing king. Perhaps he was right. Who knew whose side anyone was really on these days? Though the King's Chosen were sworn to the protection of the king, that was no guarantee that they were, in fact, on Rothbold's. If we were only going by what people were *supposed* to do, one might expect the queen to be on the king's side also, and we all knew that wasn't the case.

Once outside the walls of Whitehaven, the Hawk drew Ecfirrith and took my hand. Three bright slashes glowed in the air, springing from the sword's point as he wielded it and hanging like the arc of a child's sparkler. The glow flared, then coalesced into a doorway, throbbing with power. Mist swirled within the opening so that I couldn't see what was on the other side, but I didn't hesitate to follow Kyrrim through the magic gate.

A tingle of threshold magic crept over my skin as we passed through, the gate winking out of existence behind us. I found myself on a pathway in another place, the sky above bluer than the overcast skies above the palace had been, but we were still in the Realms. At the end of the pathway, a castle stood proudly on a hill.

Turning, I saw behind me a familiar town clustered around the shores of a lake that gleamed blue under the open sky. That sky sported several winged shapes, which dipped and climbed playfully in the air currents above the lake. Occasionally, the rainbow skin of one of them caught the sunlight just right and flashed like a winged jewel.

This was Squeak's home, the island of Arlo, which had started life as a regular island in the river Ivon, part of the realm of Illusion. For the last twenty years, it and all the people who called it home had been fugitives. Raised from the river by the power of Air magic on the terrible Night of Swords, it had fled the slaughter.

Ever since, the island and its inhabitants, the last survivors of the once grand Realm of Illusion, had been hiding from Summer's wrath. They flitted from Realm to Realm, seeking out the uninhabited spaces, the lonely endless miles of Ocean, the hidden forests—anywhere that they could stay hidden. For some time now, Arlo had been making its home in the depths of the Realm of Night, aided and abetted by Raven, third son of the Lord of Night and my sometime friend.

We turned our backs on the castle and headed for the little town. Squeak was here somewhere. Last time I'd seen him, he'd been in the lake, unconscious and having his burned skin soaked. I didn't know where he was now, but Morwenna's house seemed like a good place to start looking, since she was the healer in charge of his recovery.

A couple of men nodded at us as we entered the streets of the little town, but mostly, the place was quiet. It was early morning, no more than about eight o'clock. Most fae would still be up, but perhaps thinking of their beds already. I'd only been here a couple of times, so I wasn't sure which house was Morwenna's, but Kyrrim had obviously paid more attention on our last visit. He stopped outside a cheerful-looking house with bright yellow flowers nodding in the window boxes and rapped on the door.

Quick footsteps approached, and then the door was flung open. Morwenna's daughter, Lirra, stood there.

"Oh." She seemed disappointed; clearly, she'd been expecting someone else. "Hello. I thought you weren't coming until tomorrow. Squeak is still unconscious."

"We're here to speak with your parents. Are they home?"

Morwenna and her husband, Tirgen, were the de facto leaders of Arlo. There had once been a noble family living in the castle on the hill, but they had been at a gathering on the main island the night Summer attacked, and had died with the rest of Illusion's people. Now the townspeople governed themselves.

For the first time, it occurred to me to wonder what the king would think of this arrangement. The fae Realms were not a democracy. Most likely, he'd find some second or third son of a Lord and appoint him the new Lord of Illusion. Raven might even get the job, since he had already taken up the cause of the Illusionists. I smiled a little at the thought. Raven would probably be horrified.

"Yes," Lirra said. "Um, come in."

She seemed a little uncertain as she held the door open wider. Kyrrim gestured for me to precede him, so I entered and followed Lirra into a dining room where Morwenna and Tirgen were eating. The table was set for three; Lirra's meal had been abandoned at the knock on the door.

Morwenna hurriedly wiped her mouth on a napkin and stood. "Sir Knight—welcome to my home. You have caught us in the middle of dinner, but there is plenty if you would like to join us."

Kyrrim glanced at me, but I shrugged. It might be dinner time for them, but it was barely breakfast time for me and, after the events of the night, I wasn't that hungry anyway. Nor had it escaped me that Morwenna hadn't greeted me at all. My heart sank a little. Why was she being so difficult? Was this still because I'd managed to get Squeak hurt? Or had something happened to him, and she didn't want to tell me? A pit of anxiety opened in my stomach at the thought.

"No, thank you," Kyrrim said. "We're on a diurnal schedule at the moment. But, please, don't let us interrupt you."

Morwenna waved him to a seat and we all sat down, apart from Lirra, who still hovered in the doorway. Her mother still hadn't even acknowledged my existence.

I couldn't stand it any longer. "How is Squeak?"

Finally, she met my gaze, and hers burned with fury. "Not good."

A woman who didn't beat around the bush. Why was I not surprised? "But he'll live?"

She sighed, a short, exasperated sound. "Most likely, though what sort of life it will be, I don't know. Drakes need to fly."

Most likely? What did that mean? My hands began to shake, so I shoved them under my legs, crushing them against the chair. "You think he won't fly again?"

I was quite proud of how calm I sounded, though my heart quailed. Poor Squeak didn't deserve what had happened to him—all he'd been doing was trying to protect me.

Another knock on the front door interrupted us, and Lirra flew down the hallway again. "It's Durran!" she called. "See you later."

Probably a boyfriend, judging by her enthusiasm. I glanced at Kyrrim, so solid and dependable at my side, glad that he was here. He reached out and laid a comforting hand on my thigh.

"I very much doubt it," Morwenna replied. "I'm a healer, not a miracle worker. Those holes in his left wing— they're just too big. There's nothing there to work with."

She sounded angry—with herself or me? Probably me. She hadn't seemed to like me from the start, and Squeak's injury had only made it worse.

I swallowed a lump in my throat. "But that won't kill him, surely?"

"Some drakes lose their will to live when they lose the power of flight."

"I see." My mouth was dry, and I chewed uneasily at my bottom lip. Surely, that wouldn't happen to my happy little Squeak? "Can I see him?"

"Tomorrow night. He'll be waking up then, so you should be here anyway. He'll be scared and in pain, and he'll need his bondmate."

"About tonight," Kyrrim said. "The king has asked for a meeting with you."

"So soon?" She glanced at Tirgen in horror.

"It's what we wanted," her husband reminded her.

"Yes, but … we aren't ready to host the king—and the little drake requires so much of my attention." She turned the full force of her glare on Kyrrim. "It's very short notice."

"His Majesty is not expecting a gala reception," Kyrrim said, unquailing beneath the force of that glare. I guess he'd been glared at by plenty of people before. He hadn't exactly been Mister Popularity around Whitehaven during the years that the king was lost. "All he wants is a simple meeting with the leaders of your people here, to discuss our next steps in restoring Illusion to its rightful place."

Morwenna's gaze slid as if unwillingly to my face before she turned to Tirgen and began rattling off instructions: who needed to be informed, where they should host the meeting, even the specific tea set that ought to be used. He nodded at every point, taking it all in his stride.

Eventually, he held up his hands to stop the flow of words. "I'd better go and talk to Grindel at the castle before he turns in for the day."

Morwenna rose, too, her scowl as black as ever. "None of us will be getting any sleep today. We have a lot of work to do."

"Perhaps we can help you," I said, getting up, too. Not that I wanted to spend time with my aunt in her current mood, but she was looking at me as if this was all my fault, and I had to admit it stung. What did it take to please this woman? She'd wanted a meeting with the king, and we'd got her one, and now she was furious about it. "You could tell me more about our family while we work." And being busy would stop me obsessing about Squeak.

"Girl, you're no family of mine."

She held my gaze defiantly as I stared, shocked at her rejection.

Then I turned on my heel and strode from the house.

6

"Don't let it bother you," Kyrrim said before he left to go back to Whitehaven. He held my hands and stared into my eyes as if he could command my thoughts with sheer willpower. "She's upset and she's taking it out on you. She'll come around."

"Will she?" I wasn't so sure. "I wish you didn't have to go."

He drew me gently into his arms. "How else will the king get here?"

No doubt Rothbold had plenty of people who could magic him up a gate for easy travel. Kyrrim didn't need to point out that the king couldn't trust any of them the way he could trust his Hawk. Or that this meeting was supposed to be secret. Or even that he was a Knight of the Realms, with all the duties that entailed, and couldn't spend all his time holding his girlfriend's hand just because she was facing a new and hostile family.

Nor should I need handholding. I sighed and leaned in

for a kiss, then gently disengaged myself. I was a big girl. I could handle Morwenna.

"I know, I know. It's just—now my mother's gone, I don't have any family except for these people. It's like when you start a new job, you know? You want to make a good first impression on the boss."

He quirked an eyebrow at me. We stood in the small, private sitting room of the suite that had been assigned to me for the duration of my stay, by the window that overlooked the road down to the village. The sunlight hit his dark hair, bringing out its chestnut highlights and lighting his tawny eyes so that they seemed to glow with an inner fire. He was impossibly beautiful, but the expression on his face was completely bemused.

"Oh." Belatedly, it registered on me that he'd been in the king's service for the Lady alone knew how many years. Centuries, probably. "Well, maybe you *don't* know how that feels."

"Morwenna is not your boss," he pointed out, still with that adorably confused look that made me want to kiss him. Not that that was saying much. Most things made me want to kiss him.

"I know. But I was hoping to be welcomed to the family with open arms, and clearly, that isn't going to happen. I wanted her to love me, but she doesn't even like me."

"*I* like you," he said, moving closer again. "More than like you, in fact."

I smiled up at him, feeling that familiar melting sensation. When he was in the room, it was hard for me to look at anyone else. "I'm reasonably fond of you, too."

He snorted, then leaned in to steal a kiss that lasted long enough to leave me feeling dizzy. "Reasonably fond? How very exuberant of you."

"Well, okay, then," I said, as if I was doing him a great favour, though I twined my arms around his neck. "I'm *definitely* fond of you."

He tried to feign offence, but his lip twitched. "At least my ego won't get out of control with you around." He jerked my hips against his. "Just my libido."

A thrill shot through me as I felt the evidence of his arousal grind against me. I glanced behind me at the closed bedroom door, wishing we were back in his house in the mortal world, cooking breakfast together without a care in the world. And burning the bacon.

He groaned, following the direction of my glance, and rested his forehead against mine. "Do we have time for—?"

I sighed. "You know we don't. You should be back in Whitehaven by now." Suddenly fierce, I muttered into his chest, "I wish the world would just go away and leave us alone. We rescued the king—if this was a fairy tale, we'd be enjoying our happy ever after by now."

"Allegra." He tipped my head up with a finger under my chin, his gaze serious. "You *are* my happy ever after. My duty to the king might take me away more than I would like, but I will always return. The king needs me—but *I* need *you*."

He kissed me, warm and tender, and I felt something blossom in my heart. I'd been here before, in the first rosy stages of falling in love, but never with someone like Kyrrim. He made my last boyfriend look like a child. He had a gravity and maturity to him that made me feel safe, even in this unsafest of worlds. And unlike that last boyfriend, I felt sure he would always be there for me when I needed him.

"I need you, too," I whispered, my voice trembling with all the emotion that threatened to burst from me. How was it that he always seemed to know exactly the right thing to say—the thing I most needed to hear in that moment? Perhaps it was a skill that came with age, or maybe it was just him. He was a complicated man, and I knew how lucky I was to be the woman he was staring down at like that. Men like this didn't come along every day.

He smiled ruefully, and released me with obvious reluctance, dropping one last kiss on my lips. "Good. But you are right—I should be at Whitehaven. I'll see you tonight."

"See you," I said, watching until the door closed behind him. He could have gated straight out of this room, but perhaps he needed to speak to Morwenna or one of the others before he left. There was a lot to arrange before nightfall.

I sighed again. Thinking of Morwenna made me feel miserable again. What *was* her problem? Anyone would think she'd be happy to have a niece turn up out of the blue.

I gazed longingly at the closed door that led to the bedroom. I'd already checked it out. The large bed was piled with pillows and looked super comfy. I was running on very little sleep, and the thought of throwing myself onto the soft mattress and sleeping away the rest of the day was very tempting. It might even be a good idea to get some shut-eye before the king arrived, or I'd be useless from exhaustion.

But I knew that thoughts of Morwenna and my misery about her attitude would keep me awake. And I could just imagine her scathing response if she found out I'd been snoozing while everyone else ran themselves ragged getting everything ready for the big meeting. This was a huge event for the people of Arlo, and they were determined that everything should go smoothly.

Straightening my shoulders, I opened the door that Kyrrim had just gone through and went looking for something to do.

I found Grindel at last in the castle kitchens, deep in conversation with a man whose hot, flushed face suggested he was the castle cook. A bank of ovens along one wall were all in use and the temperature in the room was significantly higher than outside. Had they changed their minds and decided to put on a meal for the king? I thought we'd agreed on light refreshments.

"Hi," I said, awkwardly. Grindel was the only face I recognised among the people hard at work and the ones I'd passed on my way here. "Is there something I can do to help?"

He drew in a startled breath, and the cook looked positively horrified. Had they heard about my cooking prowess—or lack thereof—even here? "Of course not!"

"I don't have to cook or anything. I could just dust things or help wash up or something."

The cook made an instinctive gesture, as if shooing me away, and Grindel shook his head vehemently.

"No, no, no, my lady. You're a guest here. Please relax and enjoy your day. We can handle everything. Is there something I can get you?"

"No, thanks." Now it was my turn to feel horrified. The last thing I wanted to do was create more work for them. "I'm fine. You've been very … um … welcoming. I might just go for a walk."

There was a collective sigh of relief from everyone in the kitchen, and I slipped back into the hall, feeling vaguely guilty. Well, I'd tried. Perhaps I could help down in the town. That would certainly be a good place to get some information about Morwenna, at least.

It was a beautiful day outside, and I felt my spirits lift just from being out in the sunshine. My feet took me to Morwenna's house, since that was the only place in town I knew, and I knocked on the door, hoping they weren't all busy with other things.

There was such a long delay that I had decided no one was home and was turning away when Tirgen opened the door.

"Hello," he said, obviously surprised to see me again so soon.

"Hi. Is Morwenna home?"

"No. I thought she was up at the castle."

"Oh. Well, actually, I don't really want to see her at the moment."

Something softened in his expression of polite interest. "Could I come in?"

He held the door open and stepped back. "Of course. Be welcome in my house."

I followed him in. He led me not to the dining room that I'd seen last time, but through the house and out to a building separated from the main house by a small courtyard bursting with greenery. Inside was cool and dim. It wasn't very big, but there was room for two beds made up with crisp white linen and a set of cupboards that stretched the length of one wall. A workbench stood under one window.

It was a long moment before I realised that one of the beds was occupied, though not by a person. The small figure looked lost in the expanse of snowy white sheet.

"Squeak!" I gasped, and all but sprinted across the room to his side.

He was swathed in bandages all around his chest and, much more awkwardly, across his left wing. The other had some kind of unguent smeared all over it, but looked remarkably healthy—far better than when I'd last seen him. Clearly, Morwenna had worked miracles already, whatever she said about her lack of skill with wings. He was asleep or unconscious, and didn't stir at the sound of my voice, nor was there any response when I pushed my mind towards his. Just a black, empty hole where our connection had been.

I turned to Tirgen. "But why is he lying in a bed?"

Tirgen smiled. "Morwenna set this place up as a centre

of healing, though she didn't expect any of her patients to be drakes. But it's quiet and convenient, so why not? The bed keeps him comfortable and is high enough that she's not hurting her back bending over him."

Fair enough. I could just imagine Morwenna's snippy voice saying something like that. She seemed like my mother, in that practical concerns overrode all others. So far, that was the only family resemblance I'd seen.

I laid a tentative hand on Squeak's neck, behind his head, where the skin was undamaged. "And he'll wake up tomorrow?"

"So she says. She's been tapering off the drugs in preparation."

I glanced at him where he leaned against the door frame, arms crossed comfortably over his chest. "Thank you for letting me see him."

"Morwenna wouldn't approve, so it's probably best if we keep this little visit between ourselves."

I nodded. "Of course. But why did you let me?"

I was curious why someone married to a force of nature like Morwenna would stand up to her, even in such a small way. Commanding people like Morwenna often seemed to go for very passive partners. I'd had him pegged as a yes-man—though there had been that argument I'd overheard when Raven had been keeping me prisoner here, when Tirgen had taken her on over revealing Arlo to the world. And that seemed to have turned out for him. Maybe he just had subtler ways to get what he wanted.

"Morwenna has forgotten what it's like to be new to having a bondmate—it's been so long since she and Immi bonded. I knew you would be fretting about him, and I can't see how your being here would really be a problem. You may have noticed that my wife is rather fond of having her orders obeyed." He smiled again. "It's probably healthy for her not to get her own way all the time."

"Well, I appreciate it," I said, gazing down at Squeak. I hoped that when those bandages came off, he'd be as good as new, despite what Morwenna had said earlier. Seeing him looking so good gave me hope.

I couldn't believe the difference she had managed to make to the parts of him that were visible. His face and his right wing already looked as though nothing had happened to him, and that fact went a long way towards making me feel more charitable towards my difficult aunt.

I looked back at Tirgen, wondering how far I could stretch the friendship—but he seemed to have no problem with plain-speaking about his wife. "I wonder if you could answer a question for me?"

"Depends what it is," he said, still with that easy smile. "I was never very good at geography, so if you want to know the way somewhere, I'm not the man for you. Never had much cause to leave my home."

I smiled back. I liked this guy, and already felt comfortable with him. It occurred to me that he was my uncle, which gave me a warm feeling of happiness. I'd been so focused on Morwenna that I'd forgotten about the rest of the family. But I'd gained an uncle and a cousin, too, along with her. And who knew? There could be others.

"It's about Morwenna," I said, and his face assumed a

more cautious expression. "I get the feeling she doesn't like me. I don't suppose you know why?"

"Ah." The smile had gone, and he shifted his weight as if uncomfortable. "That's a bit of a tricky one. Probably best if I let her cover it."

"Oh." Damn. I'd been hoping for some insight. "It's just, it makes it very hard to work with her. I thought you might have some tips for me."

"Well … you might remember that she has just lost her sister."

I blinked, startled by such insensitivity. It was all I could do not to shout at him. "And *I* lost my mother." I managed quite a reasonable tone of voice, in the circumstances.

He blinked, too, and his gaze slid away from mine. How could he have forgotten? "Yes. Right. I'd … ah, I'm sorry." He chewed his lip, but after a moment of silence, he seemed to decide that he owed me something more, and added, in a low voice, "I think Morwenna blames you for Anawen's death."

"*Blames* me?" I drew in a deep breath. "But I had nothing to do with it! Does she blame me for leaving my mother alone in Autumn? It wasn't something I had a choice about, believe me. She threw me out."

I realised my voice had gotten shriller, until the last words were practically a cry of anguish. That was the rejected seventeen-year-old inside, baffled by her beloved mother's abrupt abandonment. It still hurt, even knowing, as I did now, that she'd done it to save me and had never actually stopped loving me.

"I'm sorry," I said, in more even tones. "It's still a sore point, as you can probably guess. But I hadn't seen my mother in four years. How can Morwenna blame me for what happened when I wasn't even there?"

He sighed and scrubbed at his face wearily. He was probably regretting the kind impulse that had let me in. "Perhaps you'd better sit down."

Since there was plenty of room, I sat on Squeak's bed, and Tirgen pulled out the chair from the work bench and turned it around, straddling it with his arms across the back of it.

"You know that Anawen fled Illusion on the Night of Swords, and hid with you in Autumn, assuming the identity of that poor Autumn woman."

"Livillia, yes." I'd uncovered Livillia's body, hidden for twenty years. All this had been explained to me before, but perhaps he needed to warm to his story. I sat and waited with as much patience as I could muster, watching his sun-browned fingers tapping anxiously at the wood of the chair's back. Obviously, skincrafting required at least some time out and about during the daylight hours.

"And then she cast you out into the mortal world when you were seventeen to protect your identity."

Hadn't I just told him that? I swallowed a fierce urge to tell him to get on with it.

"Well, after you left, she was free." Oh, nice. My face must have shown my feelings too clearly, because he hastened to clarify. "I don't mean it like that. She loved you, of course, but while you were there, she had to play her part. She'd heard rumours that other Illusionists had survived, but she hadn't been able to leave you long enough to go searching. Once you were gone, she left the cottage and set out to find out if the rumours were true."

"And she found Arlo?"

"Not immediately. And certainly not directly. But eventually, she found her way to us." His eyes no longer saw me, fixed on a memory that curved his lips into a smile. "You should have seen the two of them together—her and Morwenna, I mean. It was like they'd never been apart. Thick as thieves, the pair of them." The smile broadened. "They fought, too, though they always made up. She was a stubborn woman, your mother."

"What did they fight about?" I was fascinated by this glimpse into a family dynamic I'd never experienced.

He sobered again and met my eyes, his own troubled. "You, mostly."

"Me? What was there to fight about? I was in the mortal world, far away." But no wonder Morwenna wasn't my biggest fan, if she'd been arguing about me before she'd even met me.

"And your mother wanted you to stay there, ignorant of your heritage. She thought it was safest for you."

"And Morwenna wanted, what? To bring me here?" She hadn't sounded very keen on the idea that time I'd overheard her arguing with Raven and Tirgen, but perhaps events had changed her mind.

He sighed. "She had her reasons for wanting you here. But your mother thought they weren't good enough. At any rate, eventually, we got word that you'd managed to make it back to the Realms on your own. That you'd saved the king and you'd been asking questions around Autumn, looking for Anawen. She decided to go back to the cottage to wait for you."

I remembered that time all too well. There were only a few days between my beginning the search for my mother and her turning up in the mortal world, already dying. Not for the first time, I wondered uneasily if my search had been the cause. Suddenly, I wasn't sure if I wanted to hear the rest of this story.

"That was their biggest fight yet," Tirgen said. "Morwenna actually forbade her sister to leave Arlo. She might have known that would only encourage her. Of course, Anawen went, and she was waylaid at the cottage by Blethna Arbre, working on Summer's behalf, who also knew you were looking for your mother and had had the same idea about staking out the cottage to wait for your inevitable return."

I drew in a shaky breath. Morwenna's feelings towards me became a little clearer. In a way, I *had* caused my own mother's death.

The sky was a soft-focus study in oranges and pinks as the sun set behind the castle when the king arrived. The castle was alight, all the windows shining like a welcoming beacon into the gathering dark. It had probably never seen such a distinguished guest in all its time; it was certainly the most excitement it had experienced since the fall of Illusion twenty years before.

Raven waited at the top of the steps leading up to the main entry, and I stood next to him, my nerves jangling. Morwenna and Tirgen were on his other side, carefully pretending that I wasn't there. Well, Morwenna was, at least. Several people from the village I hadn't met—the other members of the council—were also in attendance. It wasn't every day that the king of all the Thirteen Realms came to visit.

Three familiar slashes in the shape of a doorway formed in the air, glowing against the darkness of the castle's forecourt. Mist billowed forth as the slashes pulsed and formed a magical gateway wider than the one I was used to seeing. How many people was Kyrrim bringing with him?

He was first through the gate, naked blade still in his hand, as wary as if he were stepping into enemy territory. Behind him came the king, resplendent in a white robe with deep bands of green and gold embroidery around the cuffs of the sleeves and all around the bottom of the robe. He looked like the painting of a Christian saint I'd seen once in a children's Bible, though his otherworldly beauty somewhat spoiled the impression. Considering the times they had lived in, most of the old saints probably hadn't even had all their teeth.

Morwenna descended the steps, her long gown trailing behind her. I couldn't help wondering if she had raided the wardrobe of the former mistress of this castle. The dress was literally worth a king's ransom. The whole bodice was made of rainbow drake skin, and there were more panels of it in the sleeves. But maybe that was my hurt talking. The fact that her husband was a skincrafter might also have something to do with her possession of such an expensive item of clothing. Queen Ceinwen would have been green with jealousy.

"Your Majesty," she said as she sank into a curtsey. "It thrills our hearts beyond measure to welcome you to Arlo."

"And it pleases me beyond measure to be here, gracious lady," the king replied with his customary aplomb. He took her hand and raised her to her feet.

"May I present my husband, Tirgen, and these others, all loyal subjects of yours," she went on. As she named each individual, they bowed and curtsied in turn.

Kyrrim kept his position at the king's side, one respectable step behind the royal shoulder. His eyes had sought mine as he stepped through the gate, but other than that, he made no acknowledgement of me. He was all the Hawk, now, intent on his duty to his liege lord. Not that there was likely to be any danger to the king from the good people of Arlo. In fact, he was probably safer here than in the corridors of his own palace at Whitehaven.

When the king had greeted everyone and exchanged a few words with Raven, he turned to me. I began to sink into my own curtsey, but he stopped me with a hand under my elbow.

"No need for formalities between us. Not here, at any rate." He smiled down at me, the famous blue eyes of the Brenfell line warm. He took my hand and tucked it into the crook of his elbow, then gestured to Morwenna to lead the way. "Shall we?"

Her lips tightened, presumably at the sign of the king's favour to me. But she turned as she was bid and swept through the open doors of the castle, leading our small group to the room that had been prepared for the king's arrival. Up two flights of stairs, its large windows looked out over the lake and the spectacle of the rainbow drakes cavorting in the skies above it. The last light of the setting sun caught their jewelled skin, making them twinkle like tiny acrobatic stars. Raven took charge once everyone was seated, directing the servants to fill glasses for all the guests. The Hawk served the king with his own hands.

"Thank you for meeting with us at such short notice,"

Raven said. He nodded at the servants, who left the room, closing the door softly behind them.

I refused to look at Morwenna, knowing her feelings on the brevity of the notice she'd received all too well.

"This meeting should have taken place years ago," the king replied, a fierce gleam in his blue eyes. "I would not delay it another second. Though I admit, I am curious as to your part in these proceedings, Bran."

Raven forced a smile. Bran was his real name, and the king's use of it was a subtle reminder that he was, in fact, the third son of the Lord of Night, with responsibilities of his own. Responsibilities that certainly weren't meant to include harbouring a bunch of fugitives in his father's Realm. I settled back in my chair, enjoying that rather strained smile.

"You are wondering whether my lord father lied to you. I assure you that I took every care to make sure that he knew nothing of Arlo's presence in our Realm."

"Strange that a Lord would have so little idea what was happening in his own Realm."

"My father has spent a lot of time since your disappearance in Whitehaven, sire, trying to protect your interests. And his own, of course."

The king nodded gravely. Everyone in the room understood Raven's meaning. The Lord of Night had not been paying as close attention to his own Realm as he might have, in the struggle to limit the influence of Summer at the royal Court.

"Tell me, how did you come to be Arlo's protector?"

Raven shrugged, grinning. "In the usual way. Because of a girl. I met one of Morwenna's people in the forests of Night. Not a safe place for a lady travelling alone. I offered my help, and we became friends."

The king raised a sceptical eyebrow. "And she trusted you with the enormous secret of her people's existence?"

"Not right away. Not for a long time, in fact. But we became close. In the end, I found out more by accident than anything else, but I was determined to offer what help I could."

The king nodded approvingly. "Very noble of you."

I almost snorted at the thought of Raven doing anything noble, but managed to restrain myself just in time. Though he had helped me, I still didn't entirely trust him. He was a trickster, and his motives for anything he did were usually unclear, if not downright ambiguous.

Raven himself seemed a little uncomfortable at the compliment. He glanced at Morwenna. "Perhaps we should address the question of who is to lead Illusion first?"

She scowled at him. "Plenty of time for that. We have far more pressing matters to discuss."

"Are you still in touch with the Air fae who originally helped to save Arlo?" the king asked her.

Morwenna nodded. "Several of them visit us regularly, to ensure the magics that keep us afloat are still fully operational."

That was something I hadn't considered. The thought of the island and all the people on it crashing suddenly to the earth made me shudder.

"Good. We will need to consult with them on returning Arlo to its original place."

"Sire, they say that it will take much less power on their part to settle the island than it did to raise it," Tirgen said, speaking for the first time. Well, that was good, since so many of them had died in the effort to save the island. "They also say that Earth magic will be required to fit Arlo back onto it foundations."

Rothbold frowned. "I am of Earth, of course," he said, looking thoughtful. "I shall have to consult with your Air fae to see how much power they think will be required, and whether one man alone will be capable of the task."

I could see his difficulty. It sounded like a big job, but he would have to be sure that anyone he enlisted to help him could keep a secret until he was ready to reveal it.

"Perhaps your sister, sire," I suggested. Yriell was the most powerful fae I knew, mistress of the Wilds, that dangerous remnant of old Earth that made the Greenways so perilous. It wouldn't surprise me to find that she was more powerful than her brother, the king.

The king glanced at Kyrrim questioningly, who nodded.

"The Princess Orina would be the perfect choice, sire," he said.

"I will leave it to you, then, to enlist her aid."

"Sire, when do you plan on making your move?" Raven asked.

"I see no reason to delay further." True, things with Summer weren't going to get any easier. A swift, bold move would be the king's best bet. "I think we must ensure the maximum number of witnesses to Arlo's return."

"What do you have in mind, sire?"

The king glanced at me again. "Allegra, perhaps your friend Lord Eldric wouldn't mind hosting a grand gathering. Something to commemorate the passing of Illusion, perhaps, on the twentieth anniversary of its demise."

Inwardly, I winced. That wasn't going to go down too well with Kellith, who had been the cause of Illusion's fall. Still, the king wasn't in the business of keeping his brother-in-law happy. Far from it. It was time for the Lord of Summer to learn his place in the Realms, and it wasn't on the throne.

"Will the queen …?" I trailed off, unsure how to phrase my question without giving offence. It was no secret whose side Queen Ceinwen was on.

"Leave Ceinwen to me. I'll give you a message for Lord Eldric."

Kyrrim shifted restlessly. "Sire, I'm not sure it's a good idea for Allegra to deliver the message herself. There have been several attempts on her life."

The king sighed. "I'm well aware of that, Kyrrim. I'm not suggesting she should go alone. She will have you to protect her. And also those estimable friends of hers. I would think twice myself before I crossed Willow Andrakis."

That made me smile. Willow in her full glory was indeed a terrifying sight.

Morwenna, predictably, was the only person in the room who didn't seem amused. "Speaking of protection, sire, I'm concerned about my people's safety after we return."

Almost apologetically, her husband added, "We have grown used to hiding, you see. It's a big step for us to come into the light again."

Ignoring him, Morwenna continued, "Summer won't take the loss of its stolen territory lightly. What's to stop them coming in and slaughtering us all as they did before?"

"What will stop them is that I am back, and they have no excuse, however flimsy, for their actions," Rothbold said, a hint of steel in his voice. The king was obviously still mightily pissed about the whole affair. "If they were to pull such a stunt, the Lords of the other Realms would turn on Kellith, and even his sister couldn't save him from their wrath. He would be deposed, and his family stripped of their titles. You can be sure of that. I would lead the charge myself."

"That's all well and good, but not much consolation to us, is it? We'd still be dead."

The king looked taken aback. He probably wasn't used to such plain speaking. But Morwenna was no noble, schooled since childhood in the ways of the nobility. My opinion of her rose a couple of notches.

"Then we will find some way to guarantee Summer's good behaviour."

"Hostages, perhaps?" Kyrrim suggested, a gleam in his eye.

"Perhaps." Rothbold didn't look keen. It would probably cause him all sorts of diplomatic issues. "That's something I will have to think on."

"It would have to be something like that," Morwenna persisted, "otherwise Kellith will do whatever he wants. You can't trust him."

"I assure you, dear lady, nobody knows that better than me." The king sounded a little exasperated, as well he might, given how he'd spent the last twenty years.

They talked a little more, but there didn't seem to be much we could progress on. We needed to consult with Yriell and the Air fae and get them on board, and someone needed to tell poor Eldric that he was in charge of organising some kind of memorial feast for half the Realms. As soon as possible.

Eventually, my stomach rumbled loud enough to be heard by the others, and Raven laughed and suggested we should finish with some of the delicious cakes the poor cook had been slaving over in that hot kitchen. The king agreed on another meeting in two nights' time, and the tense meeting dissolved into a more social affair.

Raven brought me a plate piled high with food, and offered it with a mocking bow. "Please eat, before that dragon in your stomach wakes fully and destroys us all."

"Very funny," I said, but I jammed the first little cake into my mouth all the same, delighting in the sweet taste that hit my tongue. It was true what they said: the food really was better in Fairyland. Fortunately, the bit about how it would bewitch you and turn you into Rip van Winkle wasn't.

Though I guess that didn't apply to me anymore, anyway. It was easy to forget I was fae, now, with as much magic as anyone in the room.

The king joined us, his plate piled nearly as high as mine. All that statesmanship must work up an appetite. "It's good to see you again, Allegra. No ill effects from your brush with the assassins, I hope?"

Lack of sleep, maybe? Certainly not loss of appetite. I bit into another cake, more decorously this time so I could actually answer the king. "I'm fine, thank you. A little worried about my friends, maybe. They're like family to me."

By now, Nevith's body would have been carried home to Spring. I hoped Willow and Sage were staying holed up in the sith, though, knowing Willow, she'd go out if she wanted to. I tried to remember when our next gig was booked for, but drew a blank. I realised with a shock that I'd even forgotten all about my own work schedule, and had probably missed more than one shift by now.

Dammit. Would I even have a job anymore once this was all over?

"And what of your new family? You have some relatives on the island here, I believe."

Raven almost choked on his cake.

I glanced at him curiously before answering the king. "Yes, Morwenna and Tirgen are my aunt and uncle."

"Actually," Raven said when he'd finished coughing, "that's not exactly true."

"What do you mean, not exactly? It either is or it isn't."

He glanced at Morwenna, but she had her back to us and was chatting animatedly to one of the other townspeople.

"Go on," said the king, frowning at Raven's hesitation.

He sighed heavily, in a kind of *why me?* "Okay. It isn't. She's no relation to you at all."

"Are you drunk? Of course she is. She's my mother's sister."

"That's the problem, see." He took a deep breath. "She's Anawen's sister all right, but Anawen is not your mother."

You could have heard a pin drop. I looked down at my
clenched fists, reliving that earth-shattering moment in
the castle on Arlo. The look of fury on the king's face, the
sympathy on Tirgen's, the complete shock plastered across
the features of my usually unshakeable knight. That last one
had been mirrored in my own expression, I was sure. I'd
felt as if my heart had stopped beating and all the blood had
frozen solid in my veins as a cold chill shuddered over me.

Then Sage exploded. "He said *what*?"

As if her words had released a spell, everyone started
shouting at once. The four of us were gathered in the
garden of Willow's sith—Willow, Sage, Rowan, and me.
Kyrrim had delivered me there, numb and shaking, an hour
earlier, before returning to the king and his duty. I waited
out the storm, the tempest raging in my own heart still
fresh, the hurt still sharp as a knife. I wished that Kyrrim
could have stayed. I felt unmoored, adrift in the world.

I looked at each of them in turn, then drew a deep

breath. "He said that I wasn't my mother's child," I repeated. It still sounded surreal, no matter how many times I heard the words.

"Then whose child are you?" asked Rowan. He was so shocked that he'd lost control of his glamour, and his antlers kept flickering in and out of existence.

"Apparently, I'm the only surviving child of Orlah and Turloch." I licked my lips. My mouth was drier than a desert, though my eyes were filled with tears. I'd already lost my mother once, and now I was losing her all over again. The pain was almost unbearable.

"Orlah?" Willow's eyes were huge. "You don't mean the sister of Lord Perony?"

I nodded miserably, unable to speak. But after another stunned moment of silence, my friends put two and two together and came up with the goods.

"That means—no, it can't." Sage was shaking her head, horror in her eyes.

"That means she's the heir of Illusion," Willow finished for her, her voice grim. "Everyone else is dead. Oh, honey, what a bloody disaster."

"What a bloody bombshell, you mean," Rowan said. "And you had no idea?"

"Of course I had no fucking idea!" I shouted. "I grew up in a cottage in the woods, for the Lady's sake. I trapped rabbits for food and my mother made all our clothes. We grew our own bloody vegetables, Rowan. Does that sound like a noble upbringing?" My voice rose with every word. Did he really think I'd been hiding this from him all these years? "You must think I'm the world's best actress. How can you possibly ask me if I had any idea?"

"Sorry, sorry." He flapped his hands at me in distressed soothing motions. "I'm just shocked."

"Not as shocked as she is," Sage said, shooting him a dirty look. "Honestly, Rowan, use the brains you were born with. Or do those antlers go all the way through that skull of yours?"

"Then who was Anawen if she wasn't your mother?" Willow asked gently.

"My nurse, apparently. When the attack started, she grabbed me and fled across the river in a little rowboat. The rest of my family was at the feast, and they were all killed. I had a brother, a few years older than me. But he was considered old enough to go to the feast with the adults."

A bleak silence greeted this news.

"No wonder Morwenna hates me," I continued. "If her sister hadn't been working as a nurse on the other island, she would have been home safe on Arlo and escaped with the rest of them. For years, Morwenna assumed she was dead. When she finally turned up again after I had left for the mortal world, Morwenna could hardly believe her good fortune. And then Anawen left again, despite Morwenna begging her to stay. You should have seen her face when she was telling us this. She blames me for Anawen's death. She told me so, straight out. Said that Anawen put me before her own family."

"But you *were* her family," Sage objected. "That's a shitty thing to say. You don't have to give birth to someone to be their mother. She had the raising of you since you were a baby. She loved you and cared for you, gave up everything for you. Don't go thinking that she wasn't your mother. She absolutely was."

She'd even killed for me, so she could take Livillia's identity and provide us a safe home, and the woman I knew was no killer. That must have been hard for her. But she'd done it, determined to protect me at any cost. I nodded gratefully at Sage. Her conviction made me feel a little better.

"What did the king say when Raven dropped this bombshell?" Willow asked. Of course her mind would go straight to the political ramifications. She was the heir of a great Realm, after all. She'd been trained to think that way.

The king's face, tight-lipped with fury, swam before my eyes again. "Oh, it's fair to say he was pretty unimpressed. 'And when did you plan on revealing this information?' he said to Morwenna, and if looks could kill, she would have been dead where she stood."

"Seems reasonable," Rowan said. "It's not as though it doesn't affect anything."

"Well, it certainly affects *me*." I couldn't keep the bitterness from my voice.

"The whole thing's bizarre." Willow shook her head. "Why on earth didn't someone say anything before? Like, as soon as you turned up on Arlo? And how long has bloody Raven known?"

"That must be why he was watching over you," Sage said, in the voice of a woman making a great realisation.

"All that time when Thing One and Thing Two were hanging around your garden, spying on you. He could have said something months ago."

It infuriated me, too, that Raven knew so much more about me and my business than I did myself. So many people had made decisions for me, decisions I'd had no part in. Decisions that had changed my life.

"Apparently, he sent the ravens to watch me after Anawen turned up on Arlo. There was some discussion about bringing me in, but they decided between them that it was best if I stayed where I was. My mother was adamant I should be left alone to enjoy the life I'd made for myself, so he kept an eye on me through his pets instead."

"And that upsets you," Rowan said, half-question, half-statement.

"Oh, for God's sake." Sage leaned over and punched him in the shoulder.

"Yes, it upsets me, Rowan. Bloody autocratic fae, thinking they know best about everything. Pushing people around like pawns. Present company excepted, of course."

"You needn't except me," Willow said drily. "I quite enjoy pushing people around like pawns. It's one of my specialties."

Sage punched her, too.

"Ow." Willow rubbed absentmindedly at her arm as she contemplated me. "But Rothbold must be happy, at least, that there's someone of the noble house left, even if they left it to the very last second to tell him so. Imagine the shit fight if he revealed Illusion still existed but it had no Lord."

She shuddered. "Nature abhors a vacuum, but fae nobility abhors one even more. There'd be no end to the jockeying for the position. This way, it's all neat and tidy."

"Except no one asked me if I wanted to be the ruler of Illusion!"

"It wouldn't exactly be a terrible lifestyle," Rowan said cautiously. "I mean, it's not as if Kellith can hate you any more than he already does, and you'd be rich, have an important place at Court"—he waved his hand airily—"all that sort of thing."

"*All that sort of thing* that I have no idea how to do and even less interest in trying? I'm just a guitarist in a band. I work at a service station, Rowan. What do I know about running a whole Realm? I would have to be the least-qualified person for the job they could possibly find."

"Except your blood qualifies you," Willow said. "And a lot of people have gone to a lot of trouble so that you could live to take this role."

"Oh, my *blood*. Like that's got anything to do with it. Morwenna would make a better Lady than I would—that's probably why she couldn't bring herself to say anything. Who wants to watch a newcomer make a mess of everything when you've been doing fine without them for the last twenty years? Hell, half the people on Arlo would probably do a better job than me. This fae system of inheritance is ridiculous. What's wrong with picking people on merit?"

They all stared at me, even Sage, with varying degrees of shock on their faces. I was preaching heresy.

"I think you've been in the mortal world too long," Rowan muttered.

"Why don't we all have a drink?" Sage suggested.

"And something to eat, too," Rowan said, looking around hopefully. "I'm starving."

"There's plenty of food in the kitchen," Willow said. "But Zinnia is still in Spring, so you'll have to help yourself."

Rowan frowned. "How about we go to The Drunken Irishman instead? We could all do with some cheering up. We need to get out and have a good time."

"It's probably safer if we stay here," I said, thinking of Nevith. "There could be assassins lurking anywhere. Better to be safe than sorry."

"Oh, come on," he urged. "It's not as if the Night Vipers are going to be staking out the street outside."

"That's true," Willow said. "Do you know how much it costs to hire those people? They're not street thugs. They only work when they have a carefully orchestrated plan."

"How do you know so much about the way the Night Vipers work?" I asked.

She shrugged. "I'm my father's heir. My education has included a lot of things that aren't public knowledge."

Rowan sat forward, his eyes lighting with interest. "Does that mean your dad has ordered a hit before?"

She regarded him coolly. "I could tell you, but then I'd have to kill you."

"Let's lay off the assassin jokes, okay?" Sage said with sudden fierceness. Of all of us, she'd been closest to Nevith, and she was right.

With his death so fresh, it wasn't in the best taste to be joking about killing people, but Willow just shrugged one elegant shoulder. Everyone had different ways of coping with their grief.

"Come on. Look at you all," Rowan said. "Not a smile among the lot of you. And we haven't had a night out together that wasn't performing in months. It'll be fun."

In the end, we agreed, just to shut him up. But by the time we arrived at The Drunken Irishman, my stomach was rumbling, so maybe it hadn't been such a bad idea after all. Willow pulled into the car park, which was only half full, and we all piled out of her big four-wheel drive and headed inside.

The usual roar of voices greeted us as we entered. No band was playing tonight, so Randall had the jukebox on, blasting out the dulcet tones of AC/DC. It was a popular spot with the local fae community, so there were a few familiar faces here, and we said hello to various people as we threaded our way across the room to an empty table. Sage went to the bar and came back with our usual orders: Chardonnay for Willow, beer for me and Rowan, and a gin and tonic for herself.

"Anyone else hungry?" Rowan asked. "My shout. What would you like?"

He took our orders and headed off to the bar, where he was soon deep in conversation with a blond girl I vaguely remembered seeing at our last gig. When he eventually returned, he brought the girl with him.

"Hey, everyone, this is Atinna. She's Winter."

"Hi, Atinna," we chorused in unison.

Atinna blinked in surprise. She was pretty, of course, being fae, in that pale and delicate way common among Winter fae. "Whoa, are you guys sisters or something?"

"Only in crime," Sage said, and Willow snorted as Rowan introduced the three of us.

Atinna's eyes widened as she realised who Willow was, but she soon got over her nerves at being in such august company and snuggled up against Rowan at the table with us.

Several people around us were already eating, and the smell of food was making my stomach rumble even louder. Fortunately, AC/DC's "Back in Black" was up to the challenge of drowning it out.

Atinna was quiet, but Rowan talked enough for both of them, and he and Sage got into one of their regular arguments. In the middle of a long and impassioned rant from Sage, I noticed Atinna's gaze had snagged on something over by the door. Was she checking out Tony, the bouncer? I looked over my shoulder, following the line of her gaze, and saw Kyrrim in the doorway, scanning the room.

I waved wildly and smiled as his eyes met mine. A thrill of happiness settled on me like a warm blanket as he made his way towards us, though no answering smile lit his face. The crowd parted for him like the Red Sea for Moses. He always seemed to have that effect on people.

He loomed at my side, scowling down at me. "What are you doing here?"

"Waiting for dinner," I said.

He bent, bringing his lips close to my ear. "This is not a safe place for you. You shouldn't be out in public like this. Come with me."

"Whoa, whoa, wait a minute there," Sage said as his hand closed on my arm, ready to haul me bodily from my seat. "Dinner's nearly ready. What's the rush?"

"This is a mistake." His face was cold as he glared down at her. "Allegra shouldn't be here."

"Relax! Who's going to attack her in front of all these witnesses? Here." She snagged an empty chair from the table next to us and shuffled over to make room for him next to me. "Sit down and pretend you're a normal person for a change. You might even like it."

Reluctantly, he took the offered seat, and Rowan smiled encouragingly at him.

"Have you eaten?" he shouted over the music. "Our food should be just about ready."

As if his words were a summoning spell, Cathy appeared carrying three plates. "Chicken burger with the lot?"

"That's me," I said, and she plunked the plate down on the table in front of me, then set the others in front of Willow and Sage before going back for the other meals.

"I ate at the palace," Kyrrim said, but I shoved a chip at him anyway. Who could resist the smell of hot chips?

He frowned as he ate it. "Needs more salt."

I rolled my eyes, but reached for the salt shaker and sprinkled a liberal helping of salt over the food. "Better?"

He snagged another one and chewed, then nodded approvingly.

"Better leave some of those for her," Willow said. "She gets feral when she's hungry."

"Your friend doesn't scare me," he said, unbending a little. Maybe he would actually relax for once. "I know all her ticklish spots."

"For God's sake," Willow said, pretending disgust. "Some of us are trying to eat here."

"I'm going to end up eating half of this anyway," he said to me, indicating the mountain of food on my plate. "You're never going to be able to finish it all on your own." Servings at The Drunken Irishman were always generous, and laced with a little touch of fae magic that kept the customers coming back for more.

"Want to bet?"

"A little thing like you?" He scoffed, clearly not believing me.

"Trust me, it takes a lot of food to power a body this amazing."

His severe expression bloomed into a smile as he leaned closer. "You won't get any argument from me on how amazing you are."

I smiled back and dropped my gaze to my plate. Silence fell as we all focused on our meals for a while—or as much silence as was possible in the middle of a busy pub. AC/DC had been replaced by Queen, another of Randall's favourites, and the place was almost full now. Kyrrim wouldn't have found a spare chair if he'd arrived much later.

Or maybe he would have. I often suspected he was

nudging things with his magic. His iron ward must be truly excellent, as he never seemed to feel the ill effects of using magic in this iron-laden mortal world the way someone like Willow did.

Involuntarily, I glanced at the silver ring on my own hand, a new addition since I'd come into my own magic. It had belonged to Kyrrim's grandmother, and he had all but forced it on me when we first discovered I was fae and needed protection from the poisonous atmosphere of the human world. I stroked my thumb across the delicate engraving on the ring. I'd thought myself human long enough to have an appreciation for rings and their significance as a gift between lovers. I didn't know exactly what he was promising with the gift of this particular ring, but he'd been most insistent that I keep it, and it had come straight from his hand to mine. That had to mean something.

I had to remember, though, that I was fae, and as long as Kellith didn't succeed in bumping me off, I could expect a long lifespan. There was no need to rush into anything, or force something that wasn't there between us. It was enough for now to enjoy his company. It gave me immense pleasure to watch him interacting with my friends, seeing how quickly they had accepted him as one of us. This was a new experience for me, as they had never approved of any of my previous boyfriends.

Once we'd all taken the edge off our hunger, conversation resumed. With Atinna here, of course, we couldn't talk about any of the pressing concerns that loomed large in my mind. But maybe that was a good thing. I felt myself relaxing more and more as time wore on and we kept the conversation light. Rowan raved about a movie he'd seen recently, and Atinna asked lots of questions about the band. It was good to pretend, at least for a moment, that such things were our only concerns, to have a break from the drama that our lives had become lately.

Atinna helped herself to a chip from Rowan's plate and pulled a face. "You were right," she said to Kyrrim, "they do need more salt." She stretched across the table to reach the salt shaker, which was still sitting beside my plate. Her hand hovered for the barest instant over my food as she did so, and the large ruby of her ring caught my eye.

In a move that made me almost jump out of my skin in shock, Kyrrim's hand shot out and grabbed her wrist. Time seemed to stop as her gaze met his, full of calculation. Rowan's burger paused halfway to his mouth, his eyes wide with surprise.

"What are you playing at?" Kyrrim growled at her. "Who sent you?"

Suddenly, all was chaos. With her free hand, she flipped the table, sending plates and glasses smashing to the floor. With the surprise her move gained her, she twisted herself free of Kyrrim's grip and fled towards the door.

Kyrrim leapt up with a roar of rage, drawing Ecfirrith in the same movement. He plunged after her. "Stop her!"

But the crowd seemed disinclined to get involved, stepping out of her way rather than trying to halt her flight. Only Tony, Randall's son, moved forward from his position at the door, a determined look on his broad face. Like his father, he was part-troll, and even in his human guise he was nearly seven feet tall and built like a truck. Atinna's slight figure stood no chance against him.

"Be careful," Kyrrim shouted, "she has a poisoned ring."

"No swords in here!" Randall roared from behind the bar, but he may as well have saved his breath, as Kyrrim didn't slow down or sheathe the sword. There were a few screams as people scrambled to get out of his way.

Tony moved to block the door, but the woman running toward him didn't falter. She lashed a blast of icy cold air at him, and his hair suddenly sparkled with ice in the dim light. I was already running after Kyrrim, but behind me, I heard a sudden gasp of indrawn breath from one of the others. It wasn't done to display magic, even here, where so many of the patrons were fae. There were still plenty of humans inside the bar, people who had no notion that magic was real, and it would be better if their ignorance on that point was preserved.

But Atinna wasn't holding back. Her Winter magic made no difference to Tony. Rocks didn't feel the cold, and trolls weren't much different. She tried to dodge past him, but there was barely anywhere to dodge. He filled almost the whole doorway on his own. He was clearly determined to keep her trapped until Kyrrim and his sword arrived on the scene.

She cast a wild look over her shoulder and found the knight almost upon her. So she dodged aside and threw her magic at the big front windows instead.

In an instant, cracks formed, as the glass was suddenly exposed to below-freezing temperatures. In her magic's wake, she leapt, right leg raised in a kick. She slammed through the window and landed in a tinkle of glass on the pavement outside, rolling to protect herself with the agility of a seasoned pro and coming smoothly to her feet. She took off down the street while the rest of us were still struggling to grasp what had just happened.

Tony and Kyrrim rushed out into the street, and Kyrrim gave chase, but he was soon back, shaking his head. I met him outside the door.

"No sign of her," he said, his face dark. "She must have gated away immediately."

"Who the hell was that?" Tony asked, scratching his big head in puzzlement.

"Good question." Kyrrim's hard gaze settled on Rowan, who was bunched up in the doorway with Sage and Willow. "Who was she, Rowan?"

My friends joined us in the street. The crowd of onlookers who threatened to follow thought better of it when Kyrrim scowled at them, deciding it might be safer to stay inside. Only Randall came out to inspect the damage to his windows.

"I only met her once before," Rowan said, a little horrified to be on the receiving end of Kyrrim's glare. At least the knight had sheathed his sword again. "I thought she was just a fan, you know? Girls love musicians."

"I thought she was someone you knew," Kyrrim raged at him. "How could you bring a stranger into Allegra's orbit *now*? Are you completely stupid?"

"There's a popular rumour going around to that effect," Willow said. Neither man paid her any attention.

"Now he's going to say *I told you so*, isn't he?" Sage said.

"The rest of you are no better." Kyrrim's glittering gaze raked us all. Even Tony and Randall, who were completely blameless in whatever he was accusing us of, looked reflexively guilty. "Going out in public as if you didn't just get attacked by the Night Vipers. Who do you think that woman was working for? She was one of them, and all she had to do was smile at Stupid here and you all accepted her without question. Clearly, there's only one thing to be done."

"What's that?" Willow asked coolly, the only one apparently not shaken by his tirade.

"Come with me," he said.

9

We didn't go far. Kyrrim marched us down the street and into an alley that I remembered quite well. It was here that I had opened my very first gate into the Wilds, my first use of the king's generous gift to me, a lowly changeling. Back when I still believed that I had no magic of my own and that I *was* a changeling.

But we were opening no gates into the Wilds tonight. Kyrrim and his magic sword were like an express ticket to anywhere you wanted to go. There was no following the shifting paths of the Greenways through dangerous territory with him around—all that it took was a few slashes of Ecfirrith through the air and bingo! You could be anywhere in either world that you wanted to be.

Tight-lipped, he led us all through the gate onto the now-familiar path leading to the castle on the hill. The others looked around with interest, since this was their first visit. It was dark, so we couldn't see any rainbow drakes playing above the lake, but my friends weren't stupid.

"Arlo, I presume?" Willow asked.

"Yes," I said, in no mood to be expansive. Yet another attempt had just been made on my life. How many more of these could I hope to live through? I glanced at Kyrrim as a sudden thought occurred to me. "I suppose she *was* trying to kill me? Not you? You were eating from my plate, too."

"I don't think there's any doubt about that," he said.

He strode off up the road towards the castle, so we followed. I'd spent so much time here lately that it was starting to feel like a second home.

"Um, Kyrrim?" Rowan sounded as if he was afraid the knight would bite his head off if he spoke. "What exactly are we doing here?"

"Parking you people somewhere that you can't get into any more trouble," he threw over his shoulder. Man, that was one grumpy Hawk.

"For how long?"

"As long as it takes."

Rowan and Willow exchanged looks. "But the band—" Rowan began.

"Doesn't matter in the slightest," Kyrrim said, before he could finish. "All that matters is keeping you idiots alive. With or without your cooperation."

We arrived at the gate and walked straight in, since there was no need for guards here. The island was a fortress, and Kyrrim the only key.

"So we're prisoners?" Willow's voice was incredulous. "Are you serious?"

Kyrrim ran lightly up the front steps and opened the door, not even bothering to reply.

She glared at him. "You can't keep us here against our wills."

Kyrrim sighed, sounding exhausted all of a sudden, and I felt a twinge of guilt at the worry I was causing him. "You can see it like that if you wish. Or you can see it as a chance to help right a terrible wrong and keep yourselves alive into the bargain. Your choice."

He pushed open the door and gestured us inside. We filed in and found some other people at last. Grindel and another man were crossing the foyer. They looked up in surprise at the sound of the door opening.

"Sir Knight! My lady." That was meant for me, of course. I managed to control my flinch, but only just. "We weren't expecting you back so soon."

Kyrrim took charge at once. "I hope you can find bedrooms for these other guests, too?"

"Of course."

"Is Raven here?"

A new voice answered from the top of the staircase. "I am, indeed. And I see you've got some friends with you." He hurried down the stairs, elegant in a blue velvet doublet over dark pants. He looked like he'd just been on his way to dinner at Court.

"I hope we're not interrupting anything?" I said.

"If you were, it would be the most welcome of interruptions. Please introduce me to your friends. The Lady Willow I already know, of course." He bowed low to Willow, who gave him a perfunctory nod.

"Hi, Bran," she said, as if deliberately trying to be as informal as possible to balance out his excess of manners.

"This is Raven," I said to Sage and Rowan.

Sage looked at him with open hostility. "The guy who kidnapped you?"

"The arsehole who destroyed my garage?" Rowan added, in tones of outrage.

Raven bowed a little mockingly to them both. "The very same." He looked at me enquiringly until I remembered my manners.

"And this is Sage and Rowan," I added.

"Lovely to meet you both," he said, a wicked gleam in his eye.

Rowan frowned. "I wish I could say the same, but that was a jerk move, blowing up my garage."

"I will, of course, pay in full for the damage I caused."

Only partially mollified, Rowan huffed, "You couldn't have found a less destructive way to warn her?"

"I shall be sure to consider all the options most carefully next time I have to save your friend from imminent death."

Willow rolled her eyes. "It seems we're going to be staying here a while."

Raven grinned. "Excellent! We can all get to know one another. I'm sure we'll be buddies in no time."

Rowan muttered something about dead bodies, but everyone chose to ignore him.

"Come and join me in the dining room. I was just about to have my midnight meal. And that will give Grindel a chance to prepare your rooms." He nodded at Grindel, who took the hint and disappeared towards the servants' quarters.

We followed him down the corridor to the dining room, where he settled everyone at the table while servants brought extra place settings. My stomach reminded me that my last meal had been interrupted, and I settled down to enjoy the food and tried not to think about the fact that that interruption had saved me from an assassin yet again.

"Was this really necessary?" I muttered to Kyrrim, once everyone had been served and the general chatter masked our conversation somewhat. "They could have stayed at Willow's sith."

"*Could* have, certainly. But would they?" Fury darkened his golden eyes again. "I can't believe you went to The Drunken Irishman. The only way you could have made it easier for the assassins to find you was if you had stood outside the gates of Whitehaven and yelled, 'Come and get me.' What were you thinking?"

I sighed. Willow had seemed so sure when she said that the Night Vipers wouldn't be lurking in wait for us. But I didn't want to pin the blame on her and put her in the firing line.

"I guess it was stupid."

He snorted, but I powered on.

"But we didn't think it would be a problem. And I don't want to spend my life hiding."

He caressed my hand under the table. "And I don't want to spend mine regretting that I didn't do enough to save you. Please, Allegra, I'm begging you. Take this seriously."

"I do, I promise you. But you can't *save me* from life. I won't be locked away and guarded like dragon's gold. I have things I need to do—and so do you. You already have a full-time job protecting the king. You can't protect me, too."

His face darkened with frustration, but it was the truth. "I can't lose you."

I squeezed his hand. "You won't."

He closed his eyes for a moment, then blew out a defeated sigh. "Will you at least stay on Arlo for now?"

"Well, the king did want me to talk to Eldric and—"

"I think we can come up with a better plan." He raised his voice. "Rowan."

"Yes?" Rowan was seated on the other side of the table, in between Willow and Sage. There was a wariness in his expression, as if he didn't quite trust Kyrrim not to bite.

"You've just been elected for the job of visiting Eldric and explaining to him that he is providing a feast for half of the kingdom. As soon as possible."

Rowan's eyes widened. "Elected? I didn't get a vote."

"It wasn't that kind of election," Kyrrim replied smoothly.

"But … but I left the Realms to get away from all that political stuff. I'm just a drummer. I don't do Lords."

"No one is asking you to *do* him," Sage said. "Just to go see him. What's the problem? Autumn is your home away from home. You visit there all the time."

"Yeah, but I don't go visiting *Lord Eldric*." He looked around for support, but found none.

"Come on, Rowan," Willow said. "You'd be perfect for the job. Just because you *do* visit Autumn all the time."

"That's right." Kyrrim nodded. "If the king sends a messenger from the palace, tongues will wag. Our enemies will know something is going on. But there is nothing more natural than a son of Autumn returning home for a visit. And if you go, Allegra can stay safe here, where the Night Vipers can't reach her."

Rowan sighed, clearly seeing the sense in Kyrrim's argument. "All right, then. But you have to tell me what to say. Won't Eldric think it's odd that the request doesn't come from the king?"

"That's easy," Raven said. "I'm sure we can get you something signed by the king. Eldric will understand why the king doesn't wish to be seen initiating a memorial for Illusion, considering his ties with Summer. And it's not Lord Eldric's place to question the king's wishes, anyway."

"So I'll just be the messenger boy?" Rowan looked relieved.

"Sure," Raven said. "It'll be easy. I could do it myself."

"No!" Willow and Kyrrim said in unison.

Raven feigned a look of hurt, putting his hand dramatically to his heart. "What? I'm good at running messages."

"You're good at causing trouble, you mean," Willow snapped. "Your little kidnapping stunt has put you on Kellith's radar. They'll be watching you."

"Does anyone else get the impression that the lady doesn't approve of me?" Raven asked the room in general. No one answered him.

"It's settled, then," Kyrrim said with satisfaction. "Rowan will go to Autumn, and the rest of you will stay here and do what you can to help the Illusionists prepare." His eyes lingered on me in particular, as if reinforcing the need for me to hide away from my enemies.

"You know," I said, "I understand you're worried, but Arlo is not this impregnable fortress you make it out to be. Sure, the place is warded against random strangers gating in, but what's to stop anyone with wings from flying in, the way Raven does? At least one of those Night Vipers that attacked the sith had Air magic. There could be others."

"First they'd have to know where we were," Raven said. "This area of Night is uninhabited and very difficult to access. No one comes here by chance."

"But it wouldn't *be* by chance, would it? The Vipers have a mission, and I bet they have plenty of resources to help them carry it out."

"So what are you saying?" Frustration was written all over Kyrrim's face. "That we should just give up and let them have you?"

"No, of course not. I'm just pointing out that Arlo may not be as safe as everyone seems to think. My hiding here is no guarantee of protection."

"Well, partying at The Drunken Irishman was no damn protection either," Kyrrim ground out, annoyed all over again. "This is the best we can do in the circumstances. If I could, I'd post a dozen guards on you, night and day, but I can't."

"Just as well, because I couldn't stand that. You're off with the king more than half the time, so you really need to give up this idea that it's your job to protect me. You're going to have to accept that the rest of us are pretty capable, too."

His eyes narrowed, but what was the point of pretending? He couldn't be everywhere at once.

"Maybe what Al is trying to say," Sage said, hastily stepping into the frosty silence, "is that we need to take the fight to Kellith. We keep dodging his bullets. Maybe we should be firing a few at him."

Raven laughed. "I like your enthusiasm, but are you seriously suggesting we should take out a Lord of the Realms?"

She eyed him challengingly. "Why not? I think he's earned it."

Kyrrim waved a dismissive hand. "Whether or not he's earned it, we don't have the resources. Do you have any idea how well protected he is?"

"Besides," Willow said, a regretful note in her voice, "it wouldn't be a good look for a bunch of people who are known to be working with the king to get involved in a plot against the queen's brother."

Raven grinned. "Yes, one plot at a time, please."

Sage folded her arms across her chest, a disappointed look on her face. "Well, it was just a suggestion. It sure would solve a lot of our problems."

Kyrrim pushed back from the table and stood up. "An excellent suggestion, too, but sadly one we can't take up." He looked around at us. "I have to get back to Whitehaven, but I have a suggestion for all of you: get some sleep."

10

The morning sun woke me. I opened one bleary eye and cursed myself for forgetting to close the curtains before I went to bed. I shut my eyes again and tried to go back to sleep, chasing a dream that had involved a naked Kyrrim and a lot of melted chocolate, but it was no use.

Once awake, my stupid brain insisted on running round and round in the same old circles. My mother's death. The many attempts on my own life. My hatred for Kellith, my worry for Squeak—all of it. How was I ever going to get out of this mess? Even when Arlo was restored to its rightful place and Illusion was no longer a lost Realm, what was to stop Kellith continuing in his efforts to kill me? Maybe that would be the one advantage of becoming the Lady of Illusion—that I'd have the kind of security that he apparently enjoyed.

Other than that, there was nothing about the prospect of ruling Illusion that appealed. I knew nothing of governing; I hadn't even known I was fae last week. And now the king expected me to just walk in and somehow know what to do? All the people of Arlo would be depending on me, and I was terrified of letting them down.

"Oh, for God's sake." I threw back the sheet and hurled myself out of bed. "Stop thinking!"

I was going to drive myself to drink if I kept this up. I had to find something to distract me from the endless agonising circling of my thoughts. Sighing, I threw on my clothes and left the room.

There was no sign of my friends downstairs. They were probably all enjoying the slumber that I should be getting, too. It wasn't as if I'd had that much sleep lately. Why couldn't I still be snoring in my bed upstairs?

I surprised a girl on a short ladder who was dusting the tops of the windows in the dining room, but no one else was there.

She clung to the top of her ladder and gazed down at me in apprehension. "Can I help you, my lady?"

I really wished everyone would stop calling me that. "Do you know where Raven is? Or any of the people who came with me last night?"

"I couldn't say, my lady. I think Raven might be down in the town with Morwenna. I don't know."

"Thanks."

Well, at least that gave me a destination. But first, some food. I wandered back down the corridor in the direction of the kitchen, guided by a delightful smell of roasting meat. The place was a hive of activity, but I managed to sneak a couple of bananas from a bowl near the door before anyone could make too much fuss at my presence.

Munching on a banana, I left the castle and headed down the hill toward the town. A handful of rainbow drakes were in the skies above the lake, reminding me painfully of Squeak's problems. The harsh caw of a raven caught my attention, and I looked around, but didn't see the birds.

My feet knew the way to Morwenna's house on their own now, though I hesitated before I knocked. This aversion to seeing Morwenna was an almost physical feeling, and I had to force myself to rap sharply on the door. What was I, twelve? She didn't like me—so what? I ought to be able to cope with that. And I refused to take on any guilt over my mother's death, whatever Morwenna thought. I had no control over what Anawen had done or not done. I hadn't even seen her in over four years before the night she'd turned up dying at Jamison's sith.

Maybe I was a coward, but I was still relieved when Lirra opened the door and not her mother.

"Hello," she said. "Are you here to see Mama? I'm sorry, but she's not here."

"Actually, I don't really know why I'm here. I was sort of looking for Raven, to see if there was something I could do to help."

"I haven't seen him."

"Ah. Well, I guess I'll go looking for him. Unless Squeak has woken up?"

She gave me a sympathetic smile. "Not yet. Mama says he should wake at dusk tonight."

"Can I see him?"

"There's no change." She stepped outside and pulled the door shut behind her. "Why don't I come and help you look for Raven?"

"Okay."

"We'll try down by the water. He might be talking to Papa."

I fell into step beside her, and we headed down the road towards the gleaming blue of the lake I could see peeking between the houses.

"Your papa is a skincrafter, right?"

"That's right."

"What exactly does a skincrafter do?"

"The drakes moult three or four times as they grow. Skincrafters collect the discarded skins and turn them into beautiful pieces of art or clothing. Or even jewellery."

"Will Squeak moult?"

She laughed. "No, Squeak is an adult. Any of the drakes you see flying are adults. They don't moult. It's only during the growing phases that the young ones moult. All their early life, the drakes are aquatic."

"So your father has to find the discarded skins in the lake?"

She nodded. "Yes, a lot of them he has to dive for. The very youngest drakes never leave the water. Those skins are very pliant, and make beautiful gloves. But, of course, they're small. When they're a year old, the drakes leave the water and spend most of their time building their muscles by climbing trees."

"So they don't have wings?"

"They have proto-wings, and as they develop, the drakes start using them to glide from tree to tree. But it takes another year at least after they've begun gliding before their wings grow strong enough to support them in true flight. They have one final moult before they're ready to take to the skies for good. These skins are worth a lot more, because they're so much bigger than the previous ones. But of course they can be hard to come by, considering they're often lodged high in the treetops."

No wonder Tirgen had such well-developed arm muscles, between diving for the young skins and climbing trees for the older ones. And that was only the first part of the job. He still had to turn the skins into something beautiful once he'd found them.

A flurry of rainbow drakes swooped overhead. I looked up and smiled at their antics as they dipped and dived, chasing each other through the air.

Lirra pointed. "Oh, look, there's Minki."

They all looked the same to me, so I didn't know which one she meant until a small blue shape detached itself from the crowd and swooped down to land on her shoulder. Minki was very pretty, her blue shading to a deep violet around her neck and down her breast. Somehow I knew without being told that this beauty was a she. Affectionate, too. She rubbed her delicate head on Lirra's cheek, in the same way that Squeak used to do to me.

The little creature chirped something in Lirra's ear, then peered at me.

Lirra laughed. "They're very curious creatures. She's

wondering who you are. It's not very often the drakes get to see new faces around here."

"Well, that will be changing soon."

"Yes. It's exciting, isn't it?"

"Mmmm," I murmured noncommittally.

She didn't appear to notice my lack of enthusiasm. "I've seen a lot of the Realms from above. But I've never been anywhere except Arlo in my whole life. I can't wait to see more of the world up close." She smiled at me. "I'm so glad you came. Finally, we're almost at the end of our exile."

"I'm sure it would have happened sooner or later."

"Maybe. But you're a real hero. First you saved the king and now you're saving us."

I glanced away, embarrassed. I certainly didn't feel like a hero. I only did what anyone else would have done in the same circumstances—it wasn't as if I could have just stood by and done nothing.

We had arrived at the lake shore near the long jetty that jutted out into the water. A handful of boats were drawn up beside the jetty, some bobbing from their painters, others pulled right up onto the small stretch of sand. There was no sign of Tirgen. I shaded my eyes and looked out over the sparkling lake. No sign of him out there, either, unless he was underwater searching for skins.

Lirra sat down on a log, picking up a small stick and throwing it out over the lake. To my surprise, Minki leapt from her shoulder and flew after the stick, catching it in mid-air before it disappeared into the water. She returned it as proudly as any golden retriever, dropping it by Lirra's feet with an expectant look in her large golden eyes. Obligingly, Lirra threw it again, and I laughed at the little creature's excitement as she took off after it once more.

Lirra looked up at me shyly. "I heard you took on Blethna Arbre without even using any magic. That must have been amazing."

I sat down beside her on the log. "Actually, it was scary. It was sheer luck that I didn't manage to get myself killed." I sighed. "And, of course, it didn't turn out so well for poor Squeak."

"No." The girl looked sombre for a moment, but then she smiled as Minki dropped the stick back at her feet. "Why did you call him Squeak, anyway?"

I laughed. "I didn't actually mean to, it just kind of happened. Someone asked me what his name was and put me on the spot. I blurted out the first thing that came to mind. Do you think it's a stupid name?"

She looked surprised. "Not at all. It suits him perfectly. I thought you had picked it because of the way he snores."

It was news to me that rainbow drakes even snored. "I've never seen him sleep before. We haven't been together very long, you know. What do you mean?"

"It's the cutest thing. When he snores, he makes this little squeaking sound with every breath he takes."

I smiled. "That *is* cute. But I feel a bit bad that he's the only drake without a proper name." I paused, wondering if I should go on. In for a penny, in for a pound, as Sage would say. "I had the feeling that your mother didn't approve of his name."

Lirra threw the stick again, but this time Minki wasn't fast enough. The stick hit the water, followed a moment later by the blue body of the drake, making a great splash. She snatched the stick up anyway, and leapt back into the air, spraying water behind her.

"Oh, no, Minki! Get off! You're all wet," Lirra objected as Minki deposited the stick at her feet again. The girl made shooing motions with her hands. "Go away and dry off."

The little drake eyed her, head tipped to one side, as if wondering whether she really meant it. Lirra resolutely ignored the stick, and after a moment, Minki leapt skyward again and went to find her friends.

"There are a lot of things my mother doesn't approve of," Lirra said. "I don't take too much notice. You shouldn't either."

We both watched the drakes cavorting above the lake in silence for a while. It was a warm morning, and looked like it would be a beautiful day.

"Isn't it about time for you to sleep?" I asked her. "You guys keep a nocturnal schedule, don't you?"

"Schedules have gone out the window," she said. "Everyone's too excited about going home."

"When things calm down, I have to get your mother to give me some more lessons in magic." Much as I would hate working with Morwenna again, I would hate even more to be unable to dispel my own illusions when I was representing the Realm.

"Are you still having trouble? Have you been practising?"

"I haven't done any magic since the fight with Blethna

Arbre." Part of that was because I had been just too busy, but another part had been nerves. Without Squeak, what would I do if I got stuck? I would hate to have to ask Morwenna for help again.

Lirra gave me a severe look that reminded me very much of her mother. "You'll never get anywhere without practice." Oh, joy, she even sounded like Morwenna. "You should be using this time to work on your skills."

"Surely there's something more helpful I could be doing." I stood up. "We should keep looking for Raven."

She didn't move from her log. "I'm sure Mama has everything under control. Really, I don't see what all the fuss is about. What is there for us to do? It's up to the Air and Earth mages to get us settled again." She shrugged. "You may as well practice. I can help you." I must have looked sceptical, because she added, "I know I'm not as good as Mama, but I do know what I'm doing."

Feeling pressured, I shrugged and sat down again. "Okay. Don't say I didn't warn you. If we have to go running to your mother for help, I'm blaming you."

She laughed. "I'm not scared of Mama. Have a little confidence in yourself. I'm sure we won't need any help. I can feel the power in you."

"You can?" I looked at her in surprise. "What does it feel like?"

"Like a fire. I can feel the warmth radiating from you. You're strong; you just have to believe it."

Awesome. She sounded like my old yoga teacher. "Then tell me what to do, sensei."

She looked puzzled. She'd probably never heard that word before. We'd have to get her some Teenage Mutant Ninja Turtles movies. That would really rock her world. "Change into someone."

"That's it? Some teacher you are."

She laughed. "Don't be such a baby. It's not hard. You've already changed into at least one other person. Your magic has that image forever now. All you have to do is want it."

The last person whose identity I had assumed was my mother. That didn't seem like a great choice in the circumstances. "What about someone new? Anyway, it's not really the changing *into* that I have a problem with. It's the changing *back*."

"Sure, if you want to." She reached up and untied the ribbon that held back the long fall of her dark hair. It slithered free around her shoulders as she drew the length of blue satin out. "Here, use this."

"Thanks." With it in my hand, I suddenly felt nervous. This magic thing was so new. I clenched the ribbon in my fist and looked down at it, as if the secrets of illusion would be revealed if only I concentrated hard enough.

"Go on," she prompted. "It's easy. Look."

In the blink of an eye, Morwenna sat next to me on the log. I jerked back in surprise, and Lirra threw back her head and let out a peal of laughter. It was the most carefree expression I had ever seen on Morwenna's stern face.

"Did I catch you by surprise? How about this one?"

Morwenna disappeared, replaced by Tirgen, complete with the brown vest and trousers he normally wore.

"I don't think I will ever get used to that, no matter how many times I see it."

"Your turn."

I nodded. She made it look so easy and, truthfully, I'd never had all that much trouble with this part. It was only my nerves about retaking my own form that held me back. I had to stop being such a wuss. Closing my eyes, I drew a deep breath and focused on the slippery feel of the ribbon in my hands, remembering how it had looked in Lirra's hair. How pretty Lirra herself looked this morning, in a dress the same shade as the ribbon, her green eyes open and friendly.

I opened my eyes. "How did I do?"

She clapped. "Wonderfully! It's just like looking in a mirror."

That seemed bizarre coming from the mouth of Tirgen, but I knew what she meant.

"Now for the hard part," I said.

She shook her head reprovingly at me. "You mean, 'now comes the part that is just as easy as the first part'. You're making this into a much bigger thing than it needs to be. Close your eyes again, if you find that helps, then simply become yourself."

If only it were that easy. I closed my eyes, sighing. Maybe she was right, and I was making too big a deal of the whole thing. Just because I'd gotten stuck once before didn't mean it always had to turn out that way. I breathed out slowly, trying to calm my racing heart. I could do this.

I pictured my own face as I saw it every morning in the

mirror—short blonde hair, blue eyes, a mouth that maybe didn't smile as much as it ought to. Pale skin, with a sprinkling of freckles across the nose.

I opened my eyes and raised a hopeful eyebrow. "Well?"

She shook her head. "Don't try so hard. Just become. Turning back into yourself should be like slipping on your most comfortable pair of pyjamas. Like getting home at the end of a long day. Try again."

Pyjamas. Okaaay. I was more a sleep-in-the-nude kind of girl, but whatever. I clasped my hands in my lap, admiring Lirra's long, shapely fingers there. I would not clench my fists. I would not fight this. I drew a deep breath and tried to find my own, comfortable skin.

"Again."

Dammit. Now I couldn't help clenching my fists. "I told you this was a bad idea. Morwenna is going to give me that glare again if I have to come begging for help."

Instantly, Tirgen's face was replaced with his wife's. "Morwenna is going to glare at you until you manage to do it on your own."

And she did, ferociously. Great. As if that was going to help.

Fists still clenched, I tried to find the warmth of that magic that Lirra said she could feel and blasted it with my frustration and anger.

"Whoa! I felt that." Glancing down at herself, now back in her own lithe form, Lirra let out a low whistle. "That was powerful. And you forced me back into my own form, too."

I looked down and found I was my own self again. Well,

it had taken a few tries, but at least I had gotten there in the end, and without having to resort to running to Morwenna for help. I wasn't sure my pride could have taken a beating like that this morning.

Lirra was still staring at me in astonishment.

"What? You look surprised. Didn't you think I could do it?"

"It's not that. Mama is the only person I've ever known who can force someone else into their true form. Your magic is far stronger than anyone realises." Her eyes shone with hero worship, and I shifted uncomfortably on the log.

"Probably just beginner's luck."

"Not luck but *blood*. You truly are the Lady of Illusion."

11

Dusk was falling as I headed back to the castle from Morwenna's house. Squeak was not yet awake, and she said it might still be an hour or two, judging by the depth of his slumber, so I decided to grab some food before the big moment.

She had been frostily polite to me every time I had run into her during the course of the day, and had even offered to let me join her family for their meal, but there was no warmth in the offer and I had no trouble declining it. She only did it because she thought she must, because I was to be her new Lady, however much that rankled her, and I had no desire to spend any more time with her than I absolutely had to.

As it turned out, there was a bonus to eating at the castle—when I found my friends gathered in the large hall of the castle, Kyrrim was with them.

He smiled as I came in. "I was just about to come look for you."

I threw my arms around his neck. "I didn't expect you back so soon. I thought the king was keeping you busy."

"I'm here on the king's business," he said, which took some of the shine off seeing him. It didn't matter how many times I reminded myself that this was his job, I still couldn't help resenting it ever so slightly every time he put his job before me. "I came to bring Rowan the letter that he needs to take to Eldric."

I glanced across at Rowan, who was looking a little nervous now that the moment was here. "Have you eaten yet?" I asked him.

"No," he said, "we were waiting for you."

"Excellent. I was hoping you'd say that. I could smell something delicious the minute I walked in the door."

"That's our dinner," Sage said with satisfaction. "I had a chat to the cook earlier and explained to him that we're not nocturnal. He said he'd throw a little something together for us."

That was another reason I hadn't accepted Morwenna's ungracious offer to eat at her house. They'd been eating porridge, when my stomach was craving dinner. They didn't eat their main meal until the wee, small hours of the morning. Being in a band meant the four of us kept some pretty late hours by human standards, but we were still mainly adapted to a diurnal rhythm. We liked to have our main meal somewhat earlier than four o'clock in the morning.

"I'll go and let you enjoy your meal," Kyrrim said.

"Can't you stay? Just for a little while?"

"You know I'd love to, but I need to visit Yriell tonight and bring her up to speed with events."

"Well, if you wait a little while, I can come with you."

He shook his head decisively. "It's safer if you stay here. And anyway, isn't Squeak waking up soon?"

That was true. Regretfully, I watched him stride from the great hall, then followed my friends to the dining room.

There, it became evident that the cook had put in rather more work than his words had suggested. This was not some small thing he'd whipped up at a moment's notice. Obviously, great care had gone into the preparation of this meal. There was a whole roasted duck in the centre of the table, covered in a rich orange glaze. An array of salads sat around it, as well as platters of sliced beef. There was also a tray of individual cakes—so many that we couldn't have eaten them all even if we'd ignored all the rest of the food on the table.

I felt a twinge of guilt. The kitchen staff must have spent hours on this—and soon they would start work again, presumably, feeding Raven and whomever else turned up for the fae main meal. We'd just created a lot of extra work for them. When were they supposed to sleep?

Sage whistled as she surveyed the groaning table. "Are we expecting another hundred people that no one's told me about? That is one hell of a lot of food."

When dinner was over, Rowan left, escorted by Raven, who was taking him down to Night so he could begin the long trek through the Wilds to Autumn. He looked nervous, but I had little thought to spare for his nerves since my own were consuming me.

Sage and Willow flanked me as we made our way down through the town to Morwenna's house. Several of the townspeople were out and about, and we received many curious looks.

"Do you reckon they're staring because we're so goddamned beautiful?" Sage asked after the third man had stopped what he was doing to watch us walk down the street.

"Obviously," Willow said, tossing her red-gold mane of curls. "Or, at least, because *I* am so goddamned beautiful. They'll probably spend the rest of the evening composing sonnets in my honour."

"It's a little unnerving, though," Sage said. "I feel like a monkey at the zoo. Can't you tell them to tone it down a bit?"

Willow glanced sidelong at me. "Allowances must be made for my adoring public. They can't help being entranced by my beauty." We all knew perfectly well they were staring at me, had been staring at me ever since my first visit to this place. They'd all known who I was before I had. But it obviously amused my friends to pretend otherwise.

They kept up this kind of stupid banter all the way to Morwenna's house. At least it took my mind off Squeak.

Tirgen opened the door at my knock and gestured for us to follow him through to the room out the back, where Morwenna already waited. Candles lined the windowsills and the long work bench, filling the room with the smell of coconut and lime and something else I couldn't quite identify. She nodded as we came in, but didn't speak.

I went straight to the bed and sat down next to Squeak. His front feet were twitching as if he were in the middle of a dream. Morwenna had removed the bandages from his left wing but she still had it strapped to his body in three places so that he couldn't move it. There were several ragged holes in the membrane, one nearly the size of my clenched fist. The edges of the hole were darkened with scar tissue, lumpy and malformed. The contrast with the smooth and healthy skin surrounding it was horrifying.

I looked at Morwenna, appalled. "Is he in pain?"

"Shouldn't be," she said. "I still have him pumped full of painkillers. That's why I have the wing immobilised. If he doesn't have the pain warning him off, he might try to use it, and that would be disastrous." Her voice was brisk and businesslike, and I wondered what it would be like to be under her care. Her bedside manner definitely needed work.

Still, she had done a wonderful job on the rest of him. I could hardly believe this was the same drake I'd left in her care three nights before. The holes in his wing were the only sign of damage left. His breast shimmered green, his jewelled hide glinting in the soft candlelight as beautifully as it had ever done—except for those three dreadful holes.

He made a muffled chirping noise in his sleep and shifted restlessly.

"Any minute now," Morwenna said, coming to my side and watching him carefully. "See the way his eyelids are twitching?"

I rested my hand gently on his emerald side. "What do you want me to do?"

"Reach out to him down your bond. He'll probably be scared and a little disoriented when he wakes. Reassure him that he's safe. It will help him to know that you're here."

Obediently, I reached out but there was still nothing at the other end of our bond. Nevertheless, I projected waves of love and reassurance as hard as I could, desperate to help the poor little guy. It was my fault he'd gotten into this mess.

"Will these holes close up any further?" I was very afraid I already knew the answer to that question, but I had to ask.

Morwenna's answer was short and sharp. "No."

I looked despairingly at the gaping holes in the gleaming perfection of Squeak's wing. "But fae healing …"

"Can't work miracles," she snapped. "Our magic heals our own bodies, but we can't transfer that to anyone else's. For that, we are left with regular healing."

"But his burns," I protested. "There's not a trace of them now. In the human world that would have taken months, and he probably still would have ended up with scars."

"Oh, we can use our magic to speed up the natural processes. But we can't force a body to do things it was never capable of in the first place. That tissue was gone. We can't conjure more out of thin air."

Squeak shifted again and then stretched from nose to tail, his four legs sticking out as straight as posts. His eyes blinked, once, twice, then opened fully, gazing at nothing in a bleary way. All of a sudden, I felt him at the end of our bond—mainly confusion, with a little bit of hunger thrown in. My own stomach, even though it had been recently filled, rumbled in sympathy.

"Hey, little buddy," I said, sending waves of love and calm down our bond. "You're awake. Welcome back."

He sat up, rather awkwardly since one wing was bound against his body, and instinctively tried to spread his wings. When the left one didn't move, I felt his confusion. It took him a moment to figure out what was going on. He sniffed doubtfully at the leather straps that held his wing still, then looked up at me and crooned softly.

"Yeah, sorry about that. We don't want you hurting yourself. No, leave it alone."

He had started to peck at the nearest strap with his sharp beak. The leather was thick, but he left indents in it. Clearly, given enough time, he could work his way through it.

"Stop him," Morwenna said. "Here, give him this." She set a bucket of water down on the floor next to me. Inside, several small fish floated, belly up.

I grabbed one and dangled it in front of the little drake. "Hey, look what I've got for you. Aren't you hungry?"

He snatched it from my hand and tore into the fish, holding it firmly between his two front feet. The fish was gone in seconds, and he looked up eagerly for more. I fed him another, happy for the diversion. Still, I sent waves of love and reassurance through our bond, hoping to keep him calm.

"How long will he have to have his wing strapped?" I muttered to Morwenna as I watched him feed.

"As long as he still has the painkillers in his system. Perhaps another couple of days. They make his behaviour unpredictable, like a drunk. He might think he can fly when he can't and get himself hurt."

"Isn't there some way we can patch those holes?" I asked, feeding the little drake another fish. My mind had turned to hot air balloons. Surely they patched those when they developed a hole? I wasn't sure what they were made of. Silk, perhaps? It must be something really strong.

She gave me a hard look. "Do you think I wouldn't have tried it already if there was? Nobody wants to see a drake who can't fly. He'll be totally dependent on you for food, protection, everything—assuming he lives and doesn't just give up." She shook her head. "It might have been kinder to let him die."

"Don't say that!" I bet she'd be singing another tune if it was her Immi who'd been hurt. Surely there must be a way to get him back into the air.

"I knew a drake once that lost half his wing in an accident," Tirgen said. "You remember, Wenna? Beden's bondmate? He never did fly again, but he took to the water like a hatchling instead. Loved to swim."

Morwenna gave him a reproving look. "That was one drake. And how many others have we seen go into a decline when they couldn't fly anymore? Don't give her false hope."

I'd take any kind of hope. I flashed Tirgen a grateful smile, then turned my attention back to Squeak. He finished the last fish and sat up straight again, extending his right wing. His little belly was distended from all the fish he'd eaten.

"What are you doing, buddy?"

He made a little whimpering sound and ducked his head to the leather straps again.

"No, leave those alone." I put my hand over the strap where he'd been picking at it.

He rubbed his head briefly against the back of my hand and then tried to nudge it out of the way.

"No."

He flapped his right wing, and I could feel the shoulder muscles of the left one straining underneath my hand as he tried to spread that one, too. He gave a clumsy hop, and would have buried his face in the mattress if my hand hadn't already been there to steady him.

"Whoa, what are you doing?"

He whined piteously and tried to leap again. This time, he put more force into it, his free wing helping him to gain lift. He launched himself awkwardly from the bed, but of course he couldn't get airborne. Fortunately, I was close enough to catch him, though it was a rather rough landing. He shrieked in pain as his injured wing slammed into my hands.

"Careful," Morwenna snapped.

"I'm trying," I snapped back. Did she think I wanted to hurt him? I tried to put him back on the bed, but he cried piteously, so I kept him in my arms.

He squirmed and shifted, opening and closing his free wing in panic. His feelings were in turmoil, despite my attempts to soothe him. Fear and confusion roiled inside him.

"Hush, little one. Hush." I held him close, rocking him gently as if he were a baby. I could feel his little heart racing, and his body trembled as he pressed against me. "You're fine. It'll all be fine. Just relax."

It *would* be fine. He *would* fly again. Somehow, I'd find a way.

12

An hour later, we were back at the castle, though there had been no light-hearted banter on our walk this time. We had stayed at Morwenna's until Squeak had fallen asleep again, the amount of food in his belly making it impossible for him to stay awake any longer. Morwenna said he would probably sleep the rest of the night, so we left, in a rather sombre mood.

We hadn't been back at the castle long when Kyrrim walked in again.

Sage looked up in surprise from the game of chess she was playing with Willow. "Back again so soon? When is Yriell coming?"

Kyrrim stalked over to the fireplace and glowered into the orange depths of the fire. "She's not. She threw me out without even letting me tell her why I was there."

I gazed at him in astonishment. "Why?" Why would Yriell throw Kyrrim out? She had quite a soft spot for him, particularly as he had been instrumental in saving her brother.

"Has something gone wrong?" Willow asked.

Kyrrim still had his back to us. "I knocked, but she wouldn't even let me in. Just yelled at me to go away."

"And you did?" Willow raised her eyebrows in disbelief.

"Not right away. I told her I was there because the king needed her. She said the king could kiss her arse."

Sage grinned. "She always did have a way with words."

"But didn't you tell her it was important?" Willow asked.

Kyrrim rounded on her, his eyes glittering dangerously. "Do you think I'm stupid? Of course I did. Or I tried to, anyway. I generally prefer not to hold important conversations at the top of my voice through three inches of solid wood. But she yelled at me to go away and said that if I didn't leave of my own accord, she would make me."

Oh, dear. That didn't sound good. "So you left?" I asked. He was still in one piece, so I assumed he must have.

"She made me. The veranda tipped me off and then the earth caught me like a wave and rolled me back down the path."

Willow blinked. "The veranda tipped you off?"

"You don't know what she's capable of," I said. "You weren't there the night we saved the king."

"No, I was busy playing whack-a-troll in the bushes outside." Willow shook her head. "How did the veranda *tip you off*, exactly?"

"She used her Earth magic to disturb the foundations. It was a violent but extremely localised earthquake, centred on me."

And he didn't look happy about it either.

"Well, I can kind of see where she's coming from," Sage said. "It was only a couple of weeks ago that she helped restore the king to his throne. She probably figures it's up to him to handle his own shit now. She's done her bit. After all, she left the Realms because she didn't want to be involved in politics. And then you come knocking on her door, demanding her aid again already? No wonder she's peeved."

Kyrrim didn't look convinced, but then, his idea of duty was a little different to most people's—as evidenced by his long search for the missing king, well after everyone else had given up hope of ever finding him or even believed he was still alive to find. "But she's a member of the royal family. She has a duty to the kingdom."

"I'm not sure you and Yriell have the same ideas about duty," I said, trying to be as diplomatic as possible. It wasn't really acceptable to tell your boyfriend that he was something of a fanatic. "Maybe if someone else goes— makes it seem more like a social visit and less of a demand."

"That could work," Sage said. "I could go. She likes me. We got drunk together at that presentation the king had where he gave us all presents for helping him."

I grinned. "I remember. We practically had to pour you into your bed. And you were sick as a dog the next day."

"But I don't think that will fly," Willow said. "If you wheedle your way in saying it's a social call and then you hit her up for help, she'll hit the roof."

My smile faded. "True. And if she was prepared to

throw Kyrrim out just for knocking on her door, who knows what she might do to you? She'd certainly never trust you again."

"But we need her," Kyrrim said. "There's no one else with her strength that we can trust."

I patted the empty space on the lounge beside me. "Come sit down. I can't think with you looming over us all like that."

He sat next to me and threw one arm around my shoulders. I snuggled in to his side. That was more like it.

"Maybe we need to come at this sideways," I said. "I could ask her to come and look at Squeak. She told me once that she owed me for saving her brother." And I'd wanted her help with Squeak anyway. Maybe she could produce the miracle that Morwenna couldn't.

Willow's eyes gleamed. "If she has acknowledged a debt, then she can't refuse if you ask her for a personal favour."

"Right!" Sage nodded excitedly. "You could ask her straight out to help ground Arlo as a favour to you. You're the Lady of Illusion—the king doesn't even have to come into it."

Damn. For a moment, I'd actually forgotten I had a personal stake in this. It was going to take me a long time to get used to the idea of ruling a Realm.

"I like it," Willow said. "It's clean, simple, and manipulative as hell. That's my kind of plan."

I squirmed a little. "It's not manipulative. She's basically a good person. She would want to help the Illusionists— even if it was just to piss off Summer—if she knew what we needed. It's just a way of getting her to listen."

"Sure." Willow smiled knowingly. "You keep telling yourself that."

Kyrrim frowned down at me. "I don't like the idea of you leaving Arlo."

I'd been on the receiving end of that glare so many times it had lost its power over me. "What? Not ever? Come on, Kyrrim, we've been over this. That's not protection, that's imprisonment."

His hand tightened on my shoulder. "I'm just trying to keep you safe."

I laid a hand on his thigh, stroking the firm muscle reassuringly. "And I would be. You'd be with me. It's just a jump from here to the national park, a quick walk through the bush, and Bob's your uncle."

Sage laughed. "Bob's your *what*, now?"

"Your uncle. Haven't you heard that expression before?"

She shook her head and looked at Willow, who shrugged. "No, I certainly have not. What does it even mean?"

"It means, like, 'and everything will fall into place'. Or, 'you can't go wrong'."

I could see Sage filing it away for future reference. Though, of course, it wasn't as much fun for her when Willow had learned the new slang at the same time. They liked to surprise each other. It was how they kept score in their so-called assimilation game.

"Where did you hear that?"

"Ricky says it all the time." With a guilty start, I realised I hadn't seen Ricky in days. He was probably wondering what on earth had happened to me by now. How many of my shifts had he had to cover while I was off playing with the fairies? I really needed to get back to work.

And then it hit me—was I rich? Maybe I didn't actually *have* to work anymore. Which was probably just as well, considering I'd be too busy running a whole Realm to have time for working the cash register in the service station.

A pang of something almost like homesickness hit me. *Don't be ridiculous. It's just a job.* No one in their right mind could possibly feel miserable because they no longer had the opportunity to work their butt off for minimum wage.

"If we could get back to the matter at hand?" Kyrrim's tone was abrupt. He wasn't as used as I was to the constant diversions that happened in any conversation with Sage.

"It's settled," I said, lifting my chin a little. Just let him try to talk me out of this. It was wonderful that he cared, but he'd spent a little too long as a Knight of the Realms. He'd gotten used to issuing orders and having them obeyed—but now he needed to learn a more cooperative style. "You're taking me to Yriell's house, and I'll persuade her to come back here. We'll barely be gone ten minutes. Once she's here, I can explain the whole thing to her."

Tawny eyes regarded me with a hint of steel. "It's settled, is it?"

"Unless you want to go back on your own and play earthquakes again? Stop trying to boss me around and admit you need help. The king needs Yriell's cooperation— which means it's your duty as his knight to make sure I go and get it. Your personal feelings don't matter."

He sighed as he stood up, but he drew his sword in a tacit admission that he was out of options. "Very well. But you must stay by my side at all times."

I smiled, letting my gaze roam over his muscled body. "Oh, I don't think that will be a problem. I'll stick to you like glue."

His lips twitched in a reluctant smile, even as his own gaze heated.

"She'll be like fleas on a dog," Sage promised.

"Or flies on a turd," Willow added.

"Charming. Your friends really have a way with words, don't they?"

⁓ ⚜ ⁓

Kyrrim had been to Yriell's house several times now, so his gate opened very close to our destination.

"Well, at least that's saved us twelve dollars fifty," I said as the gate snapped shut behind us. We stood on the bush track that led from the parking lot at the national park to Yriell's house, close by the blasted old stump that marked the place where we needed to leave the path. Yriell's wards prevented us from gating in right to her doorstep.

He cast me a frustrated look. "I wish you'd take this seriously, Allegra. I'm sure the Night Vipers are."

"I'm taking it as seriously as you could possibly wish. I assure you I have no interest in dying." I pushed past him and left the path, heading towards the thorny bushes that marked the beginning of Yriell's wards. "But we need Yriell's help and you know it. Do you honestly think the

Night Vipers are staking out every place I have ever been in my life, just on the off chance that I might turn up there?" I knew he was paranoid, but this was taking it to new levels. Losing the king on his watch had left scars.

"You need to take better care of yourself," he growled.

So that was a no, then, but he didn't want to admit it. I threw him a smile over my shoulder. "No need. I have the handsomest knight in all the Realms to take care of me now."

He scowled at me. "Sometimes I really want to smack you."

My smile widened. "Ooh, sounds promising. Maybe later."

"Don't tempt me, woman." His frustrated growl followed me as I pushed my way through the bushes, forcing myself past the wards that urged all comers to turn away. At least now that I was fae I actually *could* push past the wards. When my magic had been hidden, they'd stopped me in my tracks. Yriell certainly knew her stuff.

Kyrrim hesitated at the foot of the steps up onto Yriell's veranda, but I marched up and rapped sharply on her front door. "What's wrong? Scared she'll throw you off again?"

He joined me, a grim set to his mouth. "You wouldn't be laughing if it had happened to you. But no, I was just considering whether my presence might be a hindrance to you."

"Yriell, it's me," I called. "Are you there? Let me in."

Impatient footsteps approached the door, which was wrenched open, revealing Yriell's scowling face. "What now? I'm going to have to move if you bastards keep showing up on my doorstep wanting shit. I already told the fly-boy I wasn't interested, so you may as well save your breath."

She started closing the door on us, but I shoved my foot in the way. "Not so fast, please. I'm not here about the king. I need a favour for myself."

She opened the door again and studied me with a frown. "What kind of favour?"

"The kind that involves you coming with us," I said.

"Is this about that bondmate of yours? I heard Blethna Arbre toasted him."

I gave her a pained smile. Did she have to put it quite so bluntly? "I'd be grateful if you had a look at him, yes, but that's not what the favour is."

"What, then?"

"It would be easier if I showed you."

Kyrrim had been slouching against the railing of the veranda with his arms folded, a scowl to rival Yriell's on his face. He straightened. "It's a pretty big favour, actually. I'm not sure you'll be able to manage it."

I cut a sideways glance at him, eyebrows raised. What the hell was he doing, enraging the already grumpy fairy? I couldn't see that ending well for any of us.

Yriell drew herself up to her full height, which wasn't all that impressive, since she barely came to my shoulder. "Are you dissing me, fly-boy? I'll rip your feathers out and shove them up your—"

"I'm sure he didn't mean it that way," I said hurriedly.

"It *is* quite a big favour, but no one doubts your ability."

I may as well have saved my breath. She continued to stare daggers at Kyrrim. "Give me a minute. I'll grab a few things and then you can show me this *favour* of yours."

She left the door ajar while she went back inside. Through the open door, I could see her shoving little bottles and packets of dried herbs into a satchel willy-nilly, obviously still pissed.

"What were you thinking?" I hissed at Kyrrim.

He raised a haughty eyebrow. "It worked, didn't it? She's coming."

"She would probably have come even if you hadn't insulted her."

He shrugged, obviously not fazed by my disapproval. "The princess is very proud of her powers. The best way to get her to do something is to suggest that she might not be able to."

"You're Machiavellian, you know that, right?"

"Machiavelli has been frequently misrepresented over the centuries."

"Wait, what? You knew Machiavelli? How old are you?" I'd been thinking he was maybe one or two centuries old, but shit, if he'd been around when Machiavelli was, that made him more like five hundred.

"Don't you know it's rude to ask a fae his age?" He had a teasing smile on his lips, and I wondered belatedly if he was pulling my leg about Machiavelli. I wouldn't put it past him. I had discovered quite a playful side to the knight I had once thought so stern and dour.

"Lucky I don't care about being rude, then. How old?"

Suddenly, it seemed very important to know the answer to that question. I was twenty-two, and I'd always known that he was older than me. Considerably older than me. But five hundred years? That was some serious age gap.

He said nothing, and before I could press him for an answer, Yriell returned, her satchel slung over one shoulder.

"Let's go." She cast a smouldering glance at Kyrrim. "Lead on, fly-boy."

Kyrrim gave her a grave half bow, then turned and led the way back down her path, through the thickets of bushes and out past her wards. Once there, he quickly formed a gate in the air with his sword, and we all stepped through.

He'd brought us to a point closer to the town than normal, and we could plainly see flurries of rainbow drakes circling and diving above the lake, their jewelled skin flashing in the moonlight.

Yriell drew in a sharp breath. "This is Arlo, isn't it? You've brought me to the lost island of Illusion."

"Yes," I said. The rainbow drakes had been a bit of a giveaway.

"Makes sense. Where better to treat a rainbow drake than in Illusion? Better take me to him, though I don't know what I'll be able to do if Illusion's own healers haven't managed the job. I'm not a miracle worker."

And yet, I was hoping for a miracle. "Maybe a different point of view will help."

She gave me a sympathetic look, as if she knew I was trying to convince myself as much as her.

A pair of rainbow drakes zoomed past, squawking like seagulls fighting over a hot chip. The one in the lead had a fish in its mouth that the other obviously wanted.

"They're pretty creatures," Yriell said, her gaze following the fleeing pair as they sped down the street, dodging around the houses and up over the rooftops. "Noisy as all get-out, though."

There were drakes everywhere tonight. I watched their carefree flight with dread in my heart. How would Squeak cope if he could never rejoin his friends in the air?

We soon arrived at Morwenna's house. Lirra opened the door at our knock.

"I thought you might be coming soon. Squeak is awake again."

As soon as she said it, I realised I could feel him through our bond. Some of the dread I'd been feeling was his. I sent love down the bond, but received only a faint whisper of affection in return. I looked at Lirra in alarm. "Is he in pain?"

"You'd better come in."

We followed her through the house to the sick room out the back. Morwenna was there, grinding something in a pestle with hard, angry strokes. She said nothing as we entered, but that was all right with me. My attention was taken by the forlorn figure on the bed.

"Why is he tied up like that?" Poor Squeak was pinned down, wrapped in a sheet, which was fastened to the bed frame. A couple of holes in the sheet showed where he had tried to work himself free, but now he lay staring glassy-eyed at the ceiling, a picture of dejection.

"You weren't here," Morwenna said, managing to make it sound like an accusation, "and he wouldn't stop trying to fly, even with one wing strapped down. I'm making something now to put him back to sleep."

I hurried to the bed and stroked his shimmering green head. He trembled under my hand. "He can't stay asleep forever."

"Then maybe you should spend more time here helping him adjust instead of running off with your friends," Morwenna snapped. "Hold his mouth open for me."

I sent reassurance down our bond as I pried his jaws open, but he didn't respond. Morwenna tipped the mixture down his throat with a skill born of long practice.

"Who is this woman?" Yriell asked, eyeing her askance.

"I'm Morwenna, healer and leader of the exiles here on Arlo," Morwenna replied before I could say anything. "Who are you?"

"I'm a friend of Allegra's. I've come to look at the patient."

Morwenna bristled. "I can assure you that everything that could be done for him has been done. I have been a healer for almost a hundred years. I know what I'm doing."

"Is that so?" Yriell whistled as if impressed. "A hundred years? I've had dogs that lived longer than that."

Morwenna's face reddened, her eyes narrowing with fury, but Yriell had turned her back on her in a clear dismissal and approached the bed. Squeak's eyes had already fallen shut. Whatever was in that mixture had knocked him out cold.

"What have you given to put him under?"

"Milk of the poppy, feverfew, and some willow bark in a solution. Not that it's any of your business." Morwenna's voice was tight with anger.

"Well, at least those hundred years were well spent. You know your basics." Yriell worked at the knots that held the sheets closed then unwrapped Squeak gently. He didn't even stir at her touch.

With a mix of hope and dread in my heart, I watched her careful hands lay bare Squeak's shimmering body then gently open out his wing. Kyrrim moved to my side and took my hand in silent support, and I gave him a grateful smile.

The silence stretched as Yriell examined Squeak. I could hardly bear to look at the gaping holes, but she inspected them in silence, gently extending the wing, checking it from both sides.

Then she looked at me, and I knew straight away what the next words out of her mouth would be.

"I'm sorry, Allegra. There's nothing I can do."

"I told her that, but of course she knew better." Morwenna eyed me with her usual cold dislike.

"What is your problem?" Yriell asked in exasperation. "Are you always this bitchy or did we just come at a bad time?"

Morwenna bristled. "You dare insult me in my own house?"

"If you want to step outside, I'd be happy to insult you in the street. You may be a great healer, and you've certainly done a very nice job on his burns, but why shouldn't she seek a second opinion? This is important. He's her bondmate."

"If she cared so much about her bondmate, she wouldn't have taken him into danger. This could kill him. Most drakes go into a decline and simply wither away when they lose the power of flight. But then, she's always careless with other people's lives."

Yriell glanced down at the sleeping drake, who was clearly not a person, then back at Morwenna's angry face. "What in the name of the Silver Tree are you talking about, woman?"

"She's referring to my mother," I said, rage and resentment rising inside me. Would she never let this go?

"She was no blood of yours," Morwenna snapped.

"Do you mean Anawen?" Yriell asked, astonished.

"Yes. My sister was our new Lady's nurse. Not her mother."

Yriell shot me a look of surprise. Oops. I had planned to fill her in on that little development, but Morwenna had beaten me to it.

But Yriell wasn't finished with the other woman yet. "Anawen raised her. She killed for her. She devoted her life to Allegra's care. Lady's tits, she *told* the girl she was her mother, and Allegra spent all her life believing it. I think that qualifies her."

"Oh, Anawen would have agreed with you." Bitterness filled Morwenna's voice, and her face twisted in pain. "She was so devoted that she went to her death for her."

"*Why* did she?" This was the part I'd never understood.

"If she wanted to get a message to me, why couldn't Raven have sent one of his birds, or even come himself? Why would she risk leaving the safety of Arlo to speak to me if she didn't have to?"

"She wanted to tell you who you really were. She thought that if you knew, you could be persuaded to come to Arlo and go into hiding—you were too well-known once you rescued the king, and she was afraid of you coming to Summer's attention." Morwenna's mouth formed a hard, bitter line. "This, after months of arguing that you should be left in the mortal world, safe in the belief that you were a changeling. Suddenly, you rescued the king, and she got cold feet. Wanted to change the plan."

"Seems sensible to me," Yriell said. "She would have been safer here."

"We discussed it," Morwenna said. "But ultimately, the council decided it wasn't in our best interests. We thought it would raise too many questions if she just disappeared, after making such a public splash, but neither could we condone leaving her to roam, with the knowledge of who she was."

"Why not?" I asked.

"Because we didn't trust you to keep your magic secret. Once you knew the truth, you wouldn't be able to resist using it." She hit me with a freezing glare. "As in fact happened."

I returned her glare with interest. "So *you* refused to help my mother tell me, so she ran off to do it herself, and got herself killed in the process." Anger formed a tight knot in my throat, until I thought I might choke on it. "*You* killed her, not me."

Morwenna's face purpled with fury, but Yriell cut in before she could say anything. "Anawen was a grown woman, fully capable of making her own decisions. Nobody forced her to do what she did. There's no point apportioning out blame now—it won't bring her back."

"Do you think I wanted her to die?" I burst out, my eyes never leaving Morwenna's. "I loved her just as much as you did."

"This conversation avails us nothing," Kyrrim said. He still had a firm grip on my hand, and I was grateful for his strength at my side. He turned a fierce glare on Morwenna. "Remember who Allegra is."

"As if I could forget," Morwenna said bitterly.

"Then remember we must work together to achieve your goals," he said sharply.

Morwenna said nothing

"I could do with a drink," Yriell said. "There's nothing more for me to do here. Let's leave your bondmate to his rest and you can tell me all about this favour of yours. Clearly, you've been keeping secrets. Time to come clean, young lady."

13

"So if Anawen wasn't your mother, who was?" Yriell asked as we walked back to the castle on the hill, accompanied by Kyrrim.

"Lady Orlah, Lord Perony's sister," I said. It still didn't feel real to me. This name meant nothing, this mother who had died so long ago. I knew nothing about her or my father, or even the elder brother I'd had. All gone. All wiped out in one night of madness, my life only spared because of Anawen's quick thinking and resourcefulness. She was my true mother. Not some faceless Lady.

"Well, this puts a new spin on things, doesn't it? I suppose my royal brother knows already?"

"Yes. He was there last night when I found out."

"And this favour of yours is something to do with it, no doubt?" She eyed me with exasperation. "Honestly, I'm beginning to wish I'd never met you people. You're so damn needy."

"I tried to tell you about it earlier," Kyrrim said, a hint of accusation in his tone. "But you wouldn't listen."

"Well, I'm all ears now. Hit me with it."

We had reached the castle, and Kyrrim politely held the door open for us to enter. I could hear Willow laughing somewhere down the hallway, and I turned my footsteps in that direction. A little moral support wouldn't go astray at this point.

"We want to return Arlo to its rightful place and take back Illusion as a Realm from Summer," I said.

"That's a big ambition. I like it."

We found Sage and Willow in what I thought of as the lounge room, though it was big enough to hold a ball in. Sage was curled up in a chair by the fire, her legs tucked up under her, and she was reading aloud to Willow, who apparently found the book vastly amusing. It seemed to be something about the lineage of Night. She let forth another peal of laughter as we entered the room.

Sage snapped the book shut at sight of us, a smile lighting her face. "Your mission was successful, then? Thunderbirds are go?"

I glanced at Yriell, who hadn't actually agreed to help us yet. "Thunderbirds are in the process of discussing the details now."

I sank into a chair opposite Sage, and Yriell flopped onto the lounge next to Willow, kicking her shoes off with a grateful sigh.

"About that drink," she said.

Kyrrim immediately moved to the sideboard. "Vodka? Scotch? What would you like? I can call for wine, if you prefer that."

"I have a feeling this will be a vodka conversation. Make it a double."

I tried to put on a cheerful face, though I was feeling anything but. I had pinned all my hopes on Yriell, who had seemed all-powerful in my previous dealings with her. If she couldn't help Squeak, we were in trouble. Morwenna's words echoed in my mind: *This could kill him.* A tight knot of anxiety writhed in the pit of my stomach. When Kyrrim deposited a vodka shot in my hand I downed it in one go, hoping the warmth in my belly would loosen the knot.

"It shouldn't be too difficult," I said. "The Air mages say that anchoring Arlo back in its rightful place will require the assistance of an Earthcrafter or two. Rothbold would like your help."

"It's a sensitive matter, as you are well aware," Kyrrim said, handing Yriell her glass. "The king knows he can trust you."

And poor Rothbold couldn't say the same for many other people. Kyrrim didn't need to spell that out—Yriell was well aware of her brother's difficulties.

She took a quick gulp of vodka. "Shouldn't be too difficult, they say? And what do Air mages know about Earthcrafting?"

"Very little," Willow said, with a sly smile at Kyrrim. "But when has that ever stopped them from pontificating?"

"Sing it, sister," Yriell muttered. She downed the rest of her vodka in one long swig, then licked her lips appreciatively. "Still, I am the greatest living Earthcrafter. If Rothy and I can't handle it, I daresay the job can't be done."

"That's not exactly a ringing endorsement," I said. "Can you do it or not? There's a lot riding on this."

She shot me a sharp glance. "And this is your favour?"

I nodded.

"Then I can't say no. Don't worry, girl, I'll get your precious island back in one piece. You won't even feel a jolt, I promise. When is Rothy planning to do this?"

"Very soon," Kyrrim said. "Rowan has gone to talk to Eldric about hosting a 'memorial service' for Illusion next week. All the Lords will be there."

A wicked grin split Yriell's face. "Oh, I like it. They'll all be gathered with their serious faces on, then Arlo appears, complete with a new Lady, and Kellith has to suck it up."

"That's the plan," Sage said. "With all those witnesses, he can hardly do anything else."

"Girl, you should have led with this. I'd do it even if I didn't owe you a favour, just for the pleasure of seeing the look on Kellith's face when half his wealth disappears down the drain." She laughed and held out her empty glass to Kyrrim. "This calls for another drink."

He filled her glass again and left the vodka bottle on the side table at her elbow. That would probably save him a few trips.

Sage lifted her glass. "To wiping the smile off Kellith's face."

There was a chorus of amens as we all drank to that.

Yriell gave me a shrewd look. "What's wrong? Still worried about your bondmate? You don't seem as happy as I expected about sticking it to the Lord of Summer."

"Of course I'm worried about Squeak. What if he dies?"

"I'm sure Morwenna is exaggerating. Seems like the kind of thing she'd do, just to upset you. That woman needs her head read."

I sighed. "It's not just Squeak. This whole being the heir of Illusion thing—I just don't know if I can do it. It's certainly not what I had planned for my life."

"Of course you can do it. Oh, you'll fall on your face and stuff things up at first, but you'll learn. You don't really have a choice, do you?"

"Don't I? Surely someone else could take the job? Someone who actually had an inkling of how to run a Realm?"

Yriell reached over and patted my knee. "Welcome to adulthood. It's full of doing shit you don't want to do. Magic may be real, but that doesn't mean life is a fairy tale. You've got to take the good with the bad and learn to deal with the bits you don't like."

"There's a lot I don't like," I said darkly.

"Oh, yeah? Which bits would those be? The one where you now have this hunk of beefcake following you around adoringly? Or the one where you have the king's favour and free run of the Realms you were once locked out of? Or the one—"

"All right, all right, I get the picture."

"I forget how young you are. Life is change, sweetheart." She grinned suddenly. "Besides, how bad can it be when you get to order that cow Morwenna around? That's got to be worth something. Now, tell me what you've planned for getting Arlo home."

The conversation turned to the plans as they stood so far, my qualms brushed to one side. Easy for her to do, of course. It wasn't her life being upended. But I couldn't stop brooding on it, and let the others carry the conversation, though I noticed when Yriell said she would need to consult with her brother about the Earthcrafting. Kyrrim manfully managed not to roll his eyes at that suggestion. She seemed to have forgotten all about her annoyance at being bothered by the king for help yet again in her joy at anticipating Kellith's rage.

More vodka was drunk, and soon I found myself having trouble keeping my eyes open. The late hour coupled with the alcohol and distress over Squeak was exhausting me. Kyrrim, ever alert to my moods, noticed me yawning.

"Come, you need your sleep. You can barely keep your eyes open."

"Lightweight," Willow said.

Yriell grinned. "Don't worry, we'll finish the bottle."

Kyrrim held out his hand, and I let him pull me up. He kept my hand in his as we left the room and climbed the stairs to the bedroom. I was very conscious of his skin against mine, the warmth of his strong grip enveloping my fingers. All of a sudden, I wasn't quite as sleepy any more. I was filled with a restless urge to suck every drop of pleasure from this life that I could, before everything changed.

We reached my door, and he released my hand. "Good night." He bent his head to kiss me, but I turned aside at the last minute, his breath soft on my cheek.

"Aren't you coming in?" I leaned back against the door, feeling for the handle.

His eyes darkened, his gaze drawn to my lips. "You need to sleep."

"There's more to life than sleep. We don't have much time left."

He leaned one arm against the door behind me. The world narrowed to just this small space, the two of us alone, his body so close, his eyes boring into mine. "What do you mean?"

I gestured helplessly with one hand. "It's all going to change, isn't it? You have your work as a knight. The king keeps you busy, dancing to his every whim. I already hardly see you. And now I'll be the Lady of Illusion, Realms away from you."

Not merely in distance, either. Nobody cared who Allegra Brooks slept with, but that would change when I was a Lady. I knew enough about politics to understand that. And I had so much to learn about governing, so much work to do to rebuild this shattered Realm. I would no longer be free to jaunt around the worlds as I pleased.

"It's just us now," I continued. "And already we're only snatching stolen moments here and there. But when I'm a Lady, how can we ever make this work?" Tears pricked my eyes as I gazed up into his tawny ones, so close.

He frowned as understanding entered his gaze. "I won't lose you. We'll find a way."

"Will we?" Sure, he might think that now. But I was very afraid that reality would prove him wrong.

My expression must have given away my thoughts because he stepped closer, pressing insistently against me, as if he could force his will on me through his body. "We will. Have a little faith, my love."

I drew in a shaky breath. His love? He'd never called me that before. It was bittersweet to hear it from his lips now, when I felt that everything was ending between us. The tear escaped and trickled down my cheek.

With an oath, he swooped in and kissed it away. "No more vodka for you if it's going to make you maudlin."

I found the door handle and pushed the door open behind me, backing into the room. He followed, pressing close, never allowing a distance to open between our bodies.

"I'm not drunk," I protested. "Just … sad."

He kicked the door closed behind us. "Then let me cheer you up."

Taking my face between his hands, he began raining kisses on my eyelids, my nose, my lips—sweet butterfly kisses, tender and fleeting. I slid my hands around his waist and up under his shirt, feeling the smooth muscles of his back moving under his skin. My blood thrummed in my ears as his hands moved lower, roaming under my own shirt, bringing me suddenly to tingling life everywhere he touched. It was as if my body was an instrument, uniquely tuned to his hands, and it responded with a wild rush of elation. I pressed closer, hungry for more.

Responding to my need, his kisses deepened until we were both breathing hard, our lips clinging together as if that connection were the only thing keeping us alive. His hands roved over my body, and I dug my fingernails into the skin of his back, feeling it shiver beneath my touch. He grabbed my butt and hoisted me into the air. I wrapped my legs around him, squirming to get closer still as he carried me to the bed.

We tumbled onto the quilt, desperately ripping clothes off each other. Impatient with the buttons of my shirt, he simply ripped it open, dragging it off me in a frenzied movement, his lips plundering my exposed skin. My bra soon followed, and I threw my head back in ecstasy as he took one peaked nipple in his mouth. A roaring heat exploded through me, all the way down to my core, molten with need.

He left me briefly to take off his jeans, then he was back, hot and heavy against me. I writhed against him, lost in the feeling of skin on skin.

"Please," I begged. I couldn't wait a moment more. "Now."

A throaty growl was his only answer, but fire spread through me as he plunged into me. I wrapped my legs around him, wanting more, desperate to be closer, losing myself in the sensations he was arousing.

It was rough, almost savage in a way our lovemaking had never been before, and I gave a gasping cry as the waves of pleasure peaked and swept me away on a thrilling tide.

When I came back to myself, he had adjusted our position to cradle me against him with exquisite tenderness. I didn't speak, and neither did he, though his hands still stroked my bare flesh as though he couldn't bear to stop touching me.

After a time, we settled more comfortably. He fitted himself to my back, one arm protectively around me. Soon, his deep, steady breathing told me he was asleep.

But I lay awake long into the night, afraid that his wild, almost desperate lovemaking was a truer answer than his words. Things were changing for us, and this might be one of the last times we would be together.

The rumble of men's voices speaking in low tones woke me. Kyrrim was talking to someone who was standing in the open doorway to the room. The man was in silhouette, backlit by the bright lights of the hallway, so I couldn't tell who it was, but he only stayed a moment anyway. I was still blinking bleary eyes and trying to wake up when Kyrrim shut the door and padded back toward the bed.

"What's wrong?" I asked as he began to throw his clothes on.

"Trouble at Whitehaven. Go back to sleep."

I propped myself up on one elbow, rubbing my eyes, trying to force my brain into wakefulness. It felt as though I'd only been asleep for moments, and the effects of the vodka still lingered. "What kind of trouble?"

He pulled on his T-shirt in a smooth movement, lit by the soft moonlight that lay across the floor from the open windows. "The assassin kind."

Suddenly wide awake, I sat up. The sheet fell away from my naked breasts, and he paused momentarily in his efficient dressing, his gaze lingering on my body.

"Assassins? Who did they kill? Is the king all right?"

"Luckily, they killed no one. But the palace is in an uproar. Queen Ceinwen has taken the princess and fled to Summer to seek shelter with her brother, insisting that she won't return until Rothbold can guarantee their safety."

"But who was their target?"

"Apparently, the princess herself. I don't have many details. That was Raven; he came here to recall me to Whitehaven. The king is furious."

"No wonder the queen is in a panic if they are targeting her daughter. Was it the Night Vipers again?"

He sat down on the bed beside me to pull on his boots. "No one knows." He leaned close to press a hard kiss on my lips, followed by a soft one on each breast. My nipples tingled as he smiled ruefully at me. "I'm sorry, Allegra, I have to go. I'll come back as soon as I can, or send word."

"Of course," I said. This was clearly an emergency; the king needed him.

He took my hand, looking down at our intertwined fingers. "I never had to protect anyone but the king before, and now I'm torn. I want to go and I want to stay, but I can't do both." He pressed a kiss into my palm and added softly, "I know it bothers you that I want to protect you, but that's part of who I am. I'm afraid that's one thing that will never change."

"I know. So much for 'life is change', right?" I said, quoting Yriell from the night before.

"Well, she has a point. But not all change is bad. Remember that." He stood up, releasing my hand. "I thank the Lady every day for the change that swept you into my life."

He didn't look back, his face already set towards his duty as he left the room and closed the door softly behind him.

What time was it? I still felt groggy, as if I'd only had a couple of hours' sleep, and there was no sign of dawn yet outside the window. I lay down and tried to sleep again, but the moment had passed. My head was now too full of plots and assassins, of love and loss, and a great fear of what was to come.

After a few moments, I gave up the struggle, got up, and dressed. Then I went in search of company. Perhaps the others were still awake. I wouldn't put it past Yriell to be still up drinking. I'd never met someone with such a capacity for alcohol.

I passed a couple of servants in the corridors, but the large hall where my friends had gathered was empty now. I hesitated, wondering what to do with myself. Perhaps a walk. It was a warm night and the exercise might help clear my head.

Inevitably, my footsteps turned towards the town. A curious drake swooped about my head as I passed the first house, then whizzed off to join a group of his friends who were perched on a nearby roof, watching the comings and goings in the town like spectators from a grandstand.

Seeing the drake's easy flight, so playful and assured, tore at my heart unexpectedly. Squeak should be up there, not languishing in a sickroom, a shadow of his former self. I reached tentatively down our bond, but found nothing at the other end. Either he was asleep or he had shut me out, so I let my footsteps guide me toward the lake. I wandered along its shore for some time, listening to the chatter of the drakes and watching them dive and splash in the smooth, glassy waters beneath the setting moon.

Maybe we should bring Squeak out here, where he could see the sky and feel the wind on his face. It couldn't be doing his mood any good to be cooped up inside. I'd suggest it to Morwenna. Perhaps it would help.

As the sky began to lighten in the east, I turned my steps back up the hill toward the castle. One day soon, I would have to spend a lot of time in this town, getting to know the inhabitants, the people of my Realm. But today was not that day. At the moment, I had nothing to offer anyone but fear and frustration.

A voice hailed me as I made my way up the hill. Turning, I saw Lirra hurrying toward me, so I stopped and waited for her.

"I thought that was you," she said.

A dark foreboding filled me as I took in the downturned corners of her mouth and the shadows in her eyes.

"Is everything all right?" I asked sharply. "Is Squeak—?" I stopped, too choked with a sudden fear to complete the sentence.

"He's sleeping. But when I went to change his dressing just now, I found these." She opened her hand and showed me three glittering jewels.

I stared, uncomprehending. Even in dawn's dim light, they sparkled against her skin like diamonds. "I don't understand. Are these Squeak's?"

She nodded. "He's shed them."

"But I thought adults didn't moult."

"He's not moulting. This is different." Her eyes filled with tears, and I drew in a sharp, frightened breath at the knowledge in her gaze. "Sometimes when they … when they near the end, they lose their jewels."

"Near the end?" I choked. "How long has he got?"

She shrugged helplessly. "Three days, four days—maybe more. But not much more. Mama thinks you should come."

I turned to go with her back to the town, but then I stopped, realisation dawning on me. There was nothing I could do for him there. There was nothing anyone could do. If I was going to save him, I had to try something different.

"No. She's wrong. I have to go." I spun on my heel and began striding toward the castle.

"Where?" she called after me. "Where are you going?"

"To Whitehaven. It's his last chance."

I burst back into the castle foyer, the heavy door slamming shut behind me. "Raven? Raven!"

Was he still here? Perhaps he'd gone back to Whitehaven with Kyrrim. I should have done that, too, though Kyrrim wouldn't have been too happy about it. But now the clock was ticking, and Squeak was fast running out of time. The threat of assassins paled in comparison—not that they would have hung around the palace after their attempt on the princess failed.

I took the stairs two at a time and threw open the door of Raven's usual bedroom after a hasty knock. No sign of him. A passing servant eyed me curiously as I left the room.

"Have you seen Raven?" I demanded.

The man frowned. "I think he went down to the town to see Morwenna."

Great. I'd only just come from there. I must have missed him somewhere on the way. But at least he was still on the island. I muttered a thanks as I brushed past and hurried back down the stairs.

I'd just gained the tiled floor of the entry when the front door opened again, and the man himself walked in. Hallelujah.

"Raven! Thank the Lady."

His eyebrows rose as he shut the door behind him, a lot more gently than I had done. "I don't usually get such a fervent reception. I must admit, a man could grow to like it."

"Get me off this island," I said. "I need to get to Whitehaven."

"Not a good idea at the moment. Whitehaven is like a kicked ant's nest."

"I know, I know, the assassination attempt. It doesn't matter. I have to get there—right now."

"Why? What's wrong?"

"Have you just come from Morwenna's?"

He nodded.

"Then you've seen Squeak. Lirra says he only has a few days left."

His face took on a gentle sympathy that I'd never seen before. His default expression was two parts mocking, one part self-deprecation. It made him look younger, more real somehow, as if he wasn't playing a role for once.

He stepped forward and took both my hands in his. "I'm sorry. Truly I am."

I gazed up into his face as tears sprang to my eyes. "I have to help him."

"But how will going to Whitehaven help him?"

"The Dragon said to talk to him if Squeak needed help." Dread tore at my heart. Was I crazy for believing that anyone could do anything for Squeak now? Morwenna and Yriell, both fine healers, had said the damage was permanent. But a flicker of hope still persisted in the depths of my stubborn heart. "He said dragons were better at healing wing damage than anyone else."

"But Morwenna said—"

"I know, I know. But I have to try. I can't just sit here and do nothing if there's still a chance. Unless—" A sudden thought occurred to me. "He *is* still at Whitehaven, isn't he?"

"The Dragon? As far as I know. The king has sent a delegation headed by the Hawk to retrieve the queen and his daughter from Summer, but the rest of the knights are on high alert. As you can imagine, security at the palace has been tightened."

I squeezed his hands. "Then help me, please. I can't get off this island without you."

"That's probably something we need to fix."

"Indeed."

The wards had been loosened to allow Kyrrim to gate in and out with his magic sword, but there was still no direct access to the Wilds from Arlo for anyone. Not even for someone who was the nominal ruler of this place. I needed someone with wings to fly me down to the surface before I could use my own magic to navigate the Greenways to Whitehaven.

"But we'd have to call a council meeting and stuff around, and we just don't have that kind of time right now." *Squeak* didn't have that kind of time. "And you already have form in toting me around."

He grimaced. "You don't have to rub it in. *One* little kidnapping and everyone keeps going on about it forever."

"So you'll do it?"

"The Hawk will probably have my balls for it, but yes."

"Good." I stood on tiptoe to kiss his cheek, then raced away for the stairs. "Just hang on one minute while I grab something."

I was back a moment later, the cloak of shadows scrunched into my back pocket. Hopefully this would be a very straightforward mission, and I wouldn't need it, but the way my luck was running lately, it seemed like a good idea to bring it along. Better to have it and not need it than need it and not have it.

We stepped outside into a crisp early morning with not a hint of breeze. The air was so still it was as if the world was holding its breath. Raven looked up at the sky with the practised eye of a born flyer as we hurried across the courtyard and out through the gates. At the top of the hill, he swept me up into his arms as huge black wings burst from his back.

"Ready?" he asked.

I nodded, clutching him firmly around the neck. This certainly wasn't my favourite way to get around, but I trusted him to take care of me. My stomach dropped like a stone as he launched us skyward, the thunder of his labouring wings filling my ears.

Once he'd cleared the trees, he slipped sideways, finding an invisible breeze, and we sailed smoothly over the edge of Arlo. It was the oddest feeling to see it disappear above us.

It was so easy to forget, when you were standing on its surface, that it was floating in mid-air, buoyed up by magic. It felt so solid. Now I could look up and see the crumbling earth underneath it, the rocks and the deep roots of trees holding it all together. I shuddered and looked away. At least soon it would be back on the ground where it belonged.

The land below us was blanketed in forest—dark pines and huge spreading oaks. Here and there, a bald outcropping of rock shouldered its way through the trees, reaching for the sky above. It looked almost as wild as the Wilds themselves, and there wasn't a hint of fae habitation anywhere. Not a rooftop, nor a curl of smoke, not a cultivated field, nothing. A thin ribbon of silver glinted here and there among the trees, showing the winding course of a river, and it was towards this that Raven soared.

"Welcome to my father's Realm," he said as he set me down with a grunt of effort.

We stood on a rocky shore by the river, which looked cold and deep, its waters rushing purposefully to some point further away. Behind us, one of the great bald outcroppings of rock towered, the size of a decent office block back in Sydney. Never had I felt further from that familiar world.

"Thanks. I have to say, though, this part doesn't look all that inviting."

"That's why it made such a perfect place to hide Arlo," Raven said. "No one in their right mind ever comes here unless they absolutely have to." He gestured at the mammoth rock behind us, and I noticed a dark cave opening to one side. "Shall we?"

"In there? That looks like a really bad idea." In fact, it looked like the kind of place you'd find a fairytale monster or two lurking in the dark, all teeth and claws, just waiting for an unwary traveller to take refuge from a storm.

"Don't be such a chicken. I use this one all the time; it's a nice handy threshold. Do you want to do the honours or shall I?"

"You can." I was still gazing doubtfully at the looming mouth of the cave. "That way if you're wrong and there is something in there, it gets to eat you first."

"Nice. Glad to see you care." But he strode towards the menacing cave mouth with such insouciance that I followed, reassured. After all, we weren't actually going into the cave, just using the power of threshold magic inherent in its entry.

Sure enough, as I stepped through at Raven's back, no dark cave closed in around me. Instead, a world of trees opened, with a shimmering path leading away into the green dimness ahead.

"Stay on the path," Raven said.

"This isn't my first rodeo, thanks." My feet were glued to this sucker like you wouldn't believe. I'd lost the path once in the Wilds, and once was plenty.

Raven cast a grin at me over his shoulder. "Just thought you might need a reminder. Thing One isn't here today to lead us out of danger."

"Where *are* your little henchmen?" I asked. "I haven't seen them for a while."

Things One and Two had been almost like pets to me for a while there. They had lived in Rowan's backyard, keeping an eye on me in the mortal world. Every day, I'd fed them and talked to them, never once imagining that they were anything other than ordinary ravens.

"They're keeping very busy. My little raven friends are my eyes and ears in many a Realm. How do you think I always have the best gossip?"

A branch snapped in the forest off to my right, and I jumped reflexively. Normally, I liked forests, having grown up in one. But the Wilds were no ordinary forest and they always made me ill at ease. Already, my shoulder blades were beginning to itch, insisting that something behind me was watching. I resisted the urge to look over my shoulder, knowing I would see nothing. It was just the inherent magic of the Wilds, hostile to everything and everyone except Yriell, who treated the place like her own backyard. For the rest of us, this was no ordinary stroll through the woods.

Determinedly, I banished thoughts of the hideous dharrigals that had attacked us last time and focused on putting one foot after the other, following Raven along the path.

"And what gossip have they collected for you from Summer?" I asked, desperately trying to distract myself from my growing unease. The Greenways were unpredictable. Sometimes a trip through the Wilds could take hours, sometimes only a few moments. It depended on the power of the person who was using them, the strength of their will, and probably half a dozen other random things that no one had any control over. It was an unpredictable place. If I let it get to me this early, I'd be a raving mess by the time we made it to Whitehaven.

I'd never missed Kyrrim and his marvellous sword more.

"My birds don't fly to Summer anymore. I lost too many of them that way. Alas, Lord Kellith is not a trusting man." There was a certain grimness to his tone. He really loved those birds of his.

"What about Night Vipers? Have you heard any whisperings about them?"

"That's certainly a hot topic at the moment, especially since the attack on the palace. But there's not a lot of talk. They're old hands at flying under the radar. Not that we need spies to tell us who has paid them to come after you."

"I guess not. Everyone knows Kellith has it in for me, and he's fully capable of stooping that low, the bastard. But he wouldn't have ordered an attack on the princess, so there must be more people in play than we realised."

"I did hear some speculation that the attack might have been staged."

"What? You mean it wasn't the Vipers?"

"No, it was the Vipers, just not a genuine attack. The theory I heard was that Kellith paid for it."

I stopped walking, astonished. "Kellith paid the Vipers to *pretend* to attack the princess? Whose theory is that? Are they crazy?"

He grinned at me. "A gentleman never reveals his sources."

I shook my head, still floored by the idea. "But why would Kellith do that?"

"Don't you think it's a little convenient that his sister and niece immediately fled to his protection? Having them under his roof gives him a nice bargaining tool when the talk turns again to betrothals, doesn't it?"

"That's got to be a new low, even for him. Using his own family as hostages?"

He laughed. "Welcome to the Realms, my dear, where everyone smiles to your face and then stabs you in the back. Betrayal is practically a national sport for us fairies, didn't you know?"

He sounded bitter, as if he'd experienced betrayal up close and personal, but perhaps that was a story for another time. My hands were already full with what I was dealing with at the moment. And besides, he was the son of a Lord. He was capable of handling his own shit.

"Not all fairies are like that. Kyrrim isn't. He'd rather die than betray someone."

"Ah, well, we can't all be as perfect as the mighty Hawk."

I bristled a little. Just because he was helping me didn't mean I would put up with him bad-mouthing Kyrrim.

But he continued, "Truly, the world would be a better place if there were more men like your Hawk in it." He cast a sardonic grin over his shoulder. "Sadly, there are too many like me."

"Oh, you're full of it. You've been busy helping the Illusionists for years. There's nothing wrong with you or your morals, whatever you like to pretend."

"I didn't realise psychotherapy was on the menu for our little stroll."

"I'm just saying."

"And here I was thinking that you didn't trust me. I kidnapped you, remember? And burned down your house. I know your friend Rowan won't forgive me any time soon for that."

"Build him a new one and he'll be fine."

Something shimmered up ahead. Silver was appearing among the green leaves overhanging the path. My heart lifted with hope.

"Is that—?"

"Our destination?" As we got closer, the silver resolved into a shining archway wound about with vines, framing the end of the path. Mist crept from it like little puffs of dragon breath. "Yes, I believe it is. Thank goodness for that. You're getting so sentimental I didn't know if I could stand it much longer."

"Idiot," I said, and shoved him through the archway.

The gates of Whitehaven loomed ahead of us, silver and white and flashing with embedded jewels. The great branches of the Lady's silver tree spread their shade and shelter over all who entered. Except no one was entering now, as the gates were firmly closed. A full company of pike men were lined up on either side and archers stood atop the walls. I sure hoped the king had some other, less mundane protective measures in place. There were plenty of things in the Realms that would laugh at arrows and pikes.

Two grim-faced pike men crossed their weapons, barring Raven's way as he stepped forward.

"Your business, sir?" the captain of the guard asked.

"Bran of Night, returning on the king's business."

The guard nodded at him then offered me a perfunctory bow. "Miss Brooks. We weren't expecting to see you again so soon." There was no suspicion in his tone, only a rigorous adherence to the letter of his duty. "I'm sorry, but I must ask you both to repeat the hearth vow."

You could tell people were getting jittery when the hearth vow came out. Visitors who swore the vow were bound by their own magic not to do any harm to the members of the "hearth" they were visiting. It was one way to sort Illusionist enemies from the actual friends they might be impersonating, and it had been more common in the days before the fall of Illusion for that reason.

But its use was an inherent admission of weakness, basically saying that the owner of this hearth wasn't strong enough to protect his people without it—and it had rarely been used at the palace as a result. Clearly, Rothbold was done giving a stuff what people thought of him.

I highly doubted that any of the Night Vipers were Illusionists, but I had no problem with promising not to harm the king and his family. "I vow to bring no harm to those who call this hearth their home."

Raven repeated it after me. Once that was done, the captain signalled for the postern gate to be opened, and we were allowed through.

Guards lined the pathway that meandered through the garden, lending an unaccustomed military air to the place. Whitehaven was a castle more in name than substance. It sat amid vast acres of pleasure grounds, and its walls were barely high enough to withstand any kind of siege, but the determined faces of the guards on duty proclaimed their willingness to try.

The assassins must have give everyone a good scare. Who would have ever expected them to strike at the princess in the heart of her father's power? I still couldn't see why anyone would. I mean, she was the heir to the throne, obviously. But the curse of the Brenfells protected her just as well as it did her father. Even her grasping uncle hadn't had the balls to actually do away with the king, lest the magical curse fall upon him and his household. Anyone would know the same thing must happen to someone who assassinated the innocent princess before she could even take the throne.

It didn't make much sense, but then again, a lot of things the fae did didn't make much sense to me. Maybe Raven's mysterious source was right and it had just been a piece of political manoeuvring by Kellith, far-fetched as that seemed.

We moved briskly through the gardens and soon arrived at the grand entry to the palace itself. We trotted up the steps, finding yet more guards stationed here, and we were once again stopped and questioned.

"Do you know where we might find the Dragon?" Raven asked the leader of these guards.

"He'll be in the throne room with the king."

The route from the front doors to the throne room was fast becoming a familiar one. I had trodden it several times in the past few weeks. Inside, the palace was remarkably quiet. Admittedly, it was early morning, the time of day when most fae would be at their last meal before taking to their beds. Even so, the lack of people was surprising. I wondered how many servants the queen had taken with her on her panicked flight to Summer.

There were guards stationed at the head of the corridor that led to the throne room, and yet more outside the massive doors themselves, but they didn't stop us entering. The throne was empty when I walked in, and I looked around for the king, surprised.

He stood by the windows, and my heart rose as I realised the Dragon was with him. They were both staring at a scale model of the palace and its grounds laid out on a gigantic table. As we drew closer, I realised the model wasn't made of clay or anything so mundane, but constructed of the stuff of magic itself.

The king waved his hand, and the gleaming towers of the palace rushed closer, the building rapidly doubling in size. It looked real, as solid as anything else in the room, but it was some kind of Glamour, insubstantial as mist. Two men were taking notes as the king and the Dragon chatted. Obviously, security still weighed heavily on the king's mind.

He was so engrossed with the discussion that he didn't notice us for a long moment, though the Dragon smiled at me before returning his attention to the king.

Finally, Rothbold looked up, and a smile spread across his tired face. With a snap of his fingers, he banished the

Glamoured model of the palace then turned his attention to me. "Allegra, you are a sight for sore eyes at a difficult time."

"I was sorry to hear about the attack, sire. That must have been very frightening for the princess."

"So frightening that she and her mother have fled, until Ebos here and I can assure her that she will be safe under my roof." The smile flattened into a grim line. Clearly, the king was less than impressed with his wife's reaction.

The queen was far from being my favourite person, but I couldn't help a smidgen of sympathy for her. It was bad enough finding yourself under attack by the Night Vipers. I could only imagine how much worse it must feel when their target was your beloved only child.

"But what brings you here? Not more problems, I hope."

Poor Rothbold certainly had enough of those on his plate. "In a manner of speaking, sire. It's Squeak." I gave him a brief update on Squeak's condition and what Morwenna and Lirra had both said about his likely prognosis, then I turned to the Dragon imploringly. "Sir Dragon, you once told me the dragons know more about healing wings than anyone. Is there any hope? I'll do anything."

The Dragon glanced sideways at his king. "I couldn't say for certain without seeing him myself, but there's a very good chance that my people could help. But that means someone would have to go to them."

"And the borders of Fire have been closed for decades," the king said.

"Quite so."

I glanced from one to the other of them, my heart in my eyes. "But surely they would let you in, Sir Dragon? You're one of them. If you could take me there so that I could plead my case to them …"

The king shifted uneasily. "I'm not sure that's wise."

"Wise has nothing to do with it, sire." I knew what he meant—he was as bad as Kyrrim. He wanted me to stay safely tucked away on Arlo. I lowered my voice, conscious of the servants against the walls. "Your Majesty, you said once that you understood the bond between an Illusionist and their bondmate. You said if I needed anything to help Squeak—anything at all—you would help me. Please, sire. He has only days to live."

"You are right. I did say that." The king glanced at the Dragon. "But perhaps Ebos could go on your behalf without the need for you to risk yourself on the venture. The closest entry point is the mountains of Winter, which are dangerous territory. It would be an arduous trek to reach the borders of Fire. In fact, there may not even be enough time before Squeak …"

"Then the sooner we leave the better," I burst out.

The Dragon was shaking his head. "Sire, you know the reason I left. I am afraid my pleas would not move the Lord of Fire. To have any hope of success, I fear Allegra must plead her own case."

"I'll come with you," Raven said suddenly.

We all stared at him for a moment, perplexed.

"It will be hard enough getting my people to accept one stranger, let alone two," the Dragon said.

"Not as hard as it will be to face the Hawk and tell him I let Allegra go off alone with you. If he was here, he would never allow it."

"Out of the question," the Dragon said.

"Then swear a binding vow that you will do her no harm."

"Bran!" the king said. "What are you accusing Sir Ebos of?"

"Nothing." Raven held the Dragon's eyes. "I just want him to swear."

"Raven, what are you doing?" Was he trying to ruin my only chance for saving Squeak?

"It's all right, sire," the Dragon said. "I take no offence, though I wonder if the Lord of Night knows how passionately his son feels about the lady."

He was barking up the wrong tree entirely there. Raven had no more interest in me than I did in him. I waited in a fever of impatience while the Dragon laid his right hand on his heart and swore the traditional oath. When would they all stop talking so we could leave?

The king scowled in frustration when it was done. "I still don't like you going off like this."

"And *I* don't like knowing that my bondmate is dying when there's something I could do to save him."

Rothbold sighed, a gusty sound of resignation. "Very well. Sir Ebos, I charge you with the protection of Lady Allegra."

Whoops. No one outside our little circle knew that I was actually a Lady Allegra at this point, but the Dragon hadn't reacted. Hopefully, he would assume the king had just been seized by an excess of politeness.

"Accompany her at once to the Realm of Fire and do your best to effect a cure for her bondmate."

The Dragon bowed low. "As you wish, Your Majesty."

A gate carved from a solid chunk of ice appeared out of the leafy gloom of the Wilds on the path ahead.

"This is it," the Dragon said. "Are you ready?"

"Sooo ready." Apart from my usual uneasiness in the Wilds, we'd been walking for at least two hours, and I was wearing heavy winter gear borrowed from the princess's wardrobe. "I'm melting under this stuff."

"You'll be glad of it in a moment. The mountains of Winter have to be experienced to really be believed."

Without a backward glance, he strode through the icy gate, and I followed, sweat trickling down between my breasts underneath the heavy furs. The king had insisted I needed to be properly outfitted for the trip, so the royal wardrobe had been duly raided.

Instantly, my face was lashed by a thousand tiny knives as the temperature plunged. The Dragon was waiting on the other side, his hood pulled up and his scarf wrapped around the lower part of his face so that only his dark brown eyes were visible. He was a big man, roughly Kyrrim's height, though of a less solid build. Even so, rugged up in white furs, he looked like a yeti or perhaps a small ambulatory mountain.

I tugged up my own hood and hastily arranged the folds of my scarf across my mouth and nose. The air was so cold it hurt to breathe. Already, I couldn't feel my feet in their heavy boots.

Fine snow filled the air and blanketed everything in sight. Visibility was poor, but I could tell we were high up, even if the bracing air hadn't given that away. There was a vast sense of emptiness all around. Even the trees seemed to huddle together for company, bracing themselves against the Winter winds. Not a place I wanted to spend a great amount of time.

"How long will it take us to walk to the border with Fire?" I'd been out in winter storms once or twice before, but home was always a short walk away. Here, we were on our own, at the mercy of the elements and whatever else was lurking in the snow-blasted mountains.

"That depends a lot on the conditions. If it remains fine, something like eight to ten hours. If not ..." He let the sentence trail off.

If it remained fine? Right. I eyed the icy snow with misgiving. If this was fine, I didn't want to see anything worse. Anxiety gnawed at me. We didn't have time for mishaps. Everything had to go smoothly if I was to save Squeak.

"Eight to ten *hours*?" Usually, the Wilds were more

cooperative than that, and opened gates much closer to your actual destination.

"Dragons don't believe in half measures. When they closed the border, they extended their wards out a good long way. You can't gate in any closer than this."

"Let's get going, then, and make the most of this lovely weather."

He might have grinned at my poor attempt at humour, but I couldn't tell with his face muffled the way it was. But he nodded and began to forge a path through the snow. Fortunately, it wasn't very deep, so walking was easy enough. I followed, trusting in him to find the way, though there was no obvious trail for him to follow.

Soon, I fell into a walking dream, putting one foot after the other, occasionally stopping to swipe the frozen snow from my eyelashes or to rearrange my scarf. The unchanging landscape added to the sense that we were making no progress, lost in a world of white. Though my feet were numb, the exercise warmed me and I sweated under my heavy furs.

There was no sign of animal life, or any other life for that matter. After a couple of panting hours, I ventured to make conversation. "Who lives up here?"

He paused for a drink from his canteen while he considered the question. "Cave trolls, mostly. A few goblin clans, the odd bear."

"I've barely seen any tracks. Just a rabbit or two."

"Oh, they're here, all right. But it snows so damn often that their tracks are hidden. Plus, their camouflage is good."

He hefted the canteen for another long swig then replaced the folds of his scarf around his mouth and nodded towards a stand of tall pines a small distance away. "There's a foxhole over there, under that big tree, but you won't see much of the foxes until nightfall."

I squinted into the pale sameness of the landscape. I could barely make out the hole he was talking about; it was just a slight depression in the snow, more than half hidden behind a sparse bush. "You have sharp eyes."

He grinned. This time I could tell, despite the scarf, because of the way his eyes crinkled up. "Dragons hunt from the air. We have better eyesight even than eagles. If I was up there, I could see a mouse move from a mile away." He gazed skyward, a certain longing in his eyes.

"Why *aren't* you up there?" I asked, remembering for the first time that he had wings. "I mean, wouldn't it be easier to fly to Fire than to trudge all this way?"

"I daren't take my dragon form here, so close to Fire. It would likely send my brother into a rage, and then he would never help you."

Well, in that case, I was happy to trudge there and back. Squeak was the most important thing in this whole scenario, and I wouldn't do anything to put his chances at risk.

I eyed the Dragon as he packed his canteen away in his backpack again. "Why would taking your dragon form enrage your brother?" Probably it was none of my business, but it was a long way to walk in silence. We had to talk about something.

"Orobos sees me as a rival to his throne."

"Are you?"

"Of course not. I left Fire and pledged myself to the king to prove to him that I had no intention of usurping him."

"But?" I sensed there was a *but* coming.

"But showing my dragon form would only remind him that I am, in fact, stronger than him. It wouldn't be wise."

"Surely if you left your home, that would be proof enough that you're no threat to him?"

"You would think so, wouldn't you? I'm afraid my brother isn't entirely rational on this point."

"Is that going to be a problem for us?"

His eyes crinkled above his scarf as he smiled reassuringly at me. "I'm sure your presence will defuse the situation. And it has been a long time. Who knows? He may have gotten over it."

Several more hours passed as the sun moved overhead then began to sink towards the west. Still a light snow fell, just enough to be truly annoying. My hands as well as my feet were now numb, despite the thick gloves I wore. Kyrrim had taught me how to adjust my own body temperature with magic, and I'd been adjusting my guts out all day, but the more we walked and the more tired I got, the less effective my magic seemed to be.

We came to the saddle between two mountain peaks, and a winter wonderland was laid out below us, like something from a Christmas pageant. Of course, I might have appreciated the view better if I'd had any feeling in my fingers and toes. I began to hit my hands together and shake them, trying to urge the feeling back into them, and finally, the Dragon noticed.

"What are you doing?"

"Trying to warm up my fingers. I can't feel them any more."

He muttered something that sounded uncomplimentary and strode towards me. "Let me see."

Reluctantly, I slid off one glove, baring my frozen fingers to the Arctic wind. The tips of them were bright red, but the rest was as white as the snow itself, as if I had the hands of a dead thing stuck on the ends of my arms.

He shook his head. "Haven't you been warming yourself? Why didn't you tell me they were this bad?"

I just shrugged, too cold and miserable to come up with a sensible reply. He took off his own gloves and took my hand between both of his. They were astonishingly warm.

"Give me the other hand, too."

Obediently, I bared my other hand and watched it disappear into his clasp. "How do you stay so warm?"

"I'm a dragon. We come with our own central heating."

We stood there in the snow for several minutes as warmth and life gradually returned to my fingers. It hurt like hell, but it was a relief to get some feeling back. When he was satisfied that I wasn't going to get frostbite, he insisted on gifting me his own gloves. "Take them. I don't need them, and you obviously do."

They were too big for me, but he tightened the straps firmly around my wrists so that they stayed on, and it felt like sinking my hands into a warm bath.

I closed my eyes for a moment and savoured the blissful sensation. "Thank you, Sir Knight."

"Call me Ebos," he said, smiling. "See that peak over there with the smoke rising from it?"

I nodded. "That's where we're going?"

His eyes gleamed. "Yes. That's my home, the Realm of Fire."

My heart sank as I eyed the distance between us and the smoking peak. "It still looks a long way away."

"Don't worry, we don't have to walk all the way. Only to the border."

I glanced sideways at him. His cheeks above the scarf were pink, his eyes sparkling. Was that excitement at seeing his home again after so long? I hoped his brother wouldn't spoil this homecoming. "And where is the border?"

"At the bottom of the pass. We're more than halfway there."

Well, that was encouraging, though my shoulders were aching from the unaccustomed weight of the pack and my feet were still numb. "Great, let's eat something to celebrate. My stomach is starting to feel like my throat's been cut."

He snorted, but swung off his pack. I did the same, and we ate a hasty meal of cheese and fruit and little sweet cakes that the castle kitchen had provided.

The snow began to fall more heavily as we set off again. Several times I caught Ebos eyeing the sky with concern, and sniffing the breeze as if that would give him some kind of accurate weather forecast. The third time he did it I couldn't hold in my curiosity any longer.

"What do you smell?" My fae senses were good, but I couldn't smell anything except pine and the constant wetness of the air and the damp wool and fur around my head.

He considered me, as if weighing up whether to answer. "Cave trolls," he said finally.

I glanced around, but the snow was falling faster now, the flakes big and fat, and the day was rapidly disappearing into a featureless white mass. "Cave trolls? Where?"

He kept up a steady pace, striding through the snow as if he were on a well-worn path through the palace grounds. "Behind us a little ways. I first picked up the scent where we saw the fox hole."

"And you didn't say anything? How many trolls are we talking?"

"Probably just a small family pack."

He said that like it was a good thing. "Oh, awesome. What do we do?"

"We keep walking and hope that the weather worsens and throws them off our scent."

Seriously? Now we were hoping to be caught in a blizzard? This day was rapidly going from bad to worse. "And how likely is that to happen?"

"Not very. They are remarkably good trackers. But there are some caves further down where we can make a stand."

We walked a little further in uneasy silence. At least, it was uneasy on my side. That sense of being watched that I always had in the Wilds was back in full force, only this time there was a reason. An enormous, violent reason.

Probably a hungry one, too. Ebos seemed remarkably calm about the whole thing.

"Do you often run into cave trolls in these mountains?"

"All the time. The place is littered with them." He sounded almost cheerful. Strange man. He smiled at me, his eyes crinkling again above his scarf. "Don't worry. I can handle a single pack of trolls, no problem."

Great. As long as there *was* a single pack, and not a whole tribe of the bastards on our tail. Still, there was no sense stressing about it until I saw what we were up against. I resisted the urge to sprint down the mountainside in search of the caves, forcing myself to mimic his steady, ground-eating stride.

"Storm coming," my companion said after an endless, anxious time. My shoulders were up around my ears, hunched against an impending attack. "Fortunately, we're almost at the caves."

It was much darker now, more grey than white. I'd lost all sense of time, so I had no idea if that was because of the storm or if it was nearly nightfall again. Either way, a cave seemed like a pretty good idea. I had the sneaking suspicion that the trolls were waiting for the darkness before they closed in, and I wanted to be out of the open before that happened.

I was stumbling on unseen rocks, the darkness almost complete, when Ebos stopped. With a note of satisfaction in his voice, he said, "Here we are."

The cave was almost as hard to spot as the fox hole had been. Hidden behind a stand of scrubby pines, you would have had to have known it was there to have any chance of finding it. Obviously, the Dragon knew these mountains well.

He went first, summoning a ball of faelight, and inspected the cave. I shouldered in behind him, unwilling to be left alone outside. There was a neat pile of bones in one corner and a strong stench of some kind of animal, but it was clearly empty. It wasn't big enough for anything to hide from us. Somewhat relieved, I eased off my pack with a groan.

"Stay here," the Dragon said, dropping his own pack and drawing his sword instead.

16

For a moment, I considered doing as he said. My numb, exhausted feet wanted nothing more than to take the load off, and my back was aching from toting the pack halfway up the mountain and down again. But I could hardly let him go out to face a pack of trolls on his own, dragon or no dragon. So after a moment, I dug through my pack for my knives and moved to the cave entrance.

The blades were so cold I could feel them through the thick gloves I was wearing. They would probably fuse to my skin if I handled them with my bare flesh. Fortunately, I could be just as deadly with gloves on, even gloves that didn't fit properly.

I hefted the first knife in my hand, testing its weight and feel against the glove. It was hard to see anything outside. Beyond the scrubby pines that sheltered the cave loomed a wall of grey. Grey night, grey snow. I couldn't see the Dragon at all until he moved slightly. He was standing on the other side of the pines, half hidden among their drooping, snow-laden branches. And he was watching the way up the mountain with the fierce intensity of a predator.

We waited while the wind whistled past and whipped the snowflakes into a blinding world. It was fully dark now, and I kept blinking, hoping to clear the snow and grit from my eyes. It didn't make any difference—visibility was still poor. It was becoming harder to see the Dragon, still as a statue beneath his pine.

I blinked again and a piece of the mountain moved.

Holy shit. It was massive. This was a cave troll? I'd heard they were bigger than the regular river trolls I was used to, but this was something else.

The creature was twice the Dragon's height and maybe ten times heavier. It moved with a slow, lumbering gait, but the size of its legs meant it could still move quickly. It trailed a club behind it in the snow, gouging a deep furrow in the earth. The club was so crudely crafted, it was barely more than an uprooted tree with the branches stripped off.

I held my breath, watching the creature's slow approach. Was there only one? Even one troll this size would be a Herculean task to bring down. My little knives would barely be more than the annoying buzz of a fly to it. I glanced again at Ebos, wondering if he was as scared as I was, but he still hadn't moved, content to let the monster come to him.

Another troll emerged from the snow-tossed gloom. This one was significantly shorter and obviously female, though she was still massive, rising head and shoulders above the Dragon. And she also carried a club.

I strained my eyes against the swirling snow, trying to pierce the gloom. Another shape appeared, and then another, both troll children or perhaps adolescents, judging by their relative size. These were only the height of the Dragon himself, but both carried clubs. Looked like clubbing was a family pastime.

Papa Troll sniffed the air. He had a wide, flat nose that looked like it had been broken and spread across his face several times already. His craggy brows sheltered granite-cold eyes that surveyed the scene cautiously. His whole body was grey, and the dirty furs he wore blended right in with his stony skin. In the dark and the snow, he was almost invisible, despite his height.

I glanced back over my shoulder into the cave. I'd noticed a long, straight bone, probably a femur, in the pile of bones in the corner. Would that be a more useful weapon than my knife? Maybe a rock? Unless I could land a blade directly in his eye, I didn't see what use my knives would be in this fight. It looked like it was all on the Dragon, and that would be a very uneven contest indeed.

I drew back into the shadows of the cave as Papa Troll's gaze turned my way. Did the trolls know the cave was here? I had to assume they did. Maybe they'd been the ones who'd assembled the pile of bones. Suddenly, the cave no longer felt like such a sanctuary, but more of a trap.

I dug under my furs and withdrew the cloak of shadows from my back pocket. This seemed like an excellent time to be invisible. Quickly, I settled the cloak around my shoulders. It clung to me, clasping itself at my neck, and I winked out of existence. Well, not precisely. I could still feel the biting cold, sadly. But I couldn't be seen. I tucked the knife away and picked up the jagged leg bone, then stepped out into the whirling snow.

Papa Troll lifted his head to scent the air again. The wind had picked up, and was driving the snow almost horizontally. It brought me his rank troll stench, and I recognised it as the animal scent from inside the cave. So the trolls did know of its existence. Better to be out here in the clean air, then, with room to manoeuvre.

I circled around, putting the stand of pines where the Dragon waited between me and the group of trolls, moving very slowly. Of course I left footprints in the snow, but it took only moments for the wind to erase them after I had moved.

I hadn't realised how much warmth the dank cave had actually been providing until I stepped out into the weather again. Higher up, the wind was shrieking around the peaks, though their tops were invisible through the driving snow. The trolls didn't seem bothered by the weather. I watched uneasily as they spread out across the width of the pass and began to move forward as a group. It was as if they knew there was something ahead they couldn't yet see and they were determined to herd it before them.

One of the smaller trolls was closest to the stand of scrubby pines. The Dragon waited until the troll had almost drawn level with him before leaping out from his place of concealment. The bright blade of his sword sang through the air and a troll head went tumbling free.

It took a moment for the other trolls to realise what had happened. The headless body flopped to the ground, spewing blood, which lay obscenely bright against the pale snow. The female troll howled and sprang with surprising agility at the Dragon, her club raised for a smashing blow.

Ebos sidestepped the downward arc of her club and brought his sword around, biting into the troll's side. She roared in pain, but it barely slowed her down, and then her massive mate joined the fight.

The Dragon was in serious trouble. The giant troll's tree trunk of a club smashed down, missing Ebos by inches. He danced back, his sword flashing, but he couldn't get close enough to land a blow with those two mighty clubs clearing an arc around the trolls. The third troll began to circle around, trying to get behind the knight.

That was my cue. Moving soundlessly, I got as close as I could to the third troll. All his attention was on the fight between the knight and his parents, and he had no idea I was even there. I was so close I could smell the rank stench of his wet furs and his own horrendous body odour.

When I was close enough that I had to hold my breath against the foul stench of the troll teen, I hauled back and slammed my improvised bone bat into the back of his knees as if they were a baseball and I was swinging for the fences. He sprawled face first in the snow, and I cast aside the bone and drew my first knife.

I leapt onto the downed troll's back, knife ready; with my free hand, I reached for the greasy nest of matted hair on his head. I jerked his head back hard and leaned forward to slash his throat.

The troll teen had amazingly fast reflexes, considering his size. He couldn't see me. All he knew was that he was down with a weight on his back, and he did the first thing that popped into his rock-like skull. Unfortunately for me, it proved all too effective.

He hurled himself into a roll to one side, and I ended up on my back in the snow with a large and angry troll on top of me. The only thing I had going for me at this point was that I was still invisible. Thankfully, he scrambled back to his feet before I died of asphyxiation by troll, but it took me longer than I would have liked before I could move again. I was completely winded.

Luckily for me, he was none too bright. Seeing nothing on the ground, he began casting around, trying to find his invisible assailant. I got to my feet, wincing. Breathing was difficult, and I really hoped I hadn't cracked a rib, but I did my best to keep my breathing as quiet as possible. Admittedly, the howling of the wind was pretty good cover for any noises that I was making.

My blade had scratched the troll teen's neck and a line of bright blood was visible above his ragged furs. That was a start, but it wasn't going to be much use to the Dragon. I risked a look over my shoulder and saw he was still holding his own against the two larger trolls. But for how much longer? Papa Troll, in particular, had him dancing backwards and forwards across the snowy ground in a desperate effort to avoid the mighty sweeps of the giant club.

Teen Troll decided that if it was working for dad, it would work for him, too, even if he couldn't see his enemy. He began laying about him with his club, making wild swings in every direction. I had to drop back to the snow as one massive swing sailed over my head, narrowly missing me. The snow around me puffed into the air as I hit the deck and Teen Troll paused, his club upraised. I could almost hear the gears grinding in his head as he came to the conclusion that his invisible enemy must have caused that disturbance in the snow, and he brought the club whistling down.

Desperately, I rolled to the side, just managing to avoid becoming a snow slushy. But he was on to me now, watching for evidence of my movements in the snow. He pounced again so soon that he nearly took my head off.

Scrambling to my feet, I dived for the shelter of the trees. My nimbleness was an advantage in among the tree trunks, and he wasn't as free to swing that vicious club there. I ducked under the snow-laden boughs of the nearest pine and began to climb, hugging the trunk so as to disturb the least amount of snow.

Clearly, it hadn't occurred to him that his prey might take to the trees, for he continued to rampage around the bases of them, lashing out as best he could with his club, slamming it into the snow between the tree trunks. Great clouds of snow fountained into the air with every blow. Well, at least I had drawn him away from the Dragon.

But perhaps I could still do more. Once I had attained a height beyond the reach of his club, I settled myself securely in a fork of the tree and balanced my knife between my gloved fingertips. It would be a difficult shot, considering all the branches and pine needles between us. I bided my time, waiting for the right opportunity. I only had two knives, and I couldn't afford to waste a shot.

Finally, Teen Troll moved into the perfect position. I had a clear shot at his head. I lined up on my target and let the knife fly.

The blade buried itself into his left eye, and the troll's screech echoed around the pass, reverberating off the rocky walls.

That was enough to completely distract his mother from her battle with the knight. She loped toward him at once, holding her own injured side. The Dragon slashed at the back of her leg as she passed, no doubt hoping to hamstring her. But she flicked her club almost contemptuously and, by a lucky chance, managed to catch the tip of his sword.

In horror, I watched his sparkling sword go cartwheeling through the air. Now he was defenceless. Although the mother troll's attention was fully on her injured son, Papa Troll was business as usual. He brought his club whistling down, forcing the Dragon to dance out of reach, further away from his sword.

Papa Troll grinned, showing a mouthful of pointed yellow teeth, and stepped closer to the sword, practically on top of it. *Come and get it if you dare*, his body language said.

The Dragon was in a pickle. Any moment now, two angry, pain-maddened trolls could turn on him, and in the meantime the biggest one of all was still fighting fit, and him with no weapon at all. I drew my other knife and lined up a desperate shot, hoping to add Papa Troll to the list of the injured, but he moved just as I released the knife and it sailed harmlessly past his head.

The Dragon had evidently come to the same conclusion, as he darted forward, throwing himself onto his belly, reaching for the lost sword. The gigantic club slammed into the snow, but he rolled out of harm's way. Once, twice, the Dragon evaded the smashing blows. He had me believing he could do it. But the next blow connected.

I clapped my hands over my mouth to hold in the shout of horror as the massive club slammed into the back of the Dragon's head.

His arm was still outstretched, fingers grasping at the hilt, almost in reach. But now forever beyond him. There was no way any man could survive a blow to the head like that, fae or not.

Tears sprang to my eyes as I stared down at the unmoving body of the knight spreadeagled in the snow. Papa Troll shook his head at the sky and yelled something that must have been a cry of triumph. His mate and their child staggered back to his side, and all three of them stared down at the Dragon's body for a moment. Then, just in case there was any hope left in my heart at all, the troll picked up the knight's own sword and solemnly skewered him on it.

17

I perched in the tree, numb, while below me the two biggest trolls conversed in voices that sounded like rocks scraping together. After a time, they seemed to come to a decision, and Papa Troll picked up the body of his fallen child, then grabbed one of the Dragon's feet and set off down the path, dragging the dead knight behind him. The knight's limp body left a trail of pink, churned-up snow in its wake as his blood mixed with the white powder, the sword still standing up from his back like a flagpole. The injured teen troll shuffled after his father, one hand cradling his bloody eye, leaving Mama Troll behind.

The shrieking winds had abated somewhat, but the night was still dark and full of driven snow. I soon lost sight of them and the Dragon's body.

Mama Troll didn't do much for a while, just stood there sniffing the air. Then she began methodically pacing around the small stand of pines, kicking at the snow as she went. Great gouts of snow flew up into the night air as I watched her stomp around, gradually widening her circle out from around the pines into the pass.

In my grief and exhaustion, it took me a while to figure out what she was doing, but it dawned on me eventually that she was, in fact, searching for me. Her son must have told her about his invisible assailant, and now she was determinedly pursuing me as best she could.

How long would she keep this up? I didn't want to be stuck up this tree all night, but neither did I wish to risk being captured by climbing down while she was still in the vicinity. One of her children was dead, the other injured, and she was clearly in no mind to let the guilty party off scot-free.

I could probably manage to sneak away unseen, but, quite frankly, I didn't have the heart to risk it right now. With her on high alert, even slipping as I descended the tree could prove fatal. And I certainly didn't want to give her the idea of extending her search up into the branches. She was taller than her son, and the club she still carried could easily sweep me out of my perch if she knew I was there. So I sat and watched her, desperately channelling magic to my extremities, trying to keep from shivering.

I was beginning to rethink my decision an hour later when she still showed no signs of leaving the area. I still had a long way to go if I was to save Squeak, and the sooner I got started, the better.

My heart ached for the poor Dragon, and I dreaded giving the news of his death to the king. It wasn't my fault, but I couldn't help a niggling feeling of guilt, knowing that the Dragon would never have been in this area if not for me and my insistence on helping Squeak.

And now, perhaps even that goal was at risk. Without him, would the people of Fire even let me in? The Dragon had said we didn't have to walk all the way to the peak, that they would intercept us at the border. And yet I had only the vaguest idea where the border actually was, and no clue at all as to whether they would open their lands to me, a stranger, without the Dragon at my side.

No, that wasn't true. Actually, I had a pretty good idea that they wouldn't. The king had said that the borders of Fire had been closed for decades. Why would they make an exception for a stranger? But surely, if I told them of Squeak's need, they would relent?

And yet my heart sank further into my frozen boots as the night wore on and the she-troll continued her vigil in the pass.

I'd almost decided that I would have to risk making a break past her if I was ever to get underway again at all, when two trolls appeared out of the swirling darkness. One was Papa Troll, but the other was a newcomer. The new troll wore a necklace strung with long pointed teeth, some as long as my hand. What kind of creature had such teeth come from? I'd never seen any so big, and I'd butchered a few carcasses in my time. Surely they weren't dragon teeth? How could a troll, even one the size of Papa Troll or his friend, manage to best a dragon?

I sighed softly, laying my wool-wrapped cheek against the frigid bark of the pine tree. Why should I doubt it?

Hadn't I just seen the trolls defeat the Dragon in front of my very eyes? Clearly, it could be done.

The new troll conferred with the other two, and then they advanced on the cave behind me. They must have decided that this was where their invisible assailant was holed up. One by one, the three of them disappeared inside. The cave wasn't large; it wouldn't take long to realise that it was empty.

Sure enough, they soon reappeared. But Papa Troll was carrying my backpack. Damn, I'd forgotten that was in there—looked like there'd be no breakfast for me. The she-troll waved her arms around, indicating the ground between the walls of the pass. She was probably explaining to him how she'd searched it. The new troll gave a few desultory kicks at the snow, then walked off. After a moment, the other two followed him, and soon, they were swallowed by the night.

I sat in my tree for a while longer, wondering if this was some kind of trap. Perhaps they thought to lure me out of wherever I was hiding by pretending to leave. But the longer I sat there with nothing happening, the more I realised that I was giving them too much credit. Cave trolls were an evolutionary branch that was well and truly withering. Their smarter cousins, the river trolls, had nabbed all the brains from the family tree. No, the trolls had simply given up and it was time for me to climb down.

As it turned out, it was a good thing I had waited. I made a lot more noise climbing down the tree than I normally would, even slipping the last few feet when my fingers proved even stiffer with cold than I had expected. But I was soon on the ground, and I set off in the same direction the trolls had gone. My path lay that way, too.

I moved as quickly as I could without making too much noise, gradually working some feeling back into my arms and legs. I hadn't come this far to get caught now.

Screaming from further down the pass stopped me in my tracks. Goosebumps prickled to life up and down my arms. What the hell was going on down there? I would have expected the trolls to be celebrating their great victory over the knight, but those sounded like screams of pain and terror. Had fighting broken out among them, perhaps? Had the troll with the dragon necklace decided he wanted to keep the Dragon's sword as a trophy and Papa Troll had objected? Cave trolls were primitive creatures, and just as liable to fight to the death over a chicken wing as a sword.

Either way, perhaps it was a good thing for me. If they were too tied up in their own pursuits, they wouldn't even notice a shadow slip past.

At least walking warmed me up. I felt some life return to my heavy limbs as I trudged through the snow. I was thirsty, but my canteen had gone with my pack, and I had no wish to suck on frozen snow. I was cold enough already without swallowing a gullet full of ice.

The still falling snow had already erased the tracks of the trolls, but I was sure I was still following them. The sides of the pass were so sheer that there was really nowhere else to go, although I kept my eye open for well concealed caves.

As it turned out, the trolls were easy to find. I began to

smell smoke and a sharp, acrid stench, and soon, a turn of the pass brought me a strange sight.

To my left lay the opening of a large cave, big enough to drive a semitrailer through, although it seemed as if it had recently suffered a catastrophic enlargement. Rocks of many sizes, including some big boulders, lay scattered across the width of the pass as if some giant truck had ploughed through the ragged opening of the cave wall. The largest of these, a big black boulder, sat squarely in the centre of the pass in a shining pool of melted and then re-frozen snow. I moved closer to the boulder, using it as a shield between me and the cave entrance, and peeked inside.

Perhaps twenty trolls had gathered in the large, open cave. Dark shadows along the back and sides hinted at tunnels or smaller caves off the side. The main cave was smoky from a large cooking fire that burned in the centre. Smoke from the fire rose toward the peaked roof and disappeared somewhere into the jagged cracks of the ceiling. Two trolls in front of the cooking pot were dismembering a third, whose pale grey skin was seared black in places.

The large communal pot bobbled, and the smell of boiling meat drifted out to me. My stomach rumbled with hunger even as my instincts rebelled in horror. I could see body parts in that cauldron, and one arm looked the right size to have come from the Dragon.

I stood for a moment, frozen in horror. The trolls were going to eat him? His family wouldn't even have a body to bury, after his years of service to the Crown? It was horrific.

I gazed around the cave, recognising the troll with the dragon necklace. He was seated atop a large rock, overseeing the cooking process. Papa and Mama Troll stood nearby. Did they all live here together, or was this some kind of communal meeting hall? Weighed down with sorrow, I was about to move on when I spied a glint of silver in the dark recesses of the cave. Was that—?

Yes, it was. The Dragon's sword stood propped against a wall, discarded like a common garden rake. If the trolls had been fighting over it before, no one seemed to give a stuff about it now. My blood boiled. They killed a Knight of the Realms then ate him as if he were no more than an animal? And then they left his sword lying around as if his life and his honour had no meaning at all?

Well, we would see about that. If I couldn't retrieve his body for burial, at least I could do something about that sword. I took a few minutes longer to study the layout of the cave and the positioning of all its inhabitants. With the scent of that hideous meat cooking, they would never smell me, and the cloak of shadows meant that they wouldn't see me either. All I had to do was make sure I made no noise. Piece of cake.

I bent to gather a handful of small black rocks from around the base of the boulder that sheltered me, then I picked my way carefully across the broken ground toward the cave mouth. Once there, I hurled a rock as hard as I could toward the back of the cave. It clattered to the ground somewhere back there in the darkness and every ugly troll head in the place turned to trace the source of the noise.

I slipped into the cave and made my way toward the sword. Luckily, there were no trolls between me and it. It was the work of a moment to arrive beside the weapon. I drew in a deep, silent breath, readying myself for the next bit.

I let another stone fly, a little to the right of where the first one had landed, and once again, the trolls all looked toward the noise. Necklace Guy stood up and yelled something in the harsh troll language, probably some kind of insult, which only added to the diversion for all the others in the cave. I picked up the Dragon's weapon, careful not to let the naked blade scrape against the rock. Once I had it in my hand, of course, it became invisible, and I began the slow retreat to the cave mouth.

No one had seen me come, and no one noticed me go, either. In a few minutes, I was back outside, the Dragon's sword held carefully in both hands. A sheath would have been handy. It would be a major pain to carry it like this all the way down to the border, but the sheath had disappeared with the Dragon. Perhaps it was decorating some troll den somewhere or being turned to some other trollish purpose.

I increased my pace as I got further away from the troll cave. It would be good to have a bit of space between us if anyone did notice the theft. I kept an ear out as I marched onward, half expecting to hear a hue and cry begin behind me, but all was quiet. I had got away with it.

The Dragon had been a tall man, much taller than me, and his sword was sized to fit him. I couldn't even thrust it through my belt to carry it as the tip would have dragged along the ground. Once I was far enough away from the trolls, I removed my belt and slung it crosswise across my body. Then, very carefully, I wriggled the tip of the naked blade down through the makeshift bandolier at my back so the sword hilt was protruding above my shoulder. Accessing the sword in a hurry would be difficult, but I was hardly going to use it. It was a knight's weapon, and I was no knight. Briefly, I mourned the loss of my two daggers, which were weapons that did suit me—but at least I was still alive, and that had to count for something.

While there is life there is hope, they say, but I had very little hope that the people of Fire would help me as things stood. Perhaps if I offered them the Dragon's sword and explained what had happened—how he had died fighting to protect me, how important he felt my cause was.

Silver Tree, who was I kidding? I knew they wouldn't give a rat's arse about causes. From what the Dragon had said, his brother might not even be that upset that the knight was dead. I had to come up with a plan B, and it had to be spectacular.

I already had something in mind, of course, but it was a little bold, even for me. Could I really pull it off? There were so many things that could go wrong—even more than had gone wrong already. If I was discovered, they would probably kill me, but time was ticking away. I was acutely conscious that dawn was only hours away, which brought us another day closer to Squeak's death.

I had the power in my hands to save him. How could I let fear hold me back?

The Dragon had said the border with Fire was at the tree line and I would know it when I saw it. It had seemed an odd thing to say. Was there a customs checkpoint? I highly doubted it. And yet, when I got there, I realised he was right.

I paused at the place where the pass opened up, marvelling at the vista laid out before me. The snow still fell, still blanketed the ground ahead in pristine white, and yet it was very clear that Winter's domain was almost at an end. Just a little further down the mountainside, the world changed from white to black. Instead of shining on dazzling snow on the other side of the border, the moonlight fell on bare, black rock. It was as if a line had been drawn by an invisible hand. On one side, snow fell and frigid Winter reigned. On the other, the black rocks were dry and the air was still.

I had never seen such an obvious magical border between Realms before, though, to be fair, the only one I had ever seen before was the border between Autumn and

Illusion, which was merely a riverbank. You would never have guessed that sovereignty changed from one side of the reeds to the other. But here, there was no doubt.

The black rocks tumbled and fell down the mountainside into a broad but barren valley. Out of this valley reared two enormous volcanic peaks, their shoulders wreathed in smoke and their heads crowned in glowing red fire. These volcanoes were the heart of Fire's domain. Among the smoke, the occasional draconic shape could be seen circling the peaks. No doubt these were the watchers the Dragon had spoken of, the ones who would know when we crossed the border.

Time to make a decision once and for all. Plan A, with very little chance of success, or Plan B, with a higher chance but drastic consequences for failure?

I sighed as I studied the distant smoking peaks. I knew which one Kyrrim would want me to choose, but it wasn't that cut and dried. There were actually disastrous possibilities for each choice—it was just that the consequences fell on different parties. If I went to the dragons as I was and they refused to let me in or help me, then Squeak was doomed. If I went to them in a different form, Squeak had a chance but the danger to myself if my deception was discovered was great.

I removed the cloak of shadows, popping back into view, and tucked it away again in my back pocket. I was really only putting off the inevitable; I already knew which option I was going for. It was time to grow a set and commit.

I held out my gloved hands in front of me. These were the Dragon's gloves, and if I needed anything else of his,

his sword was strapped to my back. It should be an easy transformation. I closed my eyes and summoned a vision of Ebos: his tall, slim frame, his strong hands, the inquisitive spark in his dark brown eyes.

A ripple of magic passed over me, warming my skin. When I opened my eyes, I was significantly taller and wore the surcoat of a Knight of the Realms. I gazed down at myself in wonder, noting the snug fit of the gloves that had previously swum on my hands. My feet were shoved into the heavy leather boots of a knight.

I stamped my foot, feeling the weight and power of the movement. Shaking my head in wonder, I realised even that felt different. A heavy fall of dark hair was tied back in a rough ponytail at the back of my neck. I had done it. To any outward eyes, I was now the Dragon.

I strode down the path, trying to look the part, my head held high. I kept my eye on those winged shapes within the smoke around the distant peaks. Sure enough, as I approached the demarcation line between the Realms, one of them peeled away from the peak and flew towards me.

I stopped at the border, suddenly uncertain. Could I even cross? Would the border magic somehow know I was an imposter and not the man I appeared to be? Perhaps if the borders were closed to all comers, there was something in the magic that recognised true denizens of Fire and would zap me where I stood.

Well, at least that would be quick.

I strode across the invisible line and stopped on the other side, still thankfully in one piece.

The approaching dragon would have given even the bravest person nightmares. It was very hard to stand there, pretending nonchalance, with such a creature bearing down on me. Every self-preservation instinct in my brain was shrieking at me to run. I don't think I'd ever really appreciated just how big dragons were before. Its wingspan was truly enormous, and the closer it got, the larger it appeared. It was like standing on a runway with a 747 about to land on top of you. Only the thought of Squeak and a supreme effort of will kept me rooted to the spot as the gigantic creature settled a short distance away with one last thunderous clap of its wings.

For a long moment, we stared at each other, the dragon and I. Its eyes were golden, with vertical pupils that reminded me of Squeak, which helped settle me a little. Its scales were the colour of dried blood, yet glowed with an inner fire that made them beautiful, and the wings when they had been spread shone like stained-glass with the light behind. The massive head bent closer as the dragon inspected me. I waited, trying to appear stoic and unafraid, though I was trembling in my oversized boots. I figured the less I said, the better. That way I would have fewer lies to keep track of.

Smoke puffed from the dragon's nostrils as it spoke, its voice a deep, melodious rumble. "It's been a long time, Ebos."

"It has indeed." The dragon obviously knew who I was, or at least who I was pretending to be, which meant I should probably know its name as well, but I couldn't even tell if it was male or female. I'd have to really work the strong, silent thing.

"What brings you here, after all these years?"

That was an easy question, at least. "I come on a mission from the king. He begs Fire's aid for a dying rainbow drake."

More smoke puffed from the dragon's nostrils as it huffed a kind of laugh. "He begs, does he? And he thinks sending *you* will move Lord Orobos?"

"He thinks sending me is the only way to get an emissary into Fire at all," I said a little testily. Standing under the dragon's golden gaze was making me distinctly twitchy, and I didn't do diplomacy well when I was twitchy. Not that I was ever that great at diplomacy. "Or have you decided to reopen the borders?"

"You might be surprised," the red dragon said. "A lot of things are changing now."

Ain't that the truth. This dragon had no idea. "Will Orobos receive me?"

"I daresay he could do with a laugh. Assume your true form and come and see." The dragon spread its great, glowing wings in preparation for take-off, and I suddenly saw a terrible flaw in my plan.

I could mimic the Dragon's human form perfectly. And though I had never tried it, I was fairly certain I could even take on his actual draconic form. But that didn't mean I knew how to fly. And nothing would expose me as a sham faster.

The dragon was waiting expectantly, wings half spread.

My heart thundered as my brain raced, searching for an excuse, some kind of cover story. The Dragon had said we'd be met at the border, and of course, I'd realised we would eventually make our way to the peaks of Fire, but I hadn't given any thought as to how that would occur. A fatal flaw in my plan.

"I'm not sure I can." I gazed up into the huge golden eyes and let myself sway, just a little. "I'm not feeling quite myself."

Lord, I was such a comedian. A panicked urge to laugh nearly brought me undone.

"I had to fight off a pack of trolls …"

And then I let myself collapse in an ungainly heap on the black, rocky ground.

They say the bigger they are, the harder they fall. I discovered that was true and barely managed to stop myself wincing in pain as I smacked into the rocks. The sword hilt struck me painfully on the back of the head, but at least I managed to fall in such a way that the naked blade didn't cut me.

The dragon rumbled in protest. Even with my eyes closed, I felt the shadow as the dragon's bulk loomed over me. A strong smell of burning filled my nostrils as the dragon's breath huffed in my face. Belatedly, I wondered if this would be seen as a show of weakness that might put me at a serious disadvantage, but really, what could I do about it? There was no way I could pull off flying, so this seemed the only option.

The dragon rumbled to itself again, a deep noise that

managed to convey its dissatisfaction without any words, and then I felt its claws close around me. I focused on keeping as limp as possible. I was committed now.

Suddenly, I was snatched into the air. Air rushed around me as the dragon leapt skyward, the mighty downstrokes of its wings like thunder in my ears. Its claws were surprisingly gentle—they didn't dig into me at all, merely cradled me, clutching the damn sword like a rod of pain against my back. The sooner I could find a sheath for the thing, the better.

Successive small jerks told me the dragon was beating for height. My stomach dipped and soared uncomfortably. I was only grateful I couldn't see what was happening. I must look like a rabbit dangling from an eagle's claws. Hopefully, I wouldn't meet the usual fate of rabbits borne aloft by eagles. As long as the dragon had a good grip, I should be set. I was putting a lot of faith in those strong claws—falling from a height like this would certainly be a swift end, and that was about the best that could be said for it.

Though it had looked distant, the dragon's massive wings made short work of the flight to the volcano. I felt the change in the air as we began to descend. Squinting through half-closed lids, I saw smoke swirling about us and felt an unexpected heat. We must be flying over the crater.

That gave rise to a new worry. I might look like the Dragon, but I sure as hell wasn't flameproof the way a real dragon would be. If we were headed for the interior of an active volcano, I was literally toast. But before I could work up to more than a mild panic, the sensation of heat eased, and I realised we had dropped below the level of the crater.

The dragon landed, a little awkwardly since it had me in its front claws, and let me fall, not ungently. I judged it safe enough to recover consciousness at this point and made a show of stirring, throwing in a groan or two to emphasise my supposed weakness. I sat up and found myself on a wide, flat stretch of rock outside a cave.

This was no raggedy cave such as the cave trolls' had been. Stone pillars supported a wide portico above the landing that covered half the space, presumably so the dragons had space to land but then could quickly move undercover if the weather was bad. Stone vines covered in flowers writhed up each pillar and decorated the whole of the underside of the roof.

I stood up, trying not to look too impressed with the elegance and craftsmanship of the place. After all, the real Dragon had probably seen it many times before.

"Welcome home," the red dragon said, confirming my guess.

Behind the entry, a vast cavern stretched. Again, it was no rough cave, but carved and decorated with all manner of jewels and metalwork. The floors were tiled with intricate patterns in silver and black. Chandeliers dripping with diamonds hung from the vaulted ceiling. It looked more like the interior of a cathedral than something you would find on a bare mountainside.

I stepped forward into the entryway, marvelling at the sculptures inlaid with gold and silver and precious jewels. There were whole hunting scenes brought to life on the glittering walls. Feasts and duels, too. Dragons were everywhere, of course, their colours picked out in loving detail, encrusted with glittering stones, but there were also plenty of human shapes depicted. Presumably, these were dragons in their earthbound forms.

Uneasily, I wondered what the protocol was, and whether I was committing some faux pas in coming here as a man instead of a dragon. The Dragon had said his brother wouldn't tolerate seeing him in his dragon form, but then this red dragon had seemed surprised that I *wasn't* in dragon form. I didn't know what to think.

I glanced over my shoulder at the red dragon. "Thank you for your assistance."

"Seems like you'd better go and see the healers on your own account."

"A little rest will do me good. Are you coming?"

The dragon laughed, and the booming sound echoed around the vast empty chamber. "Has it been so long that you've forgotten the way?" It turned and spread its wings, making ready to take to the skies again. "I must return to my duty, more's the pity. I would have liked to be there to see Orobos's face when his long-lost brother returned."

The red dragon's mighty haunches bunched, and it leaped skyward. I stood watching until it soared out of sight, then sighed, more than a little daunted. I had gained the peak but I had no idea what to do now. It sounded as though I should probably present myself to Orobos, my supposed brother, but that would be tricky since I had no idea what he looked like or where to find him.

Three corridors led from the vast entry chamber. Each was as big as the others, as brightly lit and decorated. What I needed was a flashing sign that said, *Hey! This way to the throne room.* Or even, *Get your evil dragon brothers here!*

The enormity of what I was doing weighed heavily on me. Even if I managed to find Orobos, what on earth would I say to him? It wouldn't take much conversation before he realised I couldn't possibly be who I said I was.

Come to think of it, it would be better if I could avoid meeting with Orobos at all. All I wanted was a consultation with a healer, after all. Was there any chance I could sneak around this place without avoiding a diplomatic incident and find one? I sighed. Probably not. I picked one of the passageways at random and began walking.

The passage was wide enough that an adult dragon with wings at full stretch could pass with plenty of room to spare on each side. I wondered if they actually flew through these passages. I made myself walk briskly, as if I knew where I was going. Uncertainty lay like a cloak of dread on my shoulders and made me want to turn and run back the other way before I was caught.

You're doing this for Squeak, I reminded myself angrily. *Don't lose your nerve now.*

The passageway curved around to the left, passing several doors of a more human size. Where did these lead? Meeting rooms, kitchens? Perhaps private quarters? There was no way to know without opening them. I decided to walk further before I tried one. Surely there would be a place devoted to healing, as there was in other Realms. I hoped there would be some more obvious sign that I was getting close.

Another corridor crossed the one I was in, and I hesitated, peering along it. It was smaller, only human-sized, which somehow made it more welcoming. I hesitated, unsure of myself. Voices from that direction decided me. Despite my fear, I was ever conscious of time ticking away. I had to seize this opportunity by the balls and give it a damn good twist. No more skulking in empty corridors. I had to find someone to talk to.

I strode down the new corridor, arms swinging, to all intents and purposes a man with a mission. The voices died away, and I heard a door close softly. There. I rounded a corner and found a new hall, lined with doors, all closed. If I wasn't careful, I would get lost in here and wander for hours.

Where were all the dragons? Were they all out flying somewhere? Or deep in the crater of the volcano, basking in lava? The size of this place suggested that many people lived here, and yet I had seen no one, not even any guards at the entry. But I supposed there wasn't much need for guards since the borders were closed.

I laid a hand on the nearest door, frustration churning in my belly, just as the door on the other side of the corridor opened.

My mouth fell open in surprise at the sight of the person who came through it. "Jaxen? What in the seven hells are *you* doing here?"

Lord Eldric's brother stopped, his face a picture of

confusion. Belatedly, it occurred to me to wonder how well Jaxen and the real Dragon knew each other. But surely, since they were both part of the nobility, they at least knew each other's names?

Jaxen's gaze flitted across the knightly surcoat I wore and the hilt of the giant sword protruding above my shoulder, and gradually, his expression cleared. "I'm here to visit Lord Orobos … but I'm guessing you are not he. Ebos? I could well ask what *you* are doing here. Isn't this place a little dangerous for you?"

"Why should my brother's home be dangerous for me?" There must be a strong family resemblance between the dragon brothers if he had confused me with Orobos. I eyed him suspiciously. It hadn't escaped my attention that he had swiftly turned the questions on me, without giving me a proper answer. He was slippery like that. I could think of no legitimate reason that he, the younger brother of a rival Lord, should be here in a Realm that was supposedly closed to all outsiders.

He was definitely not one of my favourite people, but it was something of a relief to see a familiar face here, at least. I could make use of him. The thought brought a little smile to my face. Jaxen, the eternal layabout, would be horrified at the thought of being useful to anybody, but most especially to me, the despised changeling who didn't know her place.

"Perhaps I misunderstood." His usual insincere smile was missing the sneering note that I was used to seeing. Clearly, the Dragon warranted a little more respect than the lowly Allegra Brooks. "I was just on my way to see Lord Orobos, as it happens. Why don't you join me? Family reunions are always such fun."

I knew full well that Jaxen had no time for his own family, but I nodded as if his comment was sincere and gestured courteously for him to precede me. Might as well go with him, since I was having no luck finding a healer on my own. Time to brave the dragon in its den. "Then, by all means, lead on."

19

As it turned out, we didn't have far to go, but I was still glad of my guide. Jaxen led me back the way I'd come and down yet another dragon-sized corridor, stopping before two dragon-sized doors. He seemed very familiar with this place, which only deepened my suspicions of him.

He knocked, and a servant opened the left-hand door. No guards even here. I followed him in, only just managing to stop myself from gaping at the room inside. Bigger than Rothbold's throne room, it was domed like an ancient church, the dome lined with golden tiles. But in the centre, where a painting of God reaching down from the clouds might have been in a cathedral, it was open to the pale sky above. Dawn must be close.

The dome was exceedingly high, so the hole in the centre looked relatively small, but I was guessing it was large enough to admit a full-grown dragon. Dragging my eyes from the dome, I checked out the rest of the room. Behind an imposing black throne, a large natural cavern opened. It was the first piece of unadorned stone I had seen in the whole building, and by the heat and red glow that emitted from it, I guessed that it led directly to the heart of the volcano.

The throne itself was carved from black basalt and set with rubies. On it sat a man whose face I knew well, since it was the mirror image of the face I was currently wearing.

I caught my breath in surprise. Ebos had told me that Orobos was his brother, but he'd neglected to mention that they were twins. No wonder Jaxen had been confused. Orobos's fear that his brother might usurp him made more sense now. If Orobos was the elder, it could only be by minutes, which was a very small distinction to base an inheritance on. Clearly, they were identical, although the scowl on Orobos's face was an expression I had never seen on the dead knight's in the short time I'd known him.

Orobos had half risen from his throne at our entry, but now he subsided back into the red velvet cushions and propped one ankle on his other knee, leaning back in an effort to look relaxed. I wasn't fooled, however. I could see the tension in his shoulders and how tightly he was clenching his jaw behind his sardonic smile.

I offered him a respectful bow and waited to see what he would say. Hopefully, he wasn't as good at reading body language as I was or he might wonder why his brother was so nervous.

"Lord Jaxen," the man on the throne said. Even his voice was exactly the same deep rumble as the Dragon's which, of course, shouldn't have been a surprise and yet somehow was. "I see you've found a stray."

Jaxen bowed his head respectfully, but did nothing to hide the amused smirk on his face. He was clearly anticipating brotherly fireworks. "It's amazing what you can find wandering these halls, my lord. Perhaps a few guards are in order."

Orobos rubbed his chin, as if considering. "We dragons need no guards. Who would dare penetrate our fastness without permission?"

Who indeed? That barb was clearly aimed at me, but I only bowed again, refusing to be drawn. It did Squeak's cause no good to antagonise this man. I could eat humble pie all day if necessary and call it the most delicious meal I'd ever had. "Lord Orobos, I'm here on a mission from the king."

"Oh? So now the great line of Venes is reduced to running errands for our dear overlord? Does he give you a tip if you're especially speedy?"

Jaxen sniggered. Oh, yes, he'd be enjoying this. He was clearly a man after Orobos's heart—a bully with no concern for anything other than his own interests.

Orobos smiled at him. "Some wine, Lord Jaxen?"

"It's never too early for wine," Jaxen said, accepting a glass from a servant who came forward to pour for him.

Orobos waved him to a seat in the circle of armchairs that was off to one side of the room. Several other men sat there, but they all looked like functionaries and upper servants. Two of them had writing implements and one of them seemed to be in charge of a large stack of record books. At Orobos's nod, they hastily packed up their various belongings and quietly left the room. I wondered if I was supposed to know who any of them were, though all of them had been careful not to catch my eye.

"Wine for you, brother?" Orobos asked.

"No, thank you. I hope not to take up too much of your time. The king's business is truly urgent."

Orobos accepted wine from the servant in a jewel-encrusted golden cup. Judging by what I'd seen so far of the Realm of Fire, all the stories about dragons were true. They loved their gold and jewels. I wondered if there was a pile of treasure somewhere that Orobos liked to sleep on in dragon form, or if the over-the-top décor was enough to satisfy his draconic soul.

He drained half the cup and sat back in his throne, looking more at ease. "And what is so very urgent that the king has sent you all this way at such a time?"

His gaze flicked sideways to Jaxen. I could only imagine what Jaxen had been telling him about the times. There was certainly enough gossip flying around the Realms at the moment to keep anyone satisfied.

It still astonished me, however, to find him here. Of all people, Eldric's younger brother would have been one of the last I would pick as a confidante of the antisocial Lord of Fire—yet here he was, looking very much at home. I certainly couldn't imagine Jaxen trekking in past the cave trolls. That much effort wasn't his style, particularly as he was a Jumper. He had a built-in ability as good as Kyrrim's sword and was used to gating directly to wherever he wanted to go. But surely the wards that had forced us to make the long journey through the mountains of Winter would have foiled his ability, too?

"His Majesty begs the assistance of Fire's healers." Orobos's eyelids twitched a little at that, but I pressed on: "A rainbow drake has suffered severe wing damage and is dying."

Orobos raised an eyebrow. "A rainbow drake? But they are mere animals. What has this to do with the king?"

"Rainbow drakes form bonds with certain fae, and the bondmate of this particular drake is very dear to the king. You might recall how fond His Majesty was of Lord Perony."

Now Orobos sat up straighter on his throne. "An Illusionist is out in the open? Do they have a death wish?"

I glanced at Jaxen, who was following the conversation with eager interest. "Illusionists are not the pariahs they once were, now that the king has returned."

"And who is this brave Illusionist?

"It's that changeling bitch, isn't it?" Jaxen said. "I told you about her, Lord Orobos. The one who dug out the king from where he'd been mouldering in the mortal world."

I stared at Jaxen impassively. I wouldn't let him rile me. There was too much at stake here.

"Have you met her?" Orobos asked me.

"Of course. She is often at Court. You will see her for yourself if you come to Lord Eldric's memorial celebration."

"Ah, yes. So kind of Eldric to invite me." That explained what Jaxen was doing here, at least. Eldric often used him as a messenger. Though it still surprised me that the dragons had let him in. "How badly damaged are this drake's wings?"

"There are three holes in one wing. The largest is this size." I spread my fingers to indicate the size and shape of the rent in Squeak's wing.

Orobos nodded at one of the servants. "Go find Verrekesh. I'm sure she'll be thrilled to see our errant knight."

He looked amused, presumably at my expense. I wondered who this Verrekesh was. That smirk suggested I should know—that I should even be feeling uncomfortable right now.

Orobos's eyes gleamed. "It's been a while, hasn't it? You two will have quite a reunion."

Yep. Definitely someone I should know. He began to discuss the wine with Jaxen, comparing it to several they had had the previous night. It hadn't escaped my notice that I, unlike Jaxen, had not been offered a seat. Probably some kind of stupid power play between brothers. I was happy to stand here and be ignored, however. Orobos might think he was insulting me, but it was a hell of a lot easier than trying to engage in a verbal duelling match when I had no idea what I was doing. Standing around with my mouth shut meant that I wasn't giving away my ignorance. And every minute was bringing that healer closer.

Finally, the door opened, and a beautiful woman with honey-gold hair in a long braid down her back almost to her knees entered the room. She wore loose white pants of some kind of soft, drapey fabric like silk with a long sky-blue top over them. Her feet were bare apart from the rings on her toes. More jewels sparkled at her throat and in her ears, though her hands were unadorned. If she was the healer, she probably needed to keep them scrubbed.

I wasn't sure what I'd been expecting, but this wasn't it. When I thought of healers, I thought of sensible shoes and nurses' uniforms, or older women like Yriell and Morwenna. There was something exotic about this woman that made me think of tales of genies and sorcerers. Perhaps it was the way that long braid swayed as she moved, or the jewels sparkling on her toes.

When at last my gaze found her face, I discovered dark brown eyes full of storms. The look she was giving me was not friendly.

Orobos glanced between us, a look of amusement on his face. "Well, aren't you going to say hello?"

The woman glared at him. "What is *he* doing here?" Her tone was flat and unfriendly.

"He's come all this way to beg a favour for a mere animal," Orobos sneered. "Can you believe it? Palace life has taken the dragon fire from my brother."

"An animal? Do I look like a veterinarian?" She came to stand between me and the throne. Though her back was to her Lord, she was clearly aligning herself with Orobos against me.

I smothered an urge to beg on Squeak's behalf. I could sense that these proud dragons wouldn't respond well. They were more likely to throw me out as beneath their contempt than be moved by my bondmate's plight.

"The animal in question is a rainbow drake, the beloved bondmate of one of the last Illusionists." There was no harm in telling them that much. It wasn't even a lie. Jaxen had clearly already filled Orobos in on my sudden appearance on the Court scene. No doubt he'd also mentioned my fight with Blethna Arbre and the fact that I was from Illusion. "The king begs your aid, since this animal was injured in defence of the Crown." That was true, too, in a roundabout sort of way.

But there was no softening in the fierce brown eyes that studied me. Uneasily, I wondered what this woman's relationship to the Dragon was and how much of a problem that would now prove to be. If only the Dragon had been more forthcoming about the kind of welcome he'd been expecting to receive here. Trying to second- and third-guess these people was doing my head in. I hated being so in the dark, but what else could I do? I had to keep soldiering on as long as there was still a chance for Squeak.

Verrekesh turned to Orobos, though she moved so she could keep me in her peripheral vision. I had the oddest feeling that she didn't want to turn her back on me. What did she expect me to do? Attack her in the middle of Orobos's throne room? "And we're now meant to jump when Rothbold says so?"

I pressed my lips shut, resisting the urge to remind her that Rothbold was her king.

"It appears that Rothbold thinks so, at least." Orobos said. He glanced at me. "How *is* our dear king these days? Finding himself secure on his throne, I hope?"

"His Majesty is well, as you will see for yourself if you accept Lord Eldric's invitation."

"You seem very eager for me to attend this memorial service. So the king has found himself a surviving Illusionist? What of it? The Realms are better off without those tricksters in them, and I see absolutely no need to grace this ridiculous service with my presence."

"Other than that the king requests it."

Orobos shrugged. "And what if he does? Our borders have been closed for fifty years. We don't need a king or any of the other Realms. We are sufficient unto ourselves."

"He is still your king." I probably should have kept my mouth shut, but I couldn't help it. He was acting as if he owed no allegiance at all to Whitehaven, just because the king had been gone for twenty years. "And now he's back, things will return to normal."

"Will they indeed? You seem very eager to bring Fire under the Brenfell thumb again, brother. What's in it for you? Has he promised you my throne in exchange for your faithful service as his lapdog?" His eyes narrowed as his voice rose. "What kind of dragon are you?"

"The kind that is loyal to the throne." I couldn't afford to show weakness in front of this man. I squared my shoulders and looked him directly in the eye. "Like all the people of Fire, I'm still a loyal subject of the King of the Realms."

"Not a loyal subject of your brother?" he roared, leaping to his feet.

"I have always been loyal to you, brother, but a man cannot serve two masters."

"You serve no one but yourself!" He roared again, this time a full-on, animalistic sound that reverberated around the high ceilings. Between one breath and the next, the man disappeared and a dragon took his place. Black as night, smoke puffing from its nostrils, its great golden eyes glared balefully at me.

I took an involuntary step back; I couldn't help it—the dragon's appearance was so unexpected. Its enormous body barely fit on the raised dais, and the black basalt throne had disappeared beneath it somewhere. Its tail cascaded down the steps, the tip lashing back and forth like the tail of an angry cat.

The dragon lowered its great horned head and spoke, its voice a deep, menacing rumble. "Ebos has only ever had one master, and his name is Ebos."

Verrekesh retreated across the floor in my direction. She didn't turn her back on the dragon now, which was probably a wise move. How had I managed to piss Orobos off so fast? Rowan would have said it was my scintillating personality, but I'd hardly said a thing.

All I wanted was a little bit of healing help. Clearly, there were deep, unresolved issues between the brothers. Would the real Dragon have fared better? I had to think so, or else why would he have suggested bringing me here? My heart thundered so hard in my chest it was a wonder that Orobos couldn't hear it. I was way out of my league here, scared to say the wrong thing and inflame the situation further.

Verrekesh reached my side. She cast a quick, scathing glance at me and hissed, "Avert your gaze, you fool."

I looked at the floor as the dragon coiled and uncoiled its great body atop the dais.

"You are alarming your guest, my lord," Verrekesh said calmly.

"This traitor is no guest of mine," the dragon roared, lashing its tail.

The tail collided with one of the advisers' chairs and sent it flying across the room to smash into kindling against the far wall. Jaxen leapt up and shrank back against the wall behind him.

Verrekesh gestured in his direction. "I meant your friend from Autumn, my lord."

The tail lashed again, and I swallowed hard, wondering if these were my last moments.

"Forgive me, Lord Jaxen," the dragon growled. "Let us resume our discussion another time." The great haunches bunched, the black wings spread, and the dragon launched itself into the air with a sound like a clap of thunder.

I caught my breath, about to start hyperventilating, my eyes never leaving the fearsome creature. But it seemed I had escaped doom after all. Orobos climbed until he gained the gap in the ceiling. He clung there for a moment on the edge of the dome, letting forth a roar and a blast of flame, then he slipped through the opening and was gone.

"Let's go," Verrekesh said, "before he comes back and lets his temper get the better of him."

She hurried to the door, and I went with her gladly. I was all for not getting eaten by enraged dragons.

20

I followed Verrekesh through the maze of passages, watching her luxuriant length of hair sway from side to side as she strode the hallways. She was a tall woman; her head topped the Dragon's shoulder and my own long stride was required to keep up with her quick, angry one. This was a woman who wore her heart on her sleeve. There was no mistaking her mood.

Finally, we entered a remote corridor, and she yanked open the door. I followed her in, closing the door behind me.

She whirled on me, her long braid flying, and slapped me hard across the face.

My jaw burned as I stared down into her furious dark eyes. "What was that for?"

Given her obvious fury, it hadn't been much of a surprise, but it was a bad beginning. Somehow, I had to get this woman to help me.

She glared at me, not giving an inch, then lunged

forward. She caught my face between her hands and plastered her lips against mine.

Now *that* did surprise me.

I froze, not knowing what to do as her tongue invaded my mouth. Her soft breasts pressed against my chest, and I experienced a moment of complete disorientation. This was *not* how my kisses usually felt. It was beyond bizarre.

But, hey! At least she didn't seem to hate me anymore. That had to be worth something, right? Awkwardly, I put my arms around her, not sure where to put my hands. But it didn't matter. My moment of confusion had lasted too long, and she pulled away, disappointment clear in those expressive dark eyes of hers.

"Forty-nine years and you won't even kiss me hello?"

I tried to smile, but it probably looked ghastly, because the disappointment in her eyes only deepened. "It's been a long while."

She folded her arms. "And so?" Clearly, that had been the wrong thing to say. "You've forgotten how to kiss? Or you no longer love your wife? Which is it?"

Holy shit. This was Ebos's wife? Somehow, the fact that he was married had slipped his mind—or hadn't he thought it important enough to mention? But his wife was apparently the healer we'd been coming to see—surely that was worth bringing up? It wasn't as if he had planned to sneak in and out without seeing her.

I stared down at her, the silence lengthening as I grasped desperately for something to say. "Neither." I rubbed my jaw.

Oh, God. Her real husband was dead. Lady forgive me! I felt the deepest shame. I should be telling her the truth, not deceiving her by coming here in a dead man's shape. But Squeak. What a hideous dilemma. At that moment, I didn't like myself very much.

"You hit me."

Oh my God, what was wrong with me? That was a stupid thing to say.

Her eyes narrowed, and then she shrugged. "I should hit you again. That's all you have to say to me, after forty-nine years? I can't believe you were stupid enough to come back here. You're lucky Orobos didn't kill you."

She moved to a sideboard and poured herself a drink, though she didn't offer one to me. I could really have done with some alcohol right now. This situation was just going from bad to worse.

She drained the cup in one gulp then set it down, her back to me. Still reeling from surprise, I took in the room. It was a large sitting room, though not large enough for a dragon, furnished in bold reds, purples, and gold. There were no windows, but several doors gave off the room, suggesting it was part of a larger suite.

Verrekesh's shoulders began to shake, and I realised belatedly that she was crying. Holy hell, could this day get any worse? I moved closer, awkward and unsure. Would she welcome my comfort or would I just make everything worse?

"Don't cry, Verrekesh." I laid a tentative hand on her shoulder, which continued to shake silently under my touch. "I'm sorry. But you know the reason I had to leave. I loved my brother too much to stay."

She shrugged my hand off impatiently. "Don't bother spinning that lie to me. I know why you really left. It was always ambition with you, wasn't it? You never loved me enough."

What lie? I was completely lost. "You could have come with me."

That was a stab in the dark, but I had to say something. I felt like the world's biggest jerk.

Her shoulders stopped shaking, and she dashed the tears from her eyes. "You know I couldn't. I am a healer of *dragons*. I had to stay where the dragons are."

She turned to face me, her eyes still bright with tears. She was extraordinarily beautiful, even for a fae, and she looked so unhappy that my heart went out to her. The Dragon must have been one stubborn bastard to be able to leave a woman like her behind. Though maybe if your brother was threatening to kill you if you stayed, that might give you a little incentive. Or whatever had happened. She seemed to be suggesting that it hadn't happened quite how the Dragon had told me.

"Then you understand about duty. You know why I had to go."

She slapped at me, but her hand stayed on my chest, toying with my surcoat. "Duty, bah! You can stop pretending. But I didn't think you'd be gone so long, Ebos. I've missed you."

"And I, you." God, this was terrible. With every word,

I was digging myself further into the hole. How could I keep pretending to be her husband? Those soulful eyes shredded my heart with guilt.

It was all for Squeak. I had to keep reminding myself of that. The Dragon had given his life so that I could save Squeak. I couldn't let my feelings of guilt stop me now. Not when I was so close.

"Have you been well?"

She shrugged. "Well enough. My bed has been cold without you."

I was getting a very definite sense that she wouldn't be averse to a little roll in the hay, and my heart all but stopped. I could not go to bed with this woman, pretending to be her husband. I couldn't go to bed with a woman while pretending to be a man, full stop. Holy hell, would that even work? How far did the illusion go?

Her hand was moving on my chest, stroking little delicate circles. I had to put a stop to this before it went any further. I laid a hand over hers, trapping it beneath my larger one.

"I can't stay. Every minute counts. I must return before the rainbow drake dies."

She pulled her hand away and stepped back, her face hardening. "You put an animal before me? I suppose I shouldn't be surprised. I was never first in your affections, was I? Your brother was right. Your first thought has always been for yourself."

I wanted to protest on the Dragon's behalf, but I needed this woman's help.

"I never deserved you, Verrekesh. I promise you, I would stay if I could, but I can't. I'm a knight now. I'm not free to follow my heart."

Was this what Kyrrim felt like every time the king called him away from my side? Because this really sucked. I didn't know this woman from a bar of soap and yet I felt like a heel for treating her this way.

"Fine. I don't know why I expected you to be any different. Forty-nine years doesn't change a person in the ways that count." She opened one of the doors and walked through. "Not when he's spent centuries learning to be an arsehole."

I followed her in, and found a room lined with shelves cut from the stone of the walls. Most held books, but some held jars and bottles of different ingredients, rather like Yriell's shelves in her cottage, though much less gruesome. There wasn't an eyeball to be seen, for which I was thankful.

Verrekesh reached down a small pot from a high shelf and tossed it to me. "There. Give that to your precious rainbow drake, and maybe we'll see you again in another forty-nine years." Her gaze met mine in challenge. "Unless I decide to choose the other brother before then."

What could I say? I covered my confusion by unscrewing the lid of the pot and sniffing at the contents, which turned out to be a pale, creamy ointment.

"I put this on his wing?" I asked. "What is this?"

"*What is this?*" she repeated in disbelief. "Are you mocking me?"

"Of course not. I'm sorry—I've been away a long time."

"Long enough to forget you're a dragon?"

She was furious again. I put the lid back on and slid it into my pocket. Maybe Morwenna would know what to do with it. I was going to give myself away if I said anything more. Clearly, it was something Ebos knew well—or should have known well.

"I'm sorry," I said again. "I must go. Will you take me back to the border?"

Her eyes flashed. "What am I, your pack mule? Just open a gate."

"But the borders are closed."

"To everyone except those with Fire in their veins." She glared at me, and my heart sank. This was going to be tricky, since I didn't come from Fire.

I needed another excuse, but it was hard to come up with something with her glaring at me like that.

"Azir told me that you walked in, but I didn't believe him. But you did, didn't you?"

I nodded, my mind scrambling for a story. She was already looking at me as if I were an imbecile, so it was no use saying I hadn't known I could open a gate. Clearly, she thought that I *should* have known—which left the question: why had the Dragon not realised that the borders were only closed to those not born of Fire? It made me wonder if he *had* known and had chosen to pretend for reasons of his own that the only way in was through Winter. But why would he have done that? Especially considering it led to his own death. It didn't make any sense.

Not that it mattered now. The Dragon was dead, and I was the one stuck here with the very annoyed female dragon glaring at me. I fell back on something similar to what the Dragon had told me. "I didn't want to suddenly appear, for fear of upsetting Orobos. I figured it was less threatening to walk in. It would give the lookouts time to notify him of my impending arrival."

She grunted, unappeased. I still needed her help. Since I wasn't of Fire, I wouldn't be able to open a gate, and then the game would be up.

"Verrekesh … my magic is near exhausted from the journey. I'm afraid if I opened a gate now, I might end up at the bottom of Ocean, or on the far side of the Realms from where I need to go. Please, would you …?"

She made a noise of frustration and flung one arm out in an impatient gesture at the open door of the room. Mist moved in the doorway, wispy and insubstantial, obscuring the view of the next room. "Go, then, you annoying man, and good riddance to you."

I looked back as I stepped over the threshold and into the Wilds, my last sight her frowning face. She could tell something fishy was going on, sure that I was tricking her somehow, but not knowing how. I didn't want to be around if she ever figured it out.

But then, something seemed fishy from my perspective, too. I couldn't believe that the Dragon hadn't known he could have gated into Fire—but I couldn't understand why he would have lied about it either. Nor was I ever likely to find out now that he was dead.

Relief washed over me as the familiar wooded path of the Greenway stretched out before me—and relief was one emotion I'd never expected to feel about the Wilds. But I'd braved the dragons' den and not only lived to tell the tale, but escaped with the means to cure Squeak as well.

I checked that the precious pot of ointment was still in my pocket, then hurried along the path towards my own personal miracle.

$$21$$

In the end, we smeared the cream all over Squeak's whole wing, just to be sure, and it truly was like a miracle. Before our very eyes, the edges of the holes quivered and crawled towards each other, new membrane appearing from nowhere.

I watched through eyes filled with tears of joy as those terrible gaping holes disappeared as if they had never been. Morwenna and I looked at each other, and for once, there was no animosity between us, only shared amazement and rejoicing.

"We'll want to keep him quiet for a few days, to make sure it's strong enough to take his weight," Morwenna said.

But I was having none of that. Squeak had his miracle, but he hadn't realised it yet. He still lay motionless, glassy eyed and miserable. I picked him up and carried him outside into the morning sun. "It's okay, buddy. You can do this—your wings are as good as new."

I had absolute faith in the magic of the dragons, and

even more faith in their pride. No self-respecting dragon was going to take it easy and limit himself to the ground for days or even weeks, just to make sure his wing really was okay. The magic would be instant and reliable.

I held Squeak up to the sun, trying to urge him skyward, sending a blast of love and reassurance down our link. I could barely feel him at the end of it anymore, but some of my excitement must have gotten through, for he stirred, then climbed from my arms onto my shoulder and tentatively spread his wings.

"That's it! You can do it!" I held a picture of him in my mind as he'd been the first time I'd seen him, one bright green spark of light among many, soaring gracefully through the skies around the castle. "You're healed. You can do it." A flock of drakes swooped overhead, chittering to each other. "Go join them."

Squeak trilled something to his friends, and a burst of emotion rushed down our link: hope, excitement, and a healthy dose of fear. Again, I urged him onward, sending memories down our link of all the times I'd seen him flying, along with love and encouragement. He stood a little straighter, thrusting out his glittering chest and spreading his wings. He bashed me in the side of the head with one of them, but I didn't care.

"Yes, Squeak. You can do it."

And then he was gone, leaping skyward with a shriek of excitement. The flock of drakes swarmed him, and he disappeared into their glittering heart. I watched him swoop and soar, my own heart full nearly to bursting.

Morwenna came to stand beside me, shading her eyes against the glare of the morning sun. "Looks as good as new," she conceded gruffly. "The Dragon didn't come back with you?"

"No." I left it at that. I felt that the king should be the first to hear of his knight's death, and yet it seemed I couldn't be spared for a visit to Whitehaven. It wasn't the kind of thing that should be sent in a message. That would be like breaking up with someone via text, only much worse. Some things just required the personal touch.

But now that Squeak was out of danger, Morwenna and the council found a million things for me to do, and the days rushed by in a whirl of meetings and preparations. A lot of them were to do with security, and how we would best protect Arlo and the Illusionists when we were once more vulnerable on the ground. Yriell was very useful in these meetings, as she had a wealth of experience to draw on.

Often, I wondered whether I was even needed, as she and Morwenna seemed to have everything well in hand, but every time I suggested leaving them for an hour or two to visit Whitehaven, one or other of them would find something else that only I could do and I was stuck again. It seemed that Kyrrim wasn't the only one trying to keep me out of Summer's reach.

Before I knew it, the day of Arlo's return had arrived. Arlo was due to make its grand entrance after sunset during the so-called memorial service. Yriell stayed on the island with the Illusionists, but the king had sent a message via

Raven requesting that my friends and I join him at Lord Eldric's hall well before the start of the official ceremonies.

Since Arlo was lurking among the mists out over the ocean until the big reveal, one of the Air mages flew us in on a tiny island no bigger than Kyrrim's home of Oldriss and delivered us safely to the Hall of Giseult in mid-afternoon. The king had already arrived the night before and was currently resting in preparation for the evening's events.

Eldric greeted us in the tree-lined hall with its silken banners of red and gold fluttering overhead. He even went so far as to kiss my cheek. "Welcome home."

"Thank you." Autumn did still feel like home to me.

Clearly, the king hadn't taken Eldric fully into his confidence as to what was about to happen at his "memorial service". I figured he'd take it in his stride, though. In fact, he'd probably be pleased to have Illusion back. The two Realms had once been quite close.

Eldric called over a page and sent him to tell the king of our arrival. "He insisted on being woken when you got here," the Lord said. "He seemed very concerned that you not miss the ceremony."

I smiled and shrugged, guilt gnawing at me. The king would probably be far less pleased to see me when I told him my news.

But it wasn't the king who appeared from one of the upstairs doorways. Kyrrim smiled down at me from the balcony, his face lighting up as his golden eyes found mine across the crowded Hall. I smiled back, feeling the familiar shock of wonder. Every time I saw him, it seemed that I had forgotten just how handsome he was. Every time, it caught me by surprise all over again, and my heart swelled to know that this amazing man had eyes only for me.

He descended the spiral stairs in quick strides and took me in his arms for an all too brief moment. "It's good to see you," he murmured into my hair, crushing me against him. Then he stepped back and said, more formally, "The king requests that you all join him."

Eldric led the way up the stairs while Kyrrim fell back, taking my hand in his.

"How's Squeak?"

At least I had one piece of good news. "Completely cured."

"Thank the Lady."

A servant admitted us to a sunny sitting room, with a green view of the canopy from its large windows. The king emerged from another door, still straightening his jacket. He looked tired, but a warm smile of welcome spread across his face at the sight of us.

"Allegra, my dear." He came forward and took my hands, kissing me on both cheeks. "And Lady Willow. Sage. Rowan." He nodded to all of them as they made their obeisance. "Lord Eldric, could I trouble you to relax your wards for the Hawk? He still has several errands to run for me, and it would be far more convenient if he could gate directly in and out of the Hall."

Lord Eldric bowed his head. "Of course, sire. I shall go and see to it at once." He bowed again and left the room.

The king gestured at the comfortable-looking lounges arrayed in front of the windows. "Sit down, sit down. I have something I need to discuss with you. Lady Willow, I wonder if I could impose on you to accept a houseguest?"

Willow blinked in surprise. "In my sith, sire? I mean, of course, Your Majesty."

"Excellent."

I perched uncomfortably on the edge of my seat. "Your Majesty, if I may interrupt for a moment, I'm afraid I have some bad news." I couldn't wait any longer. He needed to know, before he got too far in his planning.

Instantly, the king's face sobered. "Bad news? I hope your bondmate isn't …?"

"No, sire. Squeak is fine." I didn't know how to say it. This would be a massive blow to him. "It's the Dragon, sire. I'm afraid he didn't make it."

There was a terrible pause, while the king stared at me, his face grim. "Sir Ebos is dead?"

I nodded helplessly, and the king rose abruptly and moved to stare out the window, his back to the room.

"How did he die?"

I gave him a brief summary of the fight with the trolls and how I had seen body parts in the trolls' cauldron afterwards.

"This makes no sense," Kyrrim said. "Sir Ebos was a dragon. Their strength leaves that of a normal fae for dead. Dragons are nearly impossible to kill, even in their human form. A blow to the head should barely have inconvenienced him."

"They skewered him right through," I objected.

"Even so …"

"Do you think I'm making this up?"

"No, of course not. It's just perplexing. Did you note the placement of the sword? Perhaps it went through his heart?"

I shook my head. "I couldn't say."

At last the king turned. "And how did you enlist Fire's aid, if the Dragon was dead?"

"I took the Dragon's form, sire. I'm sorrier than I can say that I had to deceive them, but I saw it as Squeak's only chance. They wouldn't have listened to me if I'd gone to them in my own form."

"You think well on your feet."

I bowed my head. "Thank you, sire."

A knock on the door interrupted us.

"Enter," the king called, an impatient note in his voice.

It was the same page again. He bowed to the king. "Your Majesty, Queen Ceinwen has arrived with Her Highness, Princess Lily, and the Lord and Lady of Summer and their son."

"Excellent."

Rothbold regarded us all as the page bowed and withdrew. "I must go and greet my family. Wait here." He strode from the room, leaving the door open behind him.

Kyrrim moved to the doorway, as if he would have liked to have gone with the king, but he wouldn't disobey a direct order. I got up and went to join him. From here, we had a good view of the vast, leafy Hall. The new arrivals had taken seats at the long table on the raised dais at the far end of the Hall, where servants were offering them refreshments. Lord Kellith and his son, Merritt, rose as the king descended the stairs and offered rather perfunctory bows, while Lady Brona curtseyed.

"Kellith, Merritt, welcome." He even managed to sound sincere. Rothbold was a far better diplomat than I would ever be. He kissed Lady Brona's cheek, then the queen's and his daughter's. "I hope your journey was pleasant."

"It was swift," Kellith said, "and made all the more tolerable by the knowledge that such a happy occasion awaited us at the end of it."

"You think a memorial for a shattered Realm is a happy occasion?"

"I refer, of course, to the announcement of the engagement between your daughter and my son. I'm glad you changed your mind, brother. The children love each other very much."

"Do they, indeed?"

The king didn't look convinced, and I couldn't say that I blamed him. Merritt wasn't even looking at Lily, seemingly more interested in the contents of his wine glass. I saw no special concern for her in his eyes. It was a stark contrast to the way Kyrrim's face had lit up when he saw me, which was my yardstick for a man in love. Merritt's behaviour reminded me more of Adam's, my ex-boyfriend, who had never loved me as much as he loved himself. If Merritt had any interest in the princess at all, it was because of the status that their relationship would bring him.

"When will you announce their betrothal?" Queen Ceinwen asked.

"After the ceremony for Illusion," Rothbold replied shortly.

"Really, it seems in rather doubtful taste to tie this joyful news to such a sad occasion," Kellith said.

I rolled my eyes and glanced at Kyrrim, whose expression was stony. Sad occasion, my arse. The hide of that man. He had single-handedly all but wiped out an entire Realm, yet he felt no guilt for it. He spoke as if he was a mere observer of Illusion's demise and not its actual architect.

"He is a stain on the face of the Realms," Kyrrim muttered in a savage undertone.

"He's dog shit on the shoe of life," I agreed.

Kyrrim gave me a fierce grin. "It's time somebody scraped him off, then."

If only we could, but his position made him virtually invulnerable. Bad enough that he was the Lord of one of the greatest Realms of all, but he was also the queen's brother, and apparently soon to be even more closely tied to the royal family. I couldn't understand why the king had changed his mind about that betrothal when he'd seemed so vehemently against it before. No doubt some political game was being played, but I didn't have the experience to figure it out.

"If you would rather we delayed the announcement, your wishes can, of course, be accommodated," the king said smoothly.

Kellith was beginning to demur when Eldric appeared.

"Welcome to Autumn," he said. "Rooms have been

prepared for each of you if you would care to rest or bathe before the evening commences."

"Thank you, Eldric," the queen said. She rose from her seat. "We should begin making ready, Lily."

Obediently, the princess rose to accompany her mother from the Hall, but as they left the room, the king called his daughter back.

"A word with you first, Lily."

The queen paused, one eyebrow raised as she looked back at him.

The king made a shooing motion at her with his hands. "Go on, Ceinwen. I'll only keep her a minute, but I know how long it takes you to get ready. Go and change."

The queen gave him a hard stare, but she left the room anyway, accompanied by her brother.

"Come upstairs with me, child," the king said, and we withdrew from the doorway as he led Lily towards our room.

I lifted an eyebrow enquiringly at Kyrrim as we moved back to the couches. "Any idea what this is about?"

"Hush."

He looked toward the door, then rose and bowed politely as the king and the princess entered. Sage and I rose, too, though I eyed Kyrrim sideways as I made my curtsey. I had the feeling he knew what the king was up to but wasn't prepared to tell me.

The king shut the door behind them and waved his daughter to a seat. She made no acknowledgement of our bows or even our presence, but sat straight in her chair, hands folded in her lap, waiting demurely to discover her father's wishes.

"What did you want to see me about, Father?"

He took a wing-backed armchair opposite her and crossed one leg over the other in a relaxed pose. "We need to discuss this engagement."

"Yes?" Her tone was cautious.

"I will not allow it," the king said pleasantly, as if he hadn't just dropped a bombshell.

She sat back in shock. "Will not …? But you are announcing it this evening. We wouldn't have come otherwise."

The king's foot swung idly. "I'm well aware of that, child, but, in fact, I am doing no such thing. I'm sorry for the lie, but it was the only way to lure your mother and her repulsive brother out of Summer. You're far too young to be getting engaged to anyone, and Merritt of Summer would be the very last person I would choose for you even if you weren't. You must see how impossible this is."

"How is it impossible?" she burst out. "Merritt is the perfect man for me."

He frowned at her. "I am one hundred per cent certain that his father was responsible for abducting me and keeping me prisoner for twenty years. He deprived you of a father and me of your entire childhood."

"He didn't! That was Dansen Arbre."

"He laid waste to Illusion," the king continued implacably, "all in service of his own greed and ambition. He wants the throne for himself."

"He had his reasons for that. He thought they had killed you. You don't know him at all if you think he could kidnap his monarch—or steal his throne. He's loyal to the crown. Dansen Arbre acted without his knowledge or permission."

"If that's what you think, then you are far too young to be playing politics."

"I may be young, but I'm old enough to know who I love, and that is Merritt. I intend to marry him. Whatever his father has done or not done is nothing to do with him. You must announce the engagement tonight. You gave your word." She glared daggers at her father, her lips compressed into a furious line, hands clenched into fists in her lap.

"And that is your final word? There is nothing I can say that will sway you?"

"Nothing. I will marry Merritt or no one."

The king rose. "In that case, please give me that lovely shawl you're wearing. Sir Hawk, you have your orders."

She removed her sparkling shawl and thrust it at him, a look of confusion on her face. The king passed it to me, and I accepted it with at least as much confusion. What on earth was going on here?

When Kyrrim drew Ecfirrith, the princess's eyes widened in shock, and she stepped back abruptly. But he only made the familiar three slashes in the air, bringing a gateway shimmering into life.

"Lady Willow," the king said, "I apologise in advance for my daughter. She will not be an easy houseguest."

Willow blinked in surprise but said nothing. Probably too shocked at discovering the identity of her houseguest to comment.

The princess looked back and forth between her and Kyrrim and shook her head violently. "No. No, I'm not going anywhere with you."

"I beg to differ, Your Highness," Kyrrim said as he sheathed his sword again. Mist swirled within the gateway, bringing with it the familiar fragrances of Willow's gardens. "Don't make this any harder than it has to be."

Wildly, the princess looked around the room, searching for a friendly face in vain. "I'll scream."

"I wouldn't advise that, my dear," her father said. There was no threat in his voice, but plenty of authority.

But the princess wasn't done. "You can't force me to go anywhere I don't want to. I am a princess of the Realms."

"Of course I can," the king said dispassionately. "I am the king, and you are my subject as well as my daughter. You have been spoiled all your life, and I can't change that, but I can take steps to give you the education you should have had. You are going for an extended stay in the mortal world. It's time you experienced real life outside the bubble of the palace."

And away from the influence of Summer, though he didn't say that.

Kyrrim took her arm while she was still gaping at her father in outrage. She struggled against his grip, but she was no match for the knight. Before she quite knew what had happened, he had drawn her through the gateway and the pair of them had disappeared into the swirling mist.

We all stood in silent shock for a moment, then Willow stirred. "I guess I'd better go with them."

"Rowan, perhaps you could help, too," the king suggested.

"Me?" He looked horrified to have come to the king's notice.

"I'll need the Hawk back here," the king said, "and Lady Willow may need some support."

"Of—of course, Your Majesty." He executed an awkward bow, then he, too, stepped through the gate and disappeared.

I glanced at Sage, who looked as surprised as I felt. Rothbold had always been so charming, so welcoming to me, that I'd almost forgotten he was a fae king, which was practically the very definition of ruthlessness. It was a terrible risk he was taking, from a personal point of view. There was every chance that his daughter would never forgive him for this. They were hardly on the best of terms as it was. And he only had one child. But for the good of the kingdom and the future of his dynasty, this betrothal idea had to be put to bed once and for all. He had just demonstrated that he was more than capable of doing whatever it took to achieve that end.

The gate snapped shut, making me flinch. I glanced down at the diaphanous shawl clenched between my fingers. "But what will the queen say when she realises the princess is gone?"

"That's where you come in, Allegra. It will be your job to make sure the queen *doesn't* realise it."

I boggled at him. Was he seriously suggesting what I

thought he was? I looked at the shawl with new eyes. "But …"

"It's only for tonight," he said. "After tonight, Lily can disappear with impunity and I will face whatever consequences my wife chooses to bring." A steely glint entered his blue eyes. "But I will have no doubt left in anyone's mind about this betrothal. It must be clear to all that there is no chance of Lily ever marrying Merritt. I'm sure you can be sufficiently convincing."

Oh, Lady save me. He *was* serious. He honestly meant for me to impersonate a princess of the Realms in front of the very people who knew her best. Was he insane or just desperate?

"But what about Illusion?" Ye gods. I, Allegra Brooks, was meant to be taking centre stage tonight. How could I be in two places at once, in two *bodies* at once? This was absolute madness. "I need to be present tonight. We should get Morwenna or one of the others to take your daughter's place."

"No. No one else must know. I'm sure you'll be able to manage it." Rothbold smiled at me. "It looks like you have a busy evening ahead of you."

22

"This is crazy." I crushed the shawl in my fists, my stomach roiling with nerves. "I can't do it."

The king had left the room, leaving Sage and me staring after him in shock.

"Yes, you can," Sage said, fiercely loyal as always, though I would have been happier if there'd been a teensy bit more conviction in her voice. "You can do anything. And we'll help you any way we can."

I didn't know what she could do, but her support made me feel better. I wrapped the beautiful shawl around my shoulders, my hands shaking. This was *not* how I had expected this day to go. And my expectations of enjoying tonight had already been pretty rock-bottom to start with. I took a deep breath, trying to calm my racing heart. Rothbold was either insane or inspired, and we wouldn't know which until the night was over.

"Okay, let's do this. Watch the door for me, please. I don't want someone to come in while I'm mid-change."

Sage moved to the door and held the handle so that it wouldn't turn, watching me with avid curiosity. She'd never seen me change forms before.

Feeling a little self-conscious, I closed my eyes. Lirra said that wasn't necessary, but I found it helpful. I focused on an image of the princess as I'd just seen her, in the sparkling silver dress, her dark hair braided down her back, the diaphanous shawl draped elegantly over her pale shoulders. I felt the magic wash over me and heard Sage gasp.

"How do I look?" I opened my eyes, checking out my new form. "Did I get the dress right?"

Sage nodded. "Operation Fake Princess is a go."

"Okay." I squared my shoulders. "I'd better go find my room and start getting ready for the ceremony. Wish me luck."

She flung her arms around me and squeezed. "You won't need luck. You'll make your own."

I hugged her back, wishing she could come with me, but that would look strange, so I went downstairs and found a page to direct me to the princess's room. *My* room. I kept my face carefully expressionless, trying for Lily's natural resting bitch face. I didn't even thank the page when we arrived at the room and he opened the door, merely swept past him.

Two maids waited inside, and they leapt up and dropped into low curtseys at my entrance.

"We have everything ready, Your Highness," one said, opening a door that led into a light-filled bedroom. Another stunning dress was laid out on the massive bed, this one in a deep blue scattered with tiny pearls. "Would you like to begin?"

I nodded, and they began to undo the myriad buttons that ran down the back of the silver gown I wore. I had a sudden panic as they slid it from my shoulders that my underwear might give me away, but that had changed, too, thank the Lady.

The whole experience was so bizarre. Did the princess do nothing for herself? I held myself stiffly, not wanting to put a foot wrong, but it seemed that nothing was expected of me. The maids did everything, working in silence. Did Lily normally chat to them? They made no effort to start a conversation, so maybe not. Or perhaps they assumed she was nervous about the evening to come and the announcement of her betrothal, and so left her to her thoughts.

The dressing took longer than I could have imagined, and then they led me to a chair in front of a dressing table and proceeded to spend another eon on doing my hair. I observed the pale beautiful face in the mirror as they curled my newly black locks and piled them on my head. The shape of that face and the famed Brenfell eyes were all her father, but the hauteur was definitely the queen. There was no warmth in that blue gaze. Maybe she was a bitch to her servants, and they were glad she was ignoring them.

How did I get myself into these situations?

We were interrupted by a knock on the outer door of the suite. One of the maids put down her curling wand and went to answer it, returning with a tiny bouquet of flowers.

"From Lord Merritt, Highness."

And they were lilies. So creative of him. My lip started to curl before I remembered who I was.

"How sweet," I said as the maid carefully pinned the corsage to my breast.

The waxy flowers did nothing for the dress, which was stunning all on its own. The pearls stitched onto it and woven through my hair glowed like tiny moons. They were a slightly different colour to the creamy lilies, but just close enough so that it looked like the flower-giver had tried to match the pearls and failed. Still, the real Lily would no doubt be thrilled with the flowers.

I eyed the gorgeous dress, thanking my lucky stars that my magic would reproduce the details for me when I needed to switch between forms. I'd have no hope of remembering the placement of every individual pearl and raven lock on my own.

The door opened again, this time without anyone knocking, and the queen swept in. The maids curtseyed as she brushed my cheek with her lips.

"You look beautiful, darling. Merritt is a lucky man. Are those lilies from him?"

I nodded, hoping to avoid too much conversation. Just because my voice would sound like Lily's didn't mean I knew what to say—especially to her own mother.

"I knew that colour would suit you. You should wear it more often." She herself was in silver. It seemed to be a favourite of hers—probably because it was one of the house colours of Summer. And, of course, the other was blue, which I wore. Not very subtle of her, even though Summer's blue was a lighter shade. "Are you ready?"

"Yes. More than ready." I'd been here for hours, and night had fallen outside the windows while the maids worked on the elaborate hairstyle. The pins were already giving me a headache.

Impatience must have shown in my tone. "Not much longer to wait, darling," she said with an indulgent smile. "We have to get through your father's stupid ceremony for Illusion first, and then you will be betrothed."

The ceremony. If only the princess wasn't required to be present. Morwenna must be having a fit by now, wondering where I was. I was supposed to be there with the councillors when Arlo made its big entrance.

I followed the queen through the Hall and outside, into the grassy meadow that stood before it. There we joined the king, who was waiting with the Lord of Autumn and two of his knights. My gaze went instinctively to the Hawk, standing between the Lion and the Wolf, but I looked away hurriedly. The princess had no interest in her father's knights.

Eldric greeted the queen, bowing over her hand. "We're almost ready to leave," he told her. "Just waiting for—ah, here they are."

Lord Kellith and his wife and son joined the party.

"You look beautiful, Lily," Kellith said, raising my hand to his lips. "Merritt is truly fortunate." It was all I could do not to shudder as his lips brushed my skin. "I see you wear his flowers. An auspicious occasion for both our houses."

The king ignored him, which amused me, merely signalling to Kyrrim, who drew his sword and created a wide gateway in the air with it. The king offered his arm to Queen Ceinwen, and they stepped through the gate and disappeared into the mist. Kyrrim, the Lion, and the Wolf followed on their heels, ever vigilant.

"Shall we, my dear?" Kellith offered his arm to his lady, and they followed in the king and queen's footsteps. My knowledge of court protocol was limited, but I suspected that I, as the princess, should have gone next. Kellith really was getting too big for his boots.

Merritt bowed in front of me, extending his arm in silent invitation. I hadn't yet heard him speak. You'd think he could make some kind of effort, considering we were supposed to be spending the rest of eternity together. Strong and silent or just not that interested?

Well, soon the point would be moot. I laid my hand lightly on his arm and we walked through the gate, followed by Lord Eldric and several other notables who'd been waiting with the king's group.

Kyrrim waited on the other side, and he bowed to me, though anger smouldered in the depths of his tawny gaze at the sight of my hand on Merritt's arm. I averted my gaze. The contrast between him and Merritt was so great. As quickly as I could, I removed my hand and moved closer to the king. When the whole party had come through, Kyrrim closed the gate behind us, and for the first time, I took in our new surroundings.

We were standing on a wide road on a cleared stretch of

land, though the forest began again twenty paces or so on either side of the road. Ahead, the road dipped down to a shallow ford that crossed a wide river. To the right of the ford, the water quickly became deep again and the river opened out almost into a bay that held several small islands, hulking in the dark like crouched animals.

I drew in a sharp breath. I'd seen these before, once or twice. The cottage where I'd grown up was only a couple of hours' walk from here. These were the islands of Illusion—the ones that were left, anyway, and all of them still bore the scars of the Night of Swords.

The biggest island, Verelho, which lay closest to the ford, held the ruins of a large castle, its walls broken off like smashed teeth, blackened and cracked by fire. A handful of rainbow drakes flitted around the ruins, their brilliant skins occasionally flashing in the dark sky above. Far overhead, half a dozen Air islands hovered. One of them must be Arlo, but they were too high up and the sky was too dark to make out details. I couldn't tell which one it was.

On both sides of the road, long trestle tables were set up, ready for a feast, and people milled about, waiting for the event to commence. Smells of cooked meat and freshly baked bread drifted tantalisingly on the breeze. Fae lanterns bobbed in the air and festive picnic rugs were laid on the grass beside the river along with rows of chairs for the nobles. A bright canopy flapped above a small dais, and on it were three chairs of a more grandiose design, clearly meant for the royal family.

The king made his way to these chairs, and I followed.

Thank goodness there were only three, so I didn't have to sit next to Merritt. I barely knew the man, had never even exchanged a single word with him, yet I had already developed a violent dislike for him.

When the nobles had settled in their chairs and the crowds of commoners had found places on the picnic rugs, Lord Eldric cleared his throat.

"My lords and ladies, esteemed guests, welcome to Autumn—though tonight we are gathered to honour another Realm, the lost Realm of Illusion. Twenty years ago almost to the day, Illusion passed into history, and tonight we mourn that passing." He bowed to the king. "Sire, would you care to address us?"

The king rose to his feet and stepped down from the dais. He nodded to someone at the rear of the crowd as he did so, a barely perceptible movement. It was Raven, and he slipped away into the trees at the king's signal. A moment later, a black bird winged skyward. I watched it from the corner of my eye as it rose toward the distant islands above until it was lost in the dark.

"Friends," the king began, "we are here today to mourn the passing of a great and wonderful Realm, the Realm of the tricksters, of the shape shifters. The Realm of my dear friend Perony, may the Lady bless him and keep him."

I glanced at Kellith, who sat in the front row with a bored expression on his face, and rage filled my heart. The king continued on, lamenting the loss of his friend's Realm and all its people, and reminiscing about the good times he had spent there. He never said one word about the details of Illusion's demise, but if I had been Kellith, I would have been squirming in my seat under that blue gaze.

Kellith, of course, didn't have a conscience and appeared unaffected by it all. Merritt sat by his side, staring at the ground beneath his booted feet with obvious indifference. The only member of the family who seemed to be paying any attention to the king was Lady Brona, Kellith's wife. At least her manners were better than those of her menfolk, whatever her morals.

The canopy above me obscured part of the sky from my view, but soon, I saw a patch of darkness begin to cover the gathered throng, growing larger and larger every moment. People began to look up and whisper to one another. The king continued to speak, but now hardly anyone was paying much attention, their gaze caught by the approaching island. Eventually, it moved past the canopy, and I could clearly see that it was Arlo, hovering low and moving with some speed along the course of the river.

I glanced at Kellith and knew the minute that he realised the island's identity. His face drained of colour and he shot a quick, furious glance at the king. If looks could kill, Rothbold's life would have ended in that moment, and I flinched, suddenly wishing I had thought to bring a weapon with me.

I caught Kyrrim's eye; he had also been watching Kellith, and he gave me a reassuring nod. No need for weapons with the Hawk on guard. I relaxed, secure in the knowledge that he had the king's back.

Merritt didn't seem to understand the significance of the

island that was passing before his eyes, but Lady Brona most certainly did. Her face paled even more than her husband's had done, and she swayed in her seat a moment, as if she were about to faint.

The murmurings in the crowd had grown so loud that the king broke off his speech, turning to check the progress of the homecoming island. When he turned back to his audience, his face bore a wolfish grin.

"But behold! This tale does, in fact, have a happy ending." His voice rang out above the noise and the people stilled, all eyes turning back to him, sensing a story to come. "We are witnesses to a historic moment, my friends."

Arlo sailed over the first and largest of the islands of Illusion, its trailing roots and clods of earth barely clearing the ruined tower of the castle.

"What you see before you is a miracle in truth. Real magic, if you will. It seems Lord Kellith didn't manage to kill off all the Illusionists after all."

The crowd gasped almost as one as he so baldly named his brother-in-law as the murderer of a whole Realm, but the king continued, ignoring the look of fury on Kellith's face.

"Arlo was saved that night by the magic of Air, and now the magic of Air and Earth will return it to its rightful place."

He held up his hands as a hubbub arose among the crowd. Everyone was standing now, craning their necks to see what was happening. Arlo hovered over an empty stretch of water between two islands. This must be its original resting place. Slowly, the island began to sink. The queen stood up, so I felt justified in doing so, too, and took the opportunity to move closer to Kyrrim, who was still on guard at the rear of the dais.

Though it was quite some distance away, Arlo glowed with faelight, and I could make out figures moving on the surface of the sinking island. One of them had large black wings. That must be Raven. Probably the little knot of people gathered beside him were the Air mages. I wondered where Yriell was.

"Now I must go and assist my sister," the king said. "You are welcome to watch, if it pleases you."

As if it wouldn't please anyone to witness such a historic event. Well, anyone but Kellith and his family. The Lord of Summer glanced, white-faced with fury, at the queen, then fell into step beside her as we all hurried along the riverbank after the king.

Rothbold didn't go far. He stepped out onto the ford, and I blinked. For a moment, I thought he was walking on water, but then I realised that the earth and rock of the ford had risen up through the shallows to meet him. Without getting a drop of water on him, Rothbold made his way out into the middle of the river.

None of the nobles followed him, though not for lack of trust in his earthcrafting abilities. A sense of a historical moment in the making seemed to keep the gathered Lords and Ladies confined to the riverbank. I took a moment to run my eye over the crowd of nobles. Kellith, of course, was furious at the impending loss of his stolen territory, and had a face like a thundercloud. The queen's wasn't much better. It seemed to me that Queen Ceinwen had much preferred her husband when he was missing, presumed dead.

The Lords of Winter and Night stood together, both their faces showing more than polite interest in the proceedings. Lord Nox, Raven's father, looked positively delighted as he watched the show. My eye was drawn to a shock of red hair in the crowd—Willow's father, Lord of Spring. He and his lady were more circumspect in their enjoyment, though I got the sense that they were, indeed, enjoying it. Eldric's face was carefully expressionless; he was ever the consummate politician. But even the Lord of Day, formerly Kellith's staunchest ally, was keeping a distance from the Lord of Summer. Indeed, a noticeable gap had opened up around the Lord and Lady of Summer and their son. Silently, I exulted at this, the first nail in the coffin of Kellith's power and influence.

I turned back to Rothbold, not wanting to miss a minute of the proceedings. He had his arms outstretched, as if in welcome, as did a small figure on the island itself. Yriell. The two siblings regarded each other across the expanse of water that separated them. Some silent communication must have passed between them, for a deep rumble arose from the depths of the river and the water underneath the hovering island began to boil and bubble.

I glanced at Kyrrim, who stood on the shore closest to Rothbold, carefully blocking access to the ford. His gaze was not on his king or on the spectacle unfolding before us, but on the crowd. Ever the faithful protector, his eyes roamed over the gathered nobles, on the watch for trouble. I met that tawny gaze briefly, then turned back to the river in time to see fingers of rock thrust upward from the water.

Were the king's arms trembling? With baited breath, I watched him for signs of strain, sure that the earth and rocks that were climbing out of the water to greet the incoming island were his doing. Involuntarily, my gaze was drawn back to the island, wondering what Yriell was doing, and I realised that as the island sank ever lower towards its intended resting place, tree roots were writhing eagerly, as if they sought the water.

It seemed to me that the hovering island twisted to the right slightly, as if it were a piece in some giant puzzle that Yriell was trying to put together. Clearly, she was determined to have everything aligned just so. Straining my eyes against the darkness, I made out rocks protruding from the bottom of the island aligning with holes in the earth that Rothbold had pulled from the bottom of the lake.

The two pieces, top and bottom, slid together even closer until there was no gap to be seen between them. I half expected some kind of click as they slotted perfectly together, but if there was, it was inaudible over the sound of the earth shifting and the rocks grinding together.

I thought that was it, but then the island sank as smoothly as if it moved on rails, dropping back down toward the water so that all the earth and rock the king had raised as its foundation disappeared again beneath the surface.

A flash of green light rippled out from the island and lit

the sky, washing over the faces of the watchers, and the king lowered his arms. Arlo was finally settled.

There wasn't a peep from the watching crowd. No applause. No one moved or spoke, not even in a whisper, while Rothbold wiped the sweat from his brow. He remained standing in the middle of the ford, his face turned toward the island as if expecting something, and the crowd held its breath.

I knew what he was awaiting; the council had planned every moment of this over the last few days. Soon, the watchers were rewarded with the sight of seven beautiful barges, which appeared from the far side of the island, sliding smoothly through the dark waters of the river. Each one's prow was shaped like the head of a rainbow drake, and the drake's glittering wings swept back along the low sides of each barge. They were elegant and beautiful, though the faces of the carved drakes were drawn into a snarl that I had never seen on the face of a real one. This, too, had been carefully considered, and was the council's subtle reminder to the gathered Lords that Illusion was no longer a weak victim, but had strengths of its own. Anyone who tried to test our borders would discover that we were not unwilling to defend ourselves.

Each barge was decked out in the green and white of Illusion, and the rainbow drake banner of Lord Perony's house flew proudly from each stern. Now, at last, the gathered crowd began to murmur as if a spell had been broken, each person turning to their neighbour to remark or exclaim. I stood next to the queen and said nothing, keeping my face carefully expressionless.

"Good people," the king said as the barges drew closer. "You were promised a feast, but the location has changed." He smiled at Lord Eldric, who was standing on the shore next to Raven's father. "Your work will not be wasted, however, Eldric."

An Air mage rose from the deck of each barge. In perfect synchronisation, each mage gestured at the tables laden with the prepared feast. Like obedient ducks, the tables rose into the air and floated in an orderly line toward the island.

"They'd better not spill any of my wine," Eldric said, and the crowd laughed, releasing the built-up tension.

The king strolled back along the ford to join the rest of the nobles. "All aboard," he shouted, waving at the barges. "Our feast awaits us. I, for one, am starving. Anchoring islands is hungry work."

23

I had never seen the great hall of Arlo's castle so full before. Perhaps no one had. All the Lords and their Ladies feasted at two long tables, with the king at the head of one and the queen at the head of the other. Morwenna and Tirgen were seated at the king's table with me, but they were too far away for me to talk to. Kellith was on my right, and Willow's mother on my left. It could have been worse—at least Merritt was on the queen's table. Not that he appeared exactly inconsolable at being separated from his intended. He was already deep in conversation with a pretty woman with poppies in her hair.

The rest of the councillors and many of the Arlo folk I recognised were seated at lower tables in the vast room, which was looking a lot smaller than usual with all these people crammed into it. The rest, presumably, were outside with the retinues of the Lords. Another great feast was laid out in the courtyard under the stars for them. The great hall was large, but not large enough to accommodate everyone the king had invited.

I saw Lirra among the crowd in the hall and smiled at her before I remembered who I was supposed to be. Hastily, I schooled my expression back into Lily's habitual look of disapproval.

"Who *are* all these people?" Kellith muttered to me, surveying the tables of commoners. "And what on earth are they wearing?"

It was true that the clothes of the Illusionists weren't as grand as those of the gathered Lords and Ladies. They were also a little behind the current fashions. But that was no reason for Kellith to curl his lip like that.

"I assume they're the few Illusionists you didn't manage to kill, Uncle," I said, poisonously sweet.

He gave me a startled glance, then decided I was joking and chuckled. "Perhaps I should have tried harder, eh?"

The main course had already been cleared away, though I had barely tasted what I'd eaten. Being forced to make polite conversation over dinner with Kellith certainly hadn't done wonders for my appetite. I couldn't wait for this charade to be over so I could slip back into my own skin, though I was becoming increasingly concerned about exactly how I was supposed to manage that while still playing the role of the princess.

Maybe Lily could be "too upset" to remain at the feast after the engagement drama was over. That was my current plan, anyway, though I was screwed if the queen decided to comfort her daughter. But what were the odds of that happening? I was convinced Queen Ceinwen had a block of ice for a heart. She would have made a perfect Winter fae.

"You have a strange collection of guests here, sire." Kellith waved a silk-clad arm that encompassed all the Illusionists at the lower tables.

Morwenna gave him a hard glance from her seat halfway down our table, but she was beneath his notice. He was too busy trying to stare down the king, who was paying more attention to his wine than his brother-in-law.

"How so?" the king asked in a bored voice.

"Is this all that Illusion has to offer now? Fishermen and shopkeepers? How is it to stand as a Realm on its own? You can't have a Realm without a Lord."

"Or a Lady," the king said mildly.

Kellith waved a dismissive hand. "Semantics, Rothbold. No one of noble blood survives to take the reins of this pathetic little island. These people would be much better off remaining part of Summer."

"If you want to discuss semantics, they can hardly 'remain' a part of something they have never been part of."

"I have ruled this territory for twenty years. I'm not giving it up to a handful of peasants," Kellith blustered. "The Realms have always had hereditary rulers. If you start changing that now, you imperil your own family's claim to the throne."

He sat back and looked around at the other Lords at the table, confident that he'd made a winning argument. Some of them had probably never even heard of democracies and republics, or if they had, only as something to be feared or despised. They certainly weren't a notion to be entertained here. The fae didn't like change. A couple of faces looked troubled, and I hoped the king soon put an end to this kind of talk.

"Fortunately, we won't have to change anything, Kellith," the king said, still in that mild, vaguely uninterested tone. "As it happens, there is an heir—one last survivor who carries Lord Perony's blood in her veins."

That caught the attention of all the Lords, even the ones at the queen's table.

"An heir?" Lord Nox asked. "Who?"

"And where is she?" Kellith added.

"Lady Allegra is Lord Perony's niece," the king said. "Daughter of his sister, Orlah."

"Not in the direct line of succession, then," Kellith said at once.

Rothbold fixed Kellith with a cold look. "You didn't leave a lot of choice after your bloodbath, my Lord of Summer. But there is precedent. People with less connection to the noble line have inherited before. Even in your own House."

Kellith knew that, of course, but he was determined to put every obstacle possible in the way of the king's plans.

"If there is an heir, surely she should be here?" Willow's father asked.

"Exactly." Kellith pounced on this suggestion. "*If* there is an heir. Surely you're not speaking of your little changeling pet? Do you seriously think you can pass her off as a noble to the Lords and Ladies of the Realms?"

Kellith knew full well I was of Illusion. This seemed desperate, even for him. The reappearance of Arlo must have seriously thrown him. He had his spies so deeply embedded in the palace that he was used to knowing every little thing that was going on. The fact that we'd managed to keep such an important secret from him had left him grasping at straws.

"I don't care for your tone, my lord," the king said, finally throwing off his nonchalant air. "In fact, there are a lot of things I don't like about you, Kellith. Not least of which is your persistent ambition to betroth your son to my daughter. Lily is too young to be betrothed. I will not hear of any such talk until she is of age, and I assure you right now, in front of all these witnesses, that a match with Summer will *never* be considered, at any age."

"What?"

Another bombshell, dropped without any warning. Oh, I was enjoying this.

At the next table, Queen Ceinwen put down her cup so hard that wine sloshed over the side, staining the snowy tablecloth red. "Rothbold! What is the meaning of this?"

"You said you would announce their betrothal tonight!" Kellith's face was red with fury. "What treachery is this?"

Even Merritt was paying attention for once, probably afraid that his gravy train was chugging off into the distance without him.

"Do not speak to me of treachery!" the king thundered, his patience exhausted at last. "If you were not my wife's brother, you would be swinging from the gallows by now, you snake."

Oops. So much for diplomacy. Still, he had managed to

capture the attention of everyone in the room. Some had even frozen with their cups halfway to their mouths, astonished at this outburst from the usually controlled king.

The king glared into his enemy's eyes. "Your son will never marry my daughter."

"Surely the wishes of the princess herself count for something?" Kellith spat back.

"Indeed they do. Tell him, Lily."

All eyes turned to me. My time had finally come—it was hard not to smile. "I do not love Merritt," I said. "I never have, and I never will. I refuse to marry him."

Kellith slammed a fist down on the table, making the crockery jump. "You have enchanted her!" he roared. "There is some conspiracy at work here. Lily, what has he done to you?"

"Nothing, Uncle. I merely speak my mind at last, sure of my father's backing. I find it interesting that your mind immediately leaps to conspiracies. They say that people accuse others of their own character failings."

Kellith's outrage was drowned out by the hubbub that arose. If I'd thought his face red before, that was nothing to the shade it took on now. With any luck, the arsehole would have a stroke right here and save us all a lot of trouble.

A voice rose above the shouting, and heads began to turn towards the door. A new figure strode in, heading straight for the king, and I almost said something extremely unprincess-like when I saw who it was.

What the hell? I glanced uncertainly at the king, but he was staring at the Dragon in shock.

He wasn't half as shocked as I was, though, considering last time I'd seen this guy, he'd been deader than Saturday night at the library. Or so I'd thought. Clearly, there were more degrees of dead than I'd realised.

At any rate, he looked fighting fit as he knelt before the king.

"Ebos? I thought you were dead."

The Dragon flashed a brief smile. "It was a near thing, sire. I woke in a cave full of trolls just as they were about to add me to the cooking pot." He looked up at the king, his smile fading. "But I have failed you, sire. You charged me to protect Allegra Brooks on her quest, and she is dead."

"Allegra Brooks is dead?" Kellith echoed, a grin of triumph splitting his face. "The same Lady Allegra you were just trying to foist on us as the new Lady of Illusion, brother? Why, what a coincidence. No wonder you won't produce this so-called heir—she's dead!" He looked around at the assembled nobles. "Now my talk of conspiracy doesn't seem so far-fetched, does it, my lords?"

"Really, Uncle, have a little dignity." This was my cue. Time for Princess Lily to retire and Lady Allegra to return. I rose, ready to leave the hall and find somewhere private to transform.

Kellith caught my wrist. "Not so fast, my dear. I think your kingdom needs you."

The other Lords were murmuring to each other. Even Lord Nox looked concerned.

"This would certainly be a good time to produce this Lady Allegra," Willow's father said, and other noble heads nodded in agreement.

"I disagree," Kellith said, rising to stand at my side. I tugged at my wrist, but he wouldn't release me. "Clearly, this heir no longer exists, and the king has stooped to deceiving his loyal Lords. I fear he hasn't been the same since his long imprisonment. It's time he stepped aside in favour of his heir, Princess Lily."

He honestly thought Rothbold had cast some enchantment on the princess, and underneath she was still his. After nearly twenty years of indoctrinating her in loyalty to Summer, it was a reasonable assumption, I supposed—or it would have been, if he had been in possession of all the facts.

The great hall erupted at his suggestion, and several other Lords rose, too. It was impossible to slip away now, even if Kellith would have released me. Every eye was on me, the princess, and the mood of the room was changing, growing uglier. Many sensed they were being played somehow, though they weren't sure exactly how.

The Dragon stood in front of everyone, looking all noble and sorrowful and *alive*, the dirtbag. How the hell had he managed that? I'd been so sure he was dead. And where had he been all this time? If he was alive, why hadn't he helped me in the frozen wastes of Winter? Why had he left it until now to reappear?

The timing was dodgy, to say the least, almost as if he was working to further Summer's interests.

I was well and truly sick of the royal Court by now. It was rotten to the core, full of Summer spies and adherents wriggling like worms through a festering apple.

"I fear you are right," the Lord of Day said.

I could barely hear him over the noise, but the Lords on either side of him were nodding. Were they all so easily swayed? Maybe Summer hadn't been the only Realm that had preferred life without a king.

Further down the table, Eldric was shouting, "Allegra Brooks is *not* dead!" but no one seemed inclined to listen, too caught up in the drama at the head of the table.

"It could indeed be time for a change of monarch, if this heir cannot be produced," the Lord of Day continued. "Where is she?"

"Does she even exist?" Kellith asked, sneering.

I chewed my lip, staring helplessly at the king. If only he'd agreed to let someone else impersonate his daughter— or me, for that matter. Now his desire for secrecy threatened his crown. Better yet, my vote would have been for him *not* to have anyone impersonate the strong-willed Lily in the first place. He could have just put up with her siding with Summer. Sadly, the king didn't take votes from anyone else. Yay for the monarchy.

But none of that helped the current situation. The king caught my eye and nodded almost imperceptibly. What did that mean? Behind him, Kyrrim stood, grim-faced, ready for anything. The shouting was getting out of control and too many of the Lords were wavering, while the king merely sat there, watching. Some I had expected to side with

Kellith, because they were Summer toadies, but others seemed genuinely uncertain of the king's sanity.

I could hardly hear myself think in the uproar. Did he want me, as Lily, to denounce them? Refuse to take the throne from her father? Would anyone listen to Lily anyway if they believed Kellith's claim that she was under an enchantment?

Or did he want me to produce the heir that the room was clamouring for?

In the end, it was the smirk on the Dragon's face that decided me. He looked so pleased at the chaos his sudden miraculous return had provoked. It was all too convenient and suspicious for my liking.

"Enough!" I shouted, and the arguments began to die down as all eyes turned to me.

With Kellith still clinging to my wrist like the world's ugliest bracelet, I closed my eyes and summoned my magic, letting it burst from me in a great swell of exasperation and anger.

Gasps and even screams greeted my transformation, but when I opened my eyes, I screamed myself. A complete stranger was holding on to me.

I stared at the man in total confusion. He was small and slender, with unkempt hair and a thin, downturned mouth. He looked ridiculous in the clothes of Kellith, which had been cut for a much larger man.

Even the king was standing now, his face mirroring the shock on every face I could see. "You speak of conspiracies," he said, his voice hoarse, "but now we see an even greater one than anyone could have imagined."

At last, the man released me, stepping back as he looked around the hall for support. "She is an Illusionist!" Even his voice sounded different. "She has changed me."

"Yes, I changed you. But that was a spell of undoing. This is your true form."

"I know this man," a new voice shouted. It was Morwenna, with a look of loathing on her face such as I'd never seen before—and I'd been the target of some pretty harsh looks from Morwenna. "His name is Hedrik, and he was Lord Perony's valet."

"I thought you died on the Night of Swords," Tirgen said, outraged. "Almost everyone else on Verelho perished that night."

"I knew I had seen him before," the king said. "And all these years, he has been posing as a Lord of the Realms."

"But where is Lily?" the queen asked, in horrified tones. "And my brother?"

"And my husband?" Lady Brona asked, but her voice was so faint no one else heard her but me. She was looking up at the man she'd thought was her husband with a completely blank expression, as if the deception was too great to take in.

I knew how she felt. All this time, the Lord of Summer had actually been an Illusionist? I could barely wrap my head around it.

"Lily is quite safe," the king said. "But Kellith …"

"How could you?" Morwenna demanded, her eyes flashing as she faced the stranger. "You've persecuted our people for twenty years—practically driven us to the point of extinction—and you were one of us? How could you do it?"

Panicked, the man looked around the great hall, finding not a single friendly face among the whole gathering. Kyrrim strode toward him, sword drawn, and he lost his nerve entirely and tried to bolt for the door.

Morwenna's hand shot out and grabbed his arm, pulling him up short. Tirgen took his other arm and, together, they hauled him back before the king.

"Never mind that," the queen said, pushing past me to stand right in front of the man. "*Where is my brother?*"

The king moved to stand behind her and put a hand on her shoulder. "Oh, Ceinwen, don't you see? This man killed him twenty years ago. Everything he has done since then has been in an effort to hide that fact."

"Willow is going to be so pissed that she missed all the excitement," Sage said.

We were sitting on the grass by the lake, watching the sun rise for the first time over Arlo since it had returned home. The really strange part was that there was now a view of Verelho rising in the background beyond the lake and, past that, the waving forests of Autumn on the distant bank of the river. I'd gotten used to the endless vista of sky from here, and it was odd to think that Arlo was finally grounded, back in its rightful place.

I nodded. "There hasn't been that much excitement in Faerie since …"

"Since we brought the king home."

"So not that long at all, really."

Sage laughed. "Girl, you are just a magnet for trouble."

"Pot, meet kettle."

Raven appeared out of the gloom, hands in his pockets. "Who's a magnet for trouble? Who must I challenge for the crown of king of misrule?"

"Allegra," Sage said, shifting over to make room for him.

He laughed and sat down beside her. "In that case, I admit defeat."

"How's everything back at the castle?" I asked. "It was too intense for me. I had to take a walk."

"The king has everything under control."

Right. In the heat of the moment, it hadn't even occurred to the queen to question *why* I'd been impersonating her daughter, but I bet that topic had come up by now. I had decided it was prudent to be well away before it did.

"I suppose the Hawk is still with him?"

"All his knights are still on high alert."

I snorted. "Then who's watching the Dragon?" I was still bitter about that. He'd abandoned me in the mountains of Winter. I'd actually mourned the ungrateful bastard, thinking he was dead, while he had disappeared somewhere for days. "When the dust settles, someone better find out where he's been. I don't trust him anymore." Which was a shame, because I'd quite liked him, despite Kyrrim's misgivings.

"The timing of his return from the dead was highly suspicious," Raven agreed. "Though vastly entertaining. You people certainly know how to put on a show. I'd expected fireworks, but you went above and beyond."

"How was I to know that I wasn't the only one in that hall pretending to be someone else?" For once, I was glad that my magic was still a little out of control. If I'd managed my own transition better, we might never have found out that Kellith was actually someone else entirely.

"I feel sorry for Kellith's family," Sage said. "Especially his wife. All these years she's been sleeping with a complete stranger."

"Probably an improvement on sleeping with Kellith," Raven said.

"He's got a point," I said, and Sage laughed. "I still can't believe he went after Illusionists the way he did, when he was one himself."

"Guess he liked being Lord of Summer," Sage said. "He had a lot to lose if his deception was ever discovered."

"And who better to find him out than a fellow Illusionist?" Raven said. "He wouldn't have felt safe until the very last one was ground beneath his heel."

"But still …" I said, shaking my head. "Everyone he had ever known … systematically murdered. That takes a special kind of psychopath."

"It must have seemed like the opportunity of a lifetime when the real Kellith fell into his power that night," Raven mused, and we all fell silent, trying to imagine it.

The smoke and fire, the screaming. So many dead, and Hedrik running for his life, or perhaps cowering in fear somewhere. And out of the chaos, a chance for life—but only if he was bold enough to seize it with both hands. Had he killed Lord Kellith, or merely stumbled across his dead body and realised the opportunity it represented? He must have kept a remarkably clear head in the circumstances.

It was just a shame that a different kind of Illusionist hadn't taken that opportunity, one who might have used it to make different choices, to end the feud between Summer and Illusion before it really took hold. So many lives could have been spared, including my mother's—both my adoptive mother and perhaps even my real one.

The sky lightened as we sat there, and I watched a flock of rainbow drakes circle over the lake, the rising sun glinting on their diamond hides. I had no trouble picking Squeak out of the crowd now. "Look at him up there, keeping up with all the others."

"You sound like a proud mother," Sage said, shading her eyes against the sun's glare.

"I'm just so happy to see him flying."

He must have felt me watching him, because he arrowed down out of the sky and landed on my knee. I stroked his head, and he warbled in contentment, rubbing his face against mine. Then he looked away and chirped a welcome.

Kyrrim stood there. The sight of him lifted my mood, though it took me a moment to realise what was different about him. And then I had it—Ecfirrith was on full display at his side, instead of hidden as it normally was. I sighed. It had been that kind of night.

"I'm surprised the king could spare you," I said.

"I'm looking for Yriell. The king wants her. Have you seen her?"

I smothered my disappointment that he'd only come on official business. "She wasn't at the feast. Said she couldn't stand the company of that many stupid people."

"Have you looked in the cellars?" Sage asked.

Raven laughed and suggested, "Perhaps at Morwenna's?"

After a rocky start, it was true that Morwenna and the

king's sister had formed a friendship of sorts, based on a mutual dislike of most of the rest of the people in the world.

"She's probably digging for dirt on Hedrik," I said.

"Does it matter?" Raven asked. "I can't see the king letting him live much beyond sunrise."

Even hating him as much as I did, I wanted to object. The idea of a fair trial for everyone was deeply ingrained in me after only a few years in the mortal world. Mainly due to TV shows, if I was honest. But the fae Realms didn't work that way. No one would be fool enough to defend what Hedrik had done, and too many people were baying for his blood—including both the king and the queen, united for once. The man's remaining life could only be measured in hours, and I couldn't say I was too sorry about that.

"Yriell loves gossip. She'll want to know everything Morwenna knows about him." I stood up, and Squeak hopped neatly from my lap to my shoulder, then took off. "I'll help you look."

As I walked off with Kyrrim, Raven moved closer to Sage, their two dark heads leaning together.

"I think he likes her," I murmured to Kyrrim.

"Who, Raven?" Not surprisingly, he seemed preoccupied. "He probably shouldn't get too attached. I heard Lord Nox was looking to arrange a marriage for him."

"Can't *anyone* fall in love with whoever they want around here?" I asked, exasperation in my voice.

"You know it's not that easy when you have other duties and responsibilities."

I couldn't tell if he was talking about Raven or himself—or me—which didn't do anything to improve my mood.

"The Lords pretty much lost interest in the question of the heir to Illusion after Kellith's big reveal, didn't they?" I said.

"They'll get back to it soon. Hedrik may have been an imposter, but he wasn't wrong. No one outside the noble houses can lead a Realm."

"What if I don't want to lead the damn Realm?" What if I just wanted to live a normal life with my friends and the man I loved?

He took my hand and kissed it. "We can't always choose our path in life. All we can do is make the best of it."

Now he sounded like Yriell. It annoyed me so much because I knew they were both right. Well, if life was change, I'd hope for a change for the better. I sighed. "Morwenna would be better at it anyway. She's been doing it for years."

"Morwenna doesn't have Lord Perony's blood," he said, in the patient tone of someone explaining something to a very small child.

"Then she can be my deputy."

He stopped and turned to face me. The early morning sun caught his tawny eyes and made them glow like topaz. "Lords and Ladies don't have deputies."

A thought occurred to me. "But they do have stewards, right?"

His eyes gleamed as his arms encircled me, pulling me firmly against him. "They do indeed."

"Then she can be steward and run the show. She'd like that."

"And what will you be doing?"

"Probably ravishing my favourite knight."

"The king might have something to say about that."

"The king *owes* me. I've saved his bacon so many times now. Surely, he can spare you now and then."

His lips dipped lower, tasted mine. "I'm not sure if knights get ravishment leave."

"I'm sure we can work something out," I said a little breathlessly. I would take whatever crumbs I could get. Nothing was sure in this world, as Kellith's—or Hedrik's— endless attempts to kill me had shown. I would do my living while I could.

He kissed me, hard, then suddenly drew back. "You are an endless delight. Not to mention an eternal temptation. But right now, I'm supposed to be finding Yriell."

He turned, pulling me along the path with him.

"Better hurry up, then. Ravishment is due to begin any moment. The Lady of Illusion commands it."

His mouth quirked in a smile. "Yes, my lady."

"Ooh, obedience! I like it."

Maybe there were some good things about being a Lady after all.

THE END

Don't miss the new series, Thirteen Realms: Thief of Souls, in which Sage takes the starring role. The first book, *Assassin's Blood*, is coming soon! For news on its release, plus special deals and other book news, sign up for my newsletter at www.marinafinlayson.com.

Reviews and word of mouth are vital for any author's success. If you enjoyed *Changeling Illusion*, please take a moment to leave a short review where you bought it. Just a few words sharing your thoughts on the book would be extremely helpful in spreading the word to other readers (and this author would be immensely grateful!).

ALSO BY MARINA FINLAYSON

MAGIC'S RETURN SERIES
The Fairytale Curse
The Cauldron's Gift

THE PROVING SERIES
Moonborn
Twiceborn
The Twiceborn Queen
Twiceborn Endgame

SHADOWS OF THE IMMORTALS SERIES
Stolen Magic
Murdered Gods
Rivers of Hell
Hidden Goddess
Caged Lightning

THIRTEEN REALMS SERIES
Changeling Exile
Changeling Magic
Changeling Illusion

ACKNOWLEDGEMENTS

Thanks once again to Mal and Jen for their beta reading, to my family in general for their support, and to my friends in the Authors' Corner for always having my back when I need help.

ABOUT THE AUTHOR

Marina Finlayson is a reformed wedding organist who now writes fantasy. She is married and shares her Sydney home with three kids, a large collection of dragon statues and one very stupid dog with a death wish.

Her idea of heaven is lying in the bath with a cup of tea and a good book until she goes wrinkly.